Clan Hero

Highland Heroes Series: Book 4

Theo Mann

Invisible Publishing Company

Highland Heroes Series

Contents

Chapter 1

Dead Betty stumbled through the dark forest trees and strained her eyes to see anything in the shadows. She spotted what looked like a pile of leaves tucked among some tree roots and went over to it.

She pushed the leaves aside to reveal a large cat curled up in a ball. His bushy striped tail covered his face.

She placed her hand on the Highland tiger's back and shook. "Reid! Reid, wake up! We have a big problem."

The cat's eyes snapped open and swiveled to look up at her. Then his head swung up and he looked around the forest with sharp, watchful eyes.

He transformed before her eyes, unfolded, and his fur sloughed off to reveal smooth skin. A young man rose to his feet where the cat had been a moment before and Reid Buchanan frowned at the surroundings. "Where the devil are we?"

"That's what I'm telling you. We're nowhere near where we were before....and it's worse. Duncan is gone—and so are Echo and Elliot. We're alone out here."

Reid rotated his head from right to left while his brain caught up with reality. "Duncan....?"

"Gone. I checked everywhere. There are no tracks or signs to show where he went. He must have magicked us here and himself.... wherever he is."

"We must go after him." Reid started to walk away.

Betty caught his arm. "We can't, Reid. You have to let him go. I know you're worried about your brother, but we have to keep going to Icemeet. We have to alert Colton and Jaimee about the new moon attack on Tyrekirk. We can't waste time looking for Duncan even if we knew where to begin."

He glared at her and then at the forest before he pursed his lips and sighed. "Ye're right, lassie. I just dinnae like to walk away when we've spent so much time and blood coming this far and coming so close to catching him."

"I feel the same way, but if he used magic to transport himself away from us, he could be anywhere in the world. He could be on another continent.... or in even another dimension. The attack on Tyrekirk is much more important."

"All right, lass. I'm with ye now. It isnae any way for a man to wake up in the morning, is it?"

She gave him a wry smirk and chuckled. "Not much. Do you want to go back to sleep or should we just get going?"

"Get going, I'd say. I'd only be dwelling on it for the rest of the night as it is." He grimaced at the stars. "We'll cover some miles and hopefully catch up on sleep once we reach Icemeet."

"How far away is it?"

"Not far. Ye remember the hilltop where we saw the battle? We can get across the Boundless near there."

The pair started walking. Betty had no idea where she was going, so Reid went in front. He talked to her over his shoulder on the way.

"I cannae wait for Colton to meet ye. I was about to say I cannae wait for Jaimee to meet ye as well, but I suppose she already kens ye. It's strange to think how all ye lassies kenned each other before now. It seems as though ye all just began here and now."

"It kind of feels that way to me, too," she murmured. "I still can't think of her as Jaimee....and about her being married. She sounds like a completely different person when you talk about her that way."

"Aye. She is a different person from who she was when she arrived. Make no mistake about that. She's the best thing that's ever happened to Colton—and to the Clan."

Betty didn't answer. She still had trouble reconciling that he was talking about Snowflake, commanding officer of the Last Division. No one was more committed than Snowflake to the Last Division's mission of isolation and retirement.

Now Jaimee was married and fully integrated into Clan Buchanan. She must be if Reid talked about her like this. He'd been talking about Jaimee since Betty first met him. He never had anything but good things to say about her....and not because of her military training and experience.

Jaimee must really have fallen hard for Colton Buchanan. Now they were mated for life and married to boot. Reid even talked about how close Jaimee was to the rest of Colton's Clansmen, especially Reid and their younger brother Duncan.

They loved her. There was no other way to put it. They loved her and she loved them. She had told them her real name because she wanted them to know everything about her. She wanted them to be her family the same way they had made her part of theirs. If that wasn't love, Betty didn't know what was.

Lily Barnett had found love in this strange version of ancient Scotland, too. She had married Grant Ritchie and now they were living as Lord and Lady Armstrong at Clan Creighton's castle of Tyrekirk in the city of Kald.

Betty couldn't imagine what would have led two members of the Last Division to abandon their mission of self-imposed exile and dedication to the poor. She would have thought such an outcome was impossible before she came to Scotland. Now everything Betty thought she knew was falling apart around her ears.

Even if, by some miracle, the Last Division could fulfill their mission to find Lady Rhona Armstrong and save her from the dark wizard hunting her, what would happen after that?

Lily and Jaimee wouldn't leave the men they loved to go back to Ironforge and a life of solitude. Why would they when they had obviously dedicated themselves to their Clans?

Now Betty and Echo Boxwood had gotten separated in this strange country. Betty didn't know where Echo was, now that Duncan Buchanan had magicked Echo and Elliot Ritchie somewhere else.

How could Betty go back to Ironforge without Lily and Jaimee.... or Echo? Snowflake wasn't Betty's commanding officer anymore. The Last Division couldn't function with only three members—if that. Ironforge and the Last Division no longer existed.

If things kept going this way, Betty might be the only one who would go back. What would she do then?

She got so absorbed in her thoughts that she barely noticed the sky lightening above the forest canopy. She jolted back to the present when Reid stepped out of the trees into a field.

She cocked her ear to listen. "What's that sound?"

"It's the battle. Come along." Reid strode across the field, started climbing a hill to the north, and he reached the top first.

As soon as Betty got near him, she realized what he was talking about. The hilltop gave a view over the Boundless.

Birds twittered in the forest canopy and pastel light shot through the clouds overhead. It was a beautiful morning, but Betty couldn't enjoy it.

A devastating battle raged on the planes beyond the estuary. The Creighton and Buchanan armies collided in a vicious clash of arms. The Creightons surged up the slopes pushing the Buchanans farther and farther from the Boundless, but that wasn't the worst part.

Almost twenty dragons circled directly over Icemeet and bombarded the outer walls with crushing fire. The last and only time Betty had seen the giant stone fortress, it had stood inviolate and immovable on the high crags above the planes.

Now the dragons had broken down the massive stone gate and half of them wheeled toward the planes chewing through the outer defenses. Several more dragons hovered over the roof assaulting the fortress to cave in the structure itself.

"Jesus!" Betty whispered. "This is bad!"

"We must get across!" Reid growled. "We must get to the fortress before the Clan evacuates."

"Evacuates—where? There is no way they can evacuate. They'll be trapped inside and the dragons will kill everyone."

"That's what they think. Come on."

He set off down the hill at a fast walk heading straight for the Boundless. He and Betty were still far enough west that no one would stop them from crossing, but Betty could see much more serious problems facing them.

She hurried to catch up with Reid. "We're going to have to fight our way inside. You realize that, right?"

"Aye. It winnae be easy, but if we...."

"It will be a lot more than not easy. It will be deadly."

He grinned at her over his shoulder. "We'll make it."

She wasn't so sure, but the only alternative was to turn around and go back to the forest, which was no alternative at all.

He marched right up to the water's edge and waded into it. They crossed in a few seconds. Then he dropped to one knee and pulled her down next to him. "Now listen here, lass. I'm going to shift and run up there. Ye'll have to keep up with me, but between us, we should make it to the entrance."

"What entrance? The gate is down. We would have to scale that big pile of rubble, and even then, we'd be running right under the dragons' fire."

"We winnae go in through the front, but it will be just as dangerous as all that. Now listen. I cannae take ye straight to the entrance or the dragons will see us go in. We must feint to the side and make them think we're trying to get in."

"Where exactly are we going?"

"There's another entrance behind the fortress. We'll go in there."

"Behind.... the fortress?" She squinted up at Icemeet. "It looks to me like the fortress seals up against the mountain. There is no 'behind the fortress'."

He laughed, but not without a healthy dose of irony. "Do ye think we'd build it without making it look that way? Of course we want our enemies to think that. Now listen, lass. Ye must keep up with me no matter what. Dinnae fall behind. If ye get caught out and I cannae find ye, ye wouldnae ever find yer way in. Understand?"

She gulped and nodded. "I understand."

"Aye. Let's go."

He stood up—or started to. Before he even got off the ground, he shifted back into a Highland tiger and rocketed away at a blinding speed. He dropped on all fours and skimmed over the rough ground racing straight into the thickest part of the battle.

Betty launched to her feet and took off after him. She never would have been able to keep up with him if the battle hadn't slowed him down.

He charged into the worst fighting. Swordsmen hacked, stabbed, and lunged on all sides. Some of them almost stepped on Reid and he veered in a desperate slalom course to get out of their way.

Betty reached him only to run into the same problem. She raised her saber and chopped her way through Creighton soldiers and lunatic Highlanders all attacking each other in fury.

The Buchanans bellowed in rage and cleaved their enemies to the marrow, but the Creightons were better armed and there were a lot more of them. They kept pushing the Buchanans back toward the mountain no matter how hard the Buchanans tried to hold their ground.

A mob of Buchanans crushed into Betty as they tried to fend off another Creighton surge. The Buchanans enveloped her and she got caught in the confusion. She had to fall in line with several huge Highlanders and lend her weapon to their efforts just to stop the Creightons from slaughtering them all.

Reid was long gone by the time she broke away. She fought her way farther up the mountain, but she still didn't see him.

She spotted a Highland tiger thirty feet to her right. The cat sprang onto a Creighton soldier's head, ripped his face to ribbons, and sprang off to slash another soldier's throat. Betty tried to fight her way toward him only to see another ten cats caught in the melee. She couldn't tell which one was Reid.

She dodged one way and then the other, but more Buchanans started shifting on all sides. Cats and men got all mixed up with each other and the noise deafened her.

The thunder of explosions got louder coming from Icemeet. The dragons leveled the outer wall with more dragons bombarding the upper keeps. Several of the highest towers toppled and hit the ground with crushing booms.

Guardsmen and archers fired up at the dragons, but the Buchanans couldn't drive them back. The situation was becoming desperate and then disaster struck.

The dragons must have made enough headway toward destroying the fortress. Half of them wheeled away, swooped toward the Boundless, and came streaking back from the Kald side. They formed a long line, stooped low to the ground, and started laying down a blistering wall of fire.

The Creighton soldiers fell back and left the Buchanans face to face with the oncoming dragons. The dragons' fire bombarded the foremost Highlanders and screams ripped through the ranks.

Betty froze in shock watching so many people meeting their deaths in such a horrific way. This was far worse than anything she ever dealt with in Afghanistan.

The next second, the Buchanans broke and ran for it. They fled in the only direction left to them and they all turned tail for Icemeet. The dragons kept advancing as they cut down hundreds of people. Their first victims created a wall of some scant protection that left just enough time and space for the survivors to make it to the mountain.

The dragons widened their formation and closed into a semi-circle. They pinned the Buchanans against the cliff. There was nowhere left to go but inside Icemeet.

Betty and the other Buchanans whirled backward and started a last, desperate scramble to get over the mounds of rubble that used to be the protective walls. The wreckage blocked the whole courtyard and the arched entrance to a passage running into the citadel.

Highlanders charged the only opening, but only one or two could get inside at a time. The others had to stand there waiting their turn as the dragons plowed through more and more people getting closer by the second.

Betty stood guard with her saber drawn, but that only left her with an unobstructed view of the disaster unfolding farther down the mountain. Thousands of bodies from both armies carpeted the plane. The dragons left a swath of scorched earth so black and dead that none of the Buchanan fallen remained. They had completely burned away.

More and more Buchanans floundered up the rubble heaps. Their Clansmen pulled them up and Betty helped shove them into the passage.

"Come on!" she shrieked to those falling behind. "Come on! You can make it!"

Her heart ached from pounding so hard. She couldn't let any more people die, but she couldn't stop it. Her dirk and saber wouldn't stop dragon fire.

She and four sturdy men hauled the last survivors onto the heap as the dragons reached the fortress. Heat blistered her cheeks. The dragons would hit her next.

She pushed four more people inside and a thunderous voice bellowed in her ear. "Get down there, lassie! Get inside—now!"

She glanced to her right to find a massive guy yelling at her. He towered over her and only he and his three comrades remained outside.

He didn't give her a chance to argue. He grabbed her, clamped his giant hand on the back of her neck, and pushed her headfirst into the hole.

A second later, he and his Clansmen dove through and landed on top of her. They all crashed to the floor in a pile as jets of fire pounded the outer wall. Some of the flames billowed through the gap and set the big guy's tartan alight, but the group still wasn't safe.

The wall imploded behind them. The explosion would have buried them in rock if they didn't claw their way out of its path in time.

A torrent of shattered stone crashed into the passage as all five scrambled to save themselves. The big guy rolled on the floor and snuffed out the flames enveloping his tartan. Smoke came from his clothes and he yanked the fabric away wincing in pain.

More pounding smashes rocked the fortress from outside, but at least now a mountain of rock protected the last remaining Buchanans from the dragons.

One of the other men turned around and came over to the big guy. "Are ye all right, Ewan?"

"Aye." He looked down at his shoulder and grimaced. He'd been burned where his tartan had been touching his neck and shoulder. "I'll survive."

His Clansman gripped his other shoulder and they all turned around to stare at the end of the passage. No one was getting out that way.

Ewan straightened up and let his eyes skim down Betty's body. He took in her clothes and nodded. "Ye'll be one of Jaimee's lassies from the future."

"You know about that?" she gasped.

"Aye. We ken all about it. Come along and we'll go find her."

Chapter 2

R eid stormed out of the keep, veered into the great hall, and back to the foyer. "Where's the lassie from the future that came in with me?"

His cousin Fletcher stared at him. "Do ye mean Jaimee?"

"Of course I dinnae mean Jaimee! I'm talking about Betty! Where is she?"

Fletcher gaped at him in stunned confusion. "Who's Betty?"

Reid spun away. "I must go back out there. I must find her."

His cousin Gavin materialized at his side along with Boyd the blacksmith and three others. They had been out on the battlefield a moment before. Now they all crowded the foyer licking their wounds and recovering from their narrow escape.

Gavin, Fletcher, and Boyd grabbed Reid and tried to hold him back. "Ye cannae go out there!" Fletcher protested. "Ye'd be burned to a crisp. The dragons are still out there."

"Leave me alone!" Reid elbowed his way through the foyer to the courtyard passageway. "I cannae leave her out there. She was with me all the way and then I lost her. If she's still out there...."

Boyd stepped in front of Reid to block his path. "I cannae let ye go out there, laddie. I've been loyal to yer father and now yer brother. Ye owe it to yer Clan to...."

"Och, stuff all that!" Reid shoved Boyd out of the way and yanked the door open.

Fletcher, Boyd, and Gavin all grabbed him and did their best to haul him back into the foyer. Reid spun around to push them away. "Get yer hands off me!"

"Ye cannae go out there!" Gavin yelled. "The dragons will kill ye for sure."

"Leave me alone!" he countered. "Do ye have any idea....?"

He ripped out of their hold and spun around to see Betty, Ewan, and three others standing in the passage. "Lassie!" he blurted out.

She charged him and threw her arms around him. "Thank God you're all right! I thought you were gone!"

His heart burst when he put his arms around her. She was alive and unhurt, but anyone could see she was badly shaken by the experience. "Aye. I was just about to go out there and try to find ye." He then frowned at the men standing behind her. "What's going on?"

Ewan jerked his thumb over his shoulder. "We got caught out by the dragons. They drove us in here. We barely got in alive."

"Have you seen Colton?" Betty interrupted. "Or Jaimee?"

"Och, I've seen them, but I havenae had a chance to speak to them about ought."

She tapped his elbow. "Come on. Let's go tell them now."

"Tell them what?" Ewan asked.

Reid turned back to him. "Get all yer men armed and ready to go back out."

"Out!" Boyd roared. "Are ye out of yer tree? It's suicide out there."

"Not there, ye mapit! Och, never mind! Come along, lass." Reid pointed at Ewan. "Ye do as I say and arm everyone."

"Does Colton ken about this?" another man asked.

"He's about to." Reid took Betty's arm, shouldered past Boyd and Fletcher, and led her inside the fortress.

The place was in chaos with dozens of armed men, women, and frightened children packed into the foyer, the great hall, the dining hall, the library, and all the other common areas at the center of the fortress.

These people had nowhere else to go, now that the keeps had all been decimated. Reid had to fight his way through and he couldn't help stepping on several feet in the process.

Betty lagged. She kept staring at everything in amazement and she slowed even more whenever she saw someone injured, crying, or in trouble. Several maids moved through the crowd treating injuries, handing out food, water, and blankets, and trying to give reassurance where they could, but there were nowhere near enough of these helpers even with dozens of Clansmen helping, too.

Reid came out of the library and saw Ewan, Boyd, and some of their other cousins come in from the passageway. They started going man to man delivering Reid's message about rearming.

Reid couldn't waste any more time in here. He pulled Betty into a side corridor leading deeper into the keep, but it was just as crowded as the hall.

"What's going on?" Betty asked. "What are all these people doing here?"

"They're preparing to evacuate. We must waylay Colton before he sends them out."

"Where will they evacuate? That man was right. You can't ask these people to go out and face those dragons."

"They winnae evacuate through the front, lassie. We have other secret ways to get out of the fortress and they'll fall back to our sanctuaries in the mountains. Ye dinnae need to worry about these people. They'll all go through to Stronghold and they'll be just grand."

She cast another pitiful glance around her. "I don't think so somehow."

"We've much more to worry about where we're concerned if we really mean to make an assault on Kald. Och, there's Colton finally."

Reid let go of her hand, waded through a particularly dense patch of his Clansmen, and forced his way through to where Colton stood. He was busy going over stacks of cartons, bundles, and crates of supplies loaded on wheeled trollies. They lined the corridor on one side and left even less space for all the people packed in shoulder to shoulder.

"I must speak to ye immediately," Reid began.

Colton didn't look up from his work. "Did ye find Duncan?"

"Aye. I found him, but he bolted and we lost him, but I must speak to ye about something much more important."

"It will have to wait until after the evacuation. I cannae spare a moment to stop now."

"It cannae wait until after the evacuation," Reid insisted. "In fact, it's critical that I explain to ye *before* the evacuation. We need every fighting man here. Ye cannae send them off just yet."

"We cannae wait." Colton went back to stacking the cartons. "If ye didnae bring Duncan in, we cannae take any more time to search for him. Now I need ye to begin taking a tally on everyone who'll evacuate so we can re-tally them when they get there."

"Didnae ye hear what I've just said?" Reid fired back. "Ye cannae send these people. All depends on our men staying here for the next assault."

Colton looked up for the first time and his black eyes met Reid's. Reid knew his brother too well not to recognize that look. Nothing would change Colton's mind.

"Assault?" Colton repeated. "There winnae be any assault unless it's a Creighton assault against us. The destruction they've already done is the only thing keeping us alive, lad. We cannae stay here."

Reid clenched his teeth. He had to convince his brother. "Listen to me, man. If ye ever hope to save these people, ye must...."

Betty stepped forward and took hold of his elbow. "Forget it. Come on. Let's see if we can find Jaimee."

Colton looked down at her and something in his iron countenance softened. "Lassie?"

She did her best to smile at him. "Hi. I've heard a lot about you. I'm Betty."

He shook her hand. "Did ye just come through, then?"

She shuffled her feet. "Not exactly. I've been with Reid in the forest for a few days. I was with Duncan and...." She looked up at Reid and the color drained from her face.

Reid took a deep breath and faced his brother. "Alastair's dead."

"Then there's naught else to be done." Colton wiped all expression from his features and went back to work. "Start tallying, lad. We must evacuate within the hour."

He moved off down the corridor and erased all awareness of Reid and Betty. Reid glared after his brother. Colton always listened to Reid and Duncan before. Colton had been becoming less and less approachable and less reasonable as the Creighton campaign escalated.

Reid fumed trying to come up with some way to reverse Colton's decision, but Colton turned his back on the pair and started dealing with the people waiting to evacuate.

Betty tugged Reid's arm again. "Come on. Let's get out of here."

Reid turned away. He didn't have to look too far to find Jaimee and he knew long before he got near her that she would be too busy to help him.

He led Betty to the old apartment that used to belong to his father, Neill Buchanan. Wounded Clansmen packed the floor with men and women working non-stop from one patient to the next.

Jaimee squatted next to a woman pressing a giant wad of bloody fabric to her face. Jaimee squeezed the woman's shoulder and then started working on the stretcher sticking out from under the woman's body.

"I dinnae need anyone to carry me," the woman insisted. "I told the lads they didnae need to waste a stretcher on me. I can still walk. Save the carrying for those that need it."

Jaimee pressed the woman's hand. "Thank you. I really appreciate it. When the time comes to evacuate, you can go out with the rest who can walk. I'm sure no one will stop you."

The woman twisted her head around and looked up at Jaimee with her one good eye. "Did ye see Callum out there, lassie? Did ye see if he made it back from the assault?"

Jaimee winced. "I didn't see. I'm sorry. It was chaos out there, but I'll look for him the very first chance I get. I'm sure he'll be just as anxious to find you as you are to find him."

"Are me children safe, lass?" The woman gulped. "Ye winnae let me children be left behind."

"Aileen has your children," Jaimee replied. "They're just fine. You'll see them once you get there."

"Thank ye, lassie," the woman choked. "Thank ye so much."

Jaimee stood up....and her features hardened when she saw Reid and Betty watching her.

She walked over to Reid and hugged him. "Thank God you made it back! Did you find Duncan?"

"We need to talk to you," Betty interjected. "It's an emergency."

Jaimee gasped when she realized Betty was there. "You! What are you doing here?"

"Liam sent me and Echo through to help finish this mission, but that isn't what we need to talk to you about. We need your help."

She bent over the next patient. "If it doesn't have anything to do with this evacuation, then it will have to wait until afterwards."

Reid threw up his hands and spun away. "This is hopeless!"

"Listen to me, Jaimee," Betty insisted. "It's absolutely critical that you don't evacuate any of the fighting men. They have to stay here."

"Forget it! We're finished. Do you get that? We'll be lucky to get everyone out alive with the dragons out there."

"Evacuating these people won't save them," Betty went on. "The Laird can use magic to track you down, and with the way the war is going, he'll wipe out the Clan sooner or later. Our only chance is to take Kald and put Duncan on the throne."

"We can't," Jaimee countered. "There is no way we can take Kald. It's a pipe dream. We can't even protect Icemeet."

"Not on your own, you can't, but with two other armies working with you, we can do this."

Jaimee stopped what she was doing and looked up. "What armies?"

Reid and Betty exchanged glances. Betty took a deep breath. What she was about to say sounded so flimsy. "We found Elliot Ritchie in the forest. We...."

Jaimee smacked her lips. "Not another Ritchie! I'm never talking to anyone named Ritchie ever again."

"Ye dinnae have to talk to him," Reid told her. "He's organizing the rebels west of Kald to coordinate with us."

"And Echo is going to Tyrekirk to convince Grant and Lily to help us from inside the castle."

Jaimee blinked from her and back to Reid. "This is insane. You know that, right?"

"What choice do we have?" Betty asked.

"For a start, we don't even have Duncan to put him on the throne. We don't even know where he is."

Reid glanced over at Betty again, but she wouldn't meet his gaze. Neither of them wanted to tell Jaimee about Duncan being out of his mind, not to mention dangerous to the people he should care about.

"Just help us talk to Colton," Betty urged. "He won't even talk to us. At least help us get him alone where we can explain all this. It would be terrible if you went to all the trouble of evacuating the men, only to have to bring them back later."

Jaimee puffed out her cheeks. "All right. I'll talk to him, but don't get your hopes up. You know how he gets when he sets his mind on something." She looked over at Betty. "Well, maybe *you* don't, but Reid does."

"Thanks," Betty exclaimed.

Jaimee walked away and Betty turned to Reid. "Well, at least she's willing to help us."

"She's right," Reid growled. "Colton winnae budge."

"Give him a chance. She's his wife. She might be able to make him see reason."

Reid snorted again. Betty didn't know Colton the way he did.

A few minutes later, Jaimee came back into the apartment. "How did it go?" Betty asked.

"About like I expected. He wouldn't even talk. He's too busy."

"What about....?" Betty began, but Jaimee wasn't listening anymore.

"I gotta go!" Jaimee exclaimed. "The evacuation is starting. I can't deal with this right now."

She hurried away, and when Reid and Betty returned to the corridor, they couldn't even get through. So many women and children pushed and shoved that Reid and Betty had to hang back and wait.

Everyone jostled and complained. Those wounded who could walk tried to join the march from the apartment. Reid and Betty had to smash themselves against the wall, but even then, no one could get through. Too many people were trying to evacuate at once.

Jaimee came back forcing her way through the packed throng. She yelled over the bubbling voices to make herself heard. "When you reach the end of the corridor, take one trolley each and take it with you into the tunnel. The trolley you take will have all your food and bedding, so if you don't take a trolley, you'll be hungry and sleeping on the floor when you get there. Every family is responsible for pulling their own supplies—no exceptions!"

Betty smiled up at Reid. "She can't stop herself from taking charge of every situation."

Reid stretched his neck to peer over the crowd. "It looks like the women and children are going first anyway. That will leave the fighting men to last. We may have a hope after all."

"Won't Colton evacuate the fighting men, too?"

"Not right away. He'll wait a bit. He winnae let anyone evacuate without their supplies, which means the evacuation will stop once this lot takes all the trolleys. No one will be able to go through the tunnel until he retrieves the trolleys and reloads them for the next wave."

"You sound like you've done this before."

"Aye. We've evacuated three times since I was born. We ken how to do it."

"Wow!" she breathed. "The Creightons must be really intent on invading."

"I dinnae ken what ye say about the Laird tracking us into the mountains. He hasnae done it yet."

"There's a first time for everything, and if he's that bent on stopping Duncan from taking the throne, he'll make sure to finish the rest of the Clan, too."

Jaimee came back down the corridor calling the same instructions. The crowd started moving slowly at first and then faster. The wounded from the apartment filed out to join the mob, and in a little while, they cleared the area.

Reid and Betty approached the corridor and saw Ewan, Callum, and some of Reid's other cousins. "Did ye rearm?" Reid asked them.

"Aye. We were just coming to check with Colton about evacuating."

Reid stiffened, but at that moment, Jaimee came back calling out again. "That's it! You can all relax. We aren't sending anyone else through."

"Can Colton talk to us now?" Betty asked.

Jaimee made a face. "How about you go ask him? I don't want to get my head bitten off."

"Who does?" Ewan joked.

"I'll go." Reid started to turn away when Colton himself approached from farther up the corridor.

He pointed to the assembled fighting men. "If ye lads havenae ought else to do, ye can go through and bring the trolleys back. We must reload them for the next wave."

"It will take at least an hour for them to unload all the trolleys and bring them through," Reid pointed out. "Perhaps ye have time to talk to us now."

Colton leveled Reid with an impenetrable stare, but when Colton glanced at Betty, he seemed to change his mind. "All right, lad. Go up to me office and I'll meet ye there." He turned to Jaimee. "Will ye please fetch our dinner and bring it up, lass? We can eat while these two talk."

Chapter 3

Jaimee stepped into Colton's office holding a tray with some food on it. She took one look at Reid and Betty talking and Betty would have to be blind not to notice the way Jaimee's expression changed.

Jaimee pinched her lips and deliberately looked away like she'd just seen something disgusting. She put the tray on the table and pulled out a chair before sitting down. She crossed her legs with all of her old businesslike stiffness, folded her hands in her lap, and looked straight in front of her like she wanted to make certain not to see Reid and Betty standing there.

Betty stared at the woman she thought was her friend. Betty had been looking forward to seeing Jaimee ever since Liam sent Betty and Echo through the time portal to this country. Now Jaimee was acting like she didn't want to know Betty at all.

What was even worse, Jaimee acted like she didn't want to know Reid, either, but that couldn't be right. He was Colton's brother and Jaimee had been acting so friendly toward both of them since Reid and Betty first made it back to Icemeet.

Did Betty do something to offend Jaimee? Had Jaimee changed her mind about the new moon assault? Would she try to convince Colton not to help out after all?

The door swung open again and Colton stormed in. He barged straight over to his desk and started wolfing down the food.

"All right, ye two," he mumbled over his shoulder with his mouth full. "I'll give ye ten minutes to say what ye have to say and then I'm sending all the Clansmen through the tunnel. What's so important?"

"The rebels in the forest west of Kald want to coordinate with us to assault Tyrekirk on the new moon," Reid began. "We've sent another one of Jaimee's lassies to the castle to speak to Grant and Lily about helping us out, too. With us attacking from this side, the rebels coming from the western forest, and hopefully Grant working inside the castle, we can unseat the Laird and put Duncan on the throne in the Laird's place."

He blurted this out in a wild rush. Betty couldn't have said it better and now Colton had all the most essential facts.

Colton went very still and quiet for a second while he stared down at his plate. Then he stopped chewing, turned around very slowly, and blinked at his brother with a wad of food still bulging in his cheek.

After what seemed like an eternity, he swallowed with difficulty and mumbled around the lump in his mouth. "Ye.... want to put Duncan.... on the throne of Armstrong? Are ye off yer bloomin' head, man?"

"I dinnae say he's in any state to rule the country and all, but this is our best chance to overthrow the Laird no matter who rules. We've got two armies coming from two different directions and...."

"Ye call this an army?!" Colton thundered. "Ye call *this* an army? How precisely do ye propose I send anyone to assault Kald across the Boundless? Tell me that. Tell me what sort of Clan Chief I'd be if I sent a single man out there right now. Dinnae talk to me about getting anywhere near the Boundless when we cannae even leave our own house!" He turned back to his plate and started muttering to himself under his breath. "As if we dinnae have enough to cope with at this hour!"

"If we let this chance go by, we may never get another one," Betty chimed in. "You can fight the Creightons all day long and wind up right back where ye started...."

"I cannae fight the Creightons at all, lass," Colton snapped over his shoulder. "Didnae ye see the state of things outside or are ye as blind as *this* dobber?" He jerked his thumb at Reid.

"I dinnae say ought about Duncan," Reid went on. "He's out of his mind and running wild God kens where, but think on it a moment, lad. We may never get anyone else to help us for the rest of...well, forever."

Colton spun around again and furrowed his brow at his brother. "Who says ought about him being out of his mind?"

"You guys are behind the latest news," Jaimee added. "Duncan was here and he was very, very sane."

Reid and Betty both whipped around to gape at her. "He was?" Betty gasped.

Jaimee nodded. "He showed up yesterday. The Laird pulled out some huge black dragon to come over here and attack us. Based on what we've seen from Grant, I'm assuming this new dragon was his brother Elliot. He started out by blowing up all our siege machines so we couldn't hit the dragons, but interestingly, he was extra careful not to hurt any people."

"And then, if ye can believe the evidence of yer own eyes—which I dinnae," Colton added, "Duncan stepped out from behind the rocks and started using magic to fight the Creighton dragons."

Reid passed his hand across his eyes. "Och!"

"Believe it," Jaimee went on, "and Duncan was very, very careful not to hit Elliot. Duncan started fighting the dragons, and as soon as Elliot saw Duncan, Elliot turned against the Creightons and started decimating them like you wouldn't believe."

"Until the Laird knocked Elliot out of the sky, that is," Colton finished.

"He what?!" Betty gasped. "He knocked Elliot...."

"Out of the sky," Jaimee repeated. "Ka-blooey. The Laird cast a spell over Elliot while he was way up in the air and shifted Elliot back into a man. Elliot crashed on the ground."

"A fall like that would have killed any ordinary man," Colton added.

"So what happened?" Betty croaked. "Is Elliot dead, then?"

"We don't know," Jaimee told her. "Duncan saw Elliot fall and then Duncan shifted into a dragon, too."

Reid's and Betty's jaws both dropped. Jaimee sat back in her chair and smirked up at them while she watched the effect this bombshell had on both of them.

"He's a big, ugly black bastard just like his brothers," Colton growled while he stuffed some more bread into his mouth. "He started fighting the dragons, but they outnumbered him. They would have killed him, so he picked up Elliot and flew away with him."

"We have no idea where Duncan is or even if he and Elliot are still alive," Jaimee told them at last.

"I wouldnae have believed the lot if I hadnae seen it with me own eyes," Colton went on. "I still dinnae believe it now."

"But this is.... this is great!" Betty exclaimed. "It means that Duncan is regaining his sanity. He has control of his magic."

"So ye kenned he had magic?" Colton countered. "What did ye see when ye found him in the forest?"

"He was totally out of control," Reid explained. "He didnae ken me and he kept attacking everybody."

"He attacked as a cat," Betty corrected. "When he used magic, he just spouted off with no rhyme or reason to it at all. He didn't even seem aware that he was doing it. It came out of his skin and hair and even from his eyes. That's how he made Elliot shift."

"So you know about Elliot, too?" Jaimee demanded. "Why didn't you tell us?"

"We didnae have time to. This is the first we've come back to Icemeet and we've been trying to talk to ye since we got here." Reid turned back to his brother. "Ye wouldnae even talk to us."

Colton blinked in stunned shock and then lowered his eyes. He stepped closer to Reid and gripped his shoulder. "I'm sorry, laddie. I shouldnae have done that. I should have heard ye out the moment ye returned."

"So what about the new moon assault?" Betty asked. "Do you still plan to send all the fighting men off to.... wherever it is you're sending them?"

Colton turned back to his tray and started eating again. He kept his back to the room and his head bowed while he chewed.

He remained silent for so long that he startled Betty out of her skin when he finally started talking. He kept his head down and his back turned. He muttered down at the floor like he might be talking to himself.

"I dinnae believe we stand a chance in Hell of putting Duncan on the throne. I would-nae have believed our Clan would ever follow a Creighton, but after the way Duncan saved us yesterday, perhaps it isnae so far-fetched as all that."

Betty's heart leapt. Without meaning to, she shot out her hand and squeezed Reid's arm. She burst into an excited grin. Was Colton going to agree to the assault after all?

Reid grinned back just as excitedly....and then she spotted Jaimee glaring at her. Betty dropped her hand instantly and her cheeks burned that Jaimee caught her doing something....

Was there something wrong with being excited that their plan was finally coming to fruition? Did Betty do something wrong by sharing that excitement with Reid?

"We dinnae ken where Duncan is nor what condition he'll be in if he's found," Colton went on. "If we're to drive the Creightons out, we must do it without considering Duncan at all."

"So do ye mean to take part in this assault?" Reid asked. "I must be frank with ye, lad. We dinnae ken if Echo and Elliot ever made it to their destinations nor if they had any success recruiting anyone. I dinnae like to put too fine a point on it, but I couldnae leave ye in any doubt about the true position. We might be doing it all on our own anyway."

Colton shrugged, picked up a cloth napkin from the tray, and started wiping his fingers and mouth. "It doesnae much matter as far as I can tell. We've naught to lose either way. If ye're right, the rebels attacking from the west will force the Creightons to withdraw from the Boundless. If we can get across and make a dent in their numbers, it would only do us some good. It's a long shot, but it's all we've got."

Chapter 4

Reid turned to leave Colton's office. Jaimee was already moving closer to Colton and Reid paused when she started talking about the evacuation. "We still have a couple hundred women, children, and old people to take down the tunnel."

"How much food do we have left?" Colton asked.

"Not enough for both Icemeet and Stronghold."

"Send everything through to Stronghold," Colton told her. "I'll stay behind here and organize the assault. Ye and Adaira look after Stronghold and hold it against all comers."

"Are you crazy?" she countered. "I'm not going to leave you here to assault Kald with a skeleton crew. I'm staying with you."

He turned to her and his features softened for the first time since all this chaos started. "I love ye too much to let ye stay. Ye'd only put yerself in danger and I need ye at Stronghold...."

"Forget it," she snapped. "Adaira can take over at Stronghold. I'm staying here."

Colton turned away with a sigh. "I dinnae fancy telling Adaira and the other archers me own self. They'll rip me head off if I leave them out of the assault."

"Did you honestly think you could get away with that?"

"Who can I send, then, if all the fighters are here?" Colton turned all the way around and saw Reid standing there.

"Dinnae even think it, lad," Reid told him. "I'm staying and no mistake."

Colton smirked at him. "Go on with ye, lad. I wasnae going to suggest that. I'd be a dead man if I did."

Jaimee didn't move. She gave Reid one of those looks he had come to understand. She was giving him a silent order to leave her alone with Colton.... for whatever reason.

Reid walked out of the office and immediately stopped when he found Betty waiting on the landing outside. "Are they finished?" Betty asked. "I need to talk to Jaimee."

Reid snorted. "They arenae finished and ye cannae talk to her—not now. Come, lass. I'll take ye where ye can get something to eat. Ye look beat."

She ran her hand across her forehead. "I guess I am. That battle really took it out of me."

"I'll show ye around Icemeet," he suggested. "Ye havenae had a chance to look around since we got in."

"I guess not."

She looked off in another direction. Reid studied her on the side. "Is ought amiss, lassie?"

"Not really. I mean.... apart from Jaimee acting weird."

"Weird?" he repeated. "How? She seemed all right to me."

"To you—of course. She wasn't all right to me."

"What do ye mean?"

"I'm not sure. She was just acting weird in Colton's office. She kept giving me dirty looks...like she was mad at me about something."

"How can she be? Ye've just arrived."

"I know. I don't understand it....and she acted like she was mad at you, too."

His eyebrows flew up. "Me! How could she be angry at me? I havenae done ought to her."

"I know. Neither have I."

He shrugged it off. "Och, she's likely on edge about the evacuation...and the siege and all. I suppose she's worried about the siege engines...."

"What about them?"

"Only that she designed them and had them built and placed them and commanded them. She came up with the whole idea and created them from scratch to defend us against the dragons. If she and Colton are right about Elliot destroying the engines.... Well, I wouldnae like to be him when she gets a hold of him."

"But she didn't sound angry about that, either," Betty countered. "You heard her and Colton. They said Elliot didn't kill anybody."

"Aye. I heard."

She cocked her head to study him. Her intense blue eyes gave him a shiver. He'd been feeling this strange energy gripping him ever since he met her.

He knew that feeling. He'd never experienced it before, but he knew it. She was his destined mate—the woman he would mate with for life. She had to be. She couldn't be anything else if she made him feel this way.

His heart fluttered at every one of her touches. Every glance of her eyes in his direction gave him a rush of superhuman strength. He could take on the whole Creighton army when she looked at him like that.

He commanded himself to stay calm. He couldn't get overexcited about this. She didn't mean anything when she looked at him that way. She came from a race that didn't mate for life. Betty wasn't even thinking about him that way.

That couldn't be right, though. Jaimee mated with Colton for life. Why couldn't Reid do the same thing with Betty?

She snapped him out of his thoughts. "What's wrong?"

"Hmm?" He glanced over at her. "Nothing's wrong. Why do you ask?"

"You were scowling just now like you were mad."

"I wasnae mad. I was just thinking."

She covered her eyes again. "I don't know what's wrong with everybody—I mean, apart from all of this."

She waved at the fortress around her. They had descended the stairs without Reid realizing it. They re-entered the foyer, but it wasn't as crowded, now that half the Icemeet population had evacuated and the other half were all down in the tunnel waiting to do the same thing.

She looked around her, stunned. Did she even know where she was? She didn't act like it.

"This is the entrance foyer," Reid began, "and that over there is the dining hall...."

She burst out laughing. "I guessed that. Thank you. You're very considerate."

"And that over there...." He motioned toward the passageway she used to enter the fortress. "That's the passage out to the courtyard...."

She laughed and her cheeks colored. She dipped her eyelashes and tried unsuccessfully to bite back her mirth. "I don't think I'll go out there if it's all the same to you."

"Och, no!"

He couldn't stop himself from gazing at her, just for a second. She looked nothing like the other four. She kept her long, curly blonde hair tied back in a loose ponytail when she first came through the time portal, but it had come even looser in the days since then.

Her pearlescent skin and piercing blue eyes made her look more like a princess than anyone he had ever met. He was used to the Buchanans' rugged beauty, not this exquisite porcelain refinement.

No one could ever mistake Betty for being fragile or delicate, though. She impressed him from her very first moments in this country—just like Jaimee and Echo. Betty was cut from the same cloth. She was tough, alert, and ready for anything.

All his problems would be solved if he could just figure out how she felt about him. Was she just being friendly or did she feel the same way?

She'd been so affectionate to him in the forest, but he still couldn't be certain. She seemed to adore him in his cat form, but that might just be her way of appreciating his shifter nature.

His acquaintance with Jaimee and then becoming her brother-in-law didn't prepare him for dealing with Betty. Betty was a different person. He might have spent a few days facing danger and hardship in the woods with her, but he still hadn't gotten to know her—not really.

He led her into the dining hall. A few loaves of bread, rinds of cheese, and bones with some meat still on them lay scattered over the tables, but no one else was around. They had all left.

Reid made a face. "This is no good at all, lassie. I'll go see what's about in the kitchen and bring ye something. Ye can go into the library until I come back. Ye dinnae want to stay in here."

"Eat—in the library? I don't think so and this is good enough. You don't need to go to any trouble because of me." She pulled up one of the benches. "Sit down. Aren't you hungry, too?"

She swung her leg over the bench, sat down, and picked up one of the bread loaves. He hesitated. Why did this surprise him? He had no reason to start treating her like a princess just because they were inside Icemeet.

Icemeet wasn't the most welcoming environment right now anyway. It wasn't as orderly or as tidy as it was when Jaimee first arrived—not that Icemeet welcomed her with open arms.

Betty pulled out her dirk and started sawing the end off the bread. "Are you sure you don't want some?" She smirked up at him and sent another thread of fire through his guts. "Are you going to stand there watching me eat it all?"

He shrugged and sat down across from her. They had been a lot closer on the way here, but for some reason, being this near her meant so much more.

They were all alone in the hall even though plenty of people kept milling around, crossing the foyer outside, and voices drifted in from multiple sides.

Betty handed him a piece of bread and grinned at him when her fingers accidentally brushed his. Was she trying to flirt with him or was she just being her usual friendly self?

She picked up one of the bones and rotated it over looking for a piece of meat big enough to cut off. "This is a lot better than we had in the forest, isn't it?"

"Listen, lassie," he began.

At that moment, Jaimee stuck her head into the dining hall. "When you two finish eating, why don't you round up the lads, take them to the great hall, and start getting them armed and trained for your big offensive? The rest of us are too busy right now."

Betty raised her eyebrows. "Lads?"

Jaimee laughed, waved at her, and walked away. "I gotta go. Finish eating and start getting everyone ready. We don't have much time."

She vanished around the corner and Betty chuckled. "Lads! She sure has changed."

"Is that weird?" Reid asked.

Betty froze with her dirk poised over the bone. "Weird?" She pronounced the word as though *he* said something weird, too.

"Ye said she was acting weird."

Betty laughed again. She looked absolutely stunning when she laughed. Reid couldn't remember Jaimee or Echo laughing like that. In fact, Reid couldn't remember anyone in his life laughing like that—ever.

"It isn't weird. It's just.... well, she's American. We don't call people 'lads'." She giggled. "You sound weird when you try to talk like us."

"Perhaps when ye've been here a wee while, ye'll call us all lads, too." Reid regretted saying the words as soon as he said them, especially when her smile froze on her face and she stared at him in blank horror.

Why did he say that out loud? Why would he assume she would stay here—a wee while or longer? He had no reason to believe that.

He shouldn't have said it, but it was too late now. It made things far more uncomfortable between them—as if anything could make it more uncomfortable than it already was.

Why did he feel so anxious and jittery around her? Everything had been great in the forest. He never had any trouble talking to her and being near her then.

Then Duncan magicked himself and the others away. As soon as Reid and Betty were alone, everything changed—for him at least. Every glance and facial expression meant the world. He couldn't stop himself from reading earth-shattering meaning into the slightest word.

She went back to cutting up the meat and didn't answer. He really stuck his foot in it. He made up his mind then and there never to open his mouth around her ever again—except that he had to when she handed him some more food.

He ate in silence. Why did he find it so difficult to talk to her all of a sudden?

She startled him out of his skin by speaking first. "So what do we have to do to get the *lads* ready?"

She laid extra emphasis on that word and he couldn't help but laugh. He found it difficult to meet her twinkling eyes without blushing. "Ye're learning, lassie."

She laughed with him. "Just don't ask me to start wearing a kilt."

"Never!"

"Why does Colton wear such fancy clothes when the rest of you don't bother?"

He shrugged. This conversation was starting to flow better than he dared to hope. "He's Clan Chief, of course. He has to primp and brush himself up. He hates it, but he must cut a finer figure than the rest of us. I tell ye, lassie, I wouldnae be Clan Chief for all the tea in China."

She nodded down at her plate. "I don't blame you. He has a lot of responsibility......" She smirked at him. "Or is it that you just don't want to wear shoes and brush your hair?"

He laughed in spite of himself. She made him ridiculously happy—but only when he was talking to her. As soon as things turned awkward and difficult, he wished he was dead. "Ye've got me number, lassie."

She put her dirk back in her belt. "Have you had enough to eat? We should probably get started on the.... lads."

"Aye. Just dinnae let them hear ye calling them that. They winnae be able to concentrate on their training if ye speak like that."

Reid's heart soared as they left the hall together. Maybe he stood a chance of winning her after all.

Chapter 5

Reid escorted Betty to the great hall, but they wound up bumping into Ewan, Fergus, Callum, and the other Clansmen on the way.

They crowded the corridors all standing around talking. "What's afoot, laddie?" Ewan asked. "We went down for the evacuation, but Colton ordered us all up here."

"He wouldnae tell us a thing," Fergus added. "The lad can get right stern when he wants to be."

"He was up to his neck in the evacuation, man!" Ewan countered. "He had to herd up dozens of wounded and crying bairns and all. I didnae like to hang about and he's been down there for hours. None of us could do the job. I'd love to see ye try."

"Can ye tell us ought, lad?" Callum asked Reid. "Why doesnae he evacuate us with the rest?"

"We're staying behind," Reid replied. "We're arming for another assault, so ye lot must all get over to the great hall. We've much to do arming and training and all."

"Training!" Fergus snorted. "What training can we do that we havenae already done? We've been fighting the Creightons tooth and nail as it is. We dinnae need any training."

"Ye tell that to Jaimee and see how she takes it," Reid replied. "In fact, I can tell ye right now how she'll take it."

"She'll say there's no such thing as enough training," Ewan replied. "That woman can find something wrong with anyone's training."

Betty laughed and all the assembled men turned to stare at her. "Ye dinnae laugh about Jaimee's training, lassie," Fergus told her. "It isnae any joke."

"I know!" she replied. "I've trained under her for years. I'm laughing because you guys are learning what we've been dealing with all along. She's a slave driver."

"She is that all over," Ewan muttered.

"So ye lads must train up or at least make her think ye are." Reid waved them away. "Let's go get started. She'll be easier on us if she sees us at it when she gets here."

"Easy!" Fergus countered. "Jaimee and 'easy' dinnae got together in one sentence, lad."

The others laughed and Betty joined in. Reid caught some of the others raising their eyebrows at her attitude, especially when she joined them to enter the hall.

The Clansmen fanned out and started their usual routine of taking off their weapons, throwing everything in piles along the outer walls, and limbering up their arms and legs.

Betty didn't notice anything out of the ordinary. She studied the tapestries and coats of arms on the walls. She didn't notice Ewan stride out into the middle of the floor.

Callum came toward him from the opposite side, and without warning, they rushed each other. They grabbed each other by the arms and shoulders, started wrestling, and Ewan laughed once before he shifted.

He changed in the blink of an eye, twisted out of Callum's grip, and rocketed at Callum's face with all his claws extended to flay his cousin alive.

Callum shifted in a flash and both tigers slammed down on the floor kicking, yowling, and doing their best to tear each other apart.

The other men gathered from all over the hall. They chanted and cupped their mouths to cheer the two on. Reid yelled out, "Take him, laddie!" before he realized that something was wrong with Betty.

She hadn't joined in with the other onlookers. She stood so far back that the Highlanders' bodies blocked her from seeing the fight, but they didn't block enough.

She stared at the two tigers with her jaw on the floor and her eyes hanging out of their sockets. The two cats twisted and flipped and contorted around each other in a blood frenzy. Ewan took the upper hand first by throwing his weight on top of Callum's light, wiry frame.

Ewan flattened his cousin and drove his fangs for Callum's throat, but Callum recovered in an instant. He let Ewan come, and when Ewan tried to give Callum the killing bite, Callum struck.

He kicked out once with his hind legs and flipped Ewan head over heel. Ewan cartwheeled over his own head and hit the floor flat on his back. Callum pounced on top of him with incredible speed, dove in, and slashed Ewan across the chest.

Ewan gave a horrendous shriek of pain and outrage, but Reid could hardly hear him over the escalating cheers of the onlookers.

Reid got caught up in the excitement and forgot about Betty for a minute. He stepped closer to the circle and bellowed down at his two cousins. "Finish him, lad! Ye've got him down!"

Callum took full advantage of his victory and attacked in a blind whirlwind. He jumped on top of Ewan and landed all four paws on Ewan's stomach. Ewan tried to defend himself, but Callum was just too fast.

He slammed his own body down on top of Ewan's sprawled form and clamped his jaws around Ewan's neck. The whole assembly exploded in cheers, laughter, and the Clansmen clapped each other on the backs as Ewan collapsed. He went limp and relaxed all his limbs in surrender.

Callum hopped off and strutted in a circle. He swished his tail in triumph and sniffed at Ewan picking himself up. Ewan shifted back into a man and limped back into the circle. His Clansmen welcomed him with congratulations and praise. Blood ran down his chest from the wound in his shoulder and Fergus handed Ewan a jar of healing ointment.

Reid remembered Betty and glanced over at her. She stood frozen and distant from everyone else....and then Reid saw Jaimee standing behind Betty.

Jaimee watched the match from the threshold, but instead of looking mad or annoyed, she was laughing with the rest.

Some of the others noticed her, too, and the laughter started to fade as she strode into the room. She surveyed them all with some of her old mischief. She wasn't angry at them for fooling around.

"Dinnae tell me ye're having us train now of all times, lassie," Fergus began. "We've just fought a royal battle outside. Give us a chance to unwind a bit."

She only laughed. "All right. I won't stop you. Who's next?"

No one moved for a second. "What about ye, lass?" Boyd called out.

A bunch of people cheered and more laughter made her blush. She grinned at all her old friends. "All right. Who wants a broken nose?"

No one moved except to shuffle their feet and look away from her.

She turned in a complete circle waiting for someone to accept her challenge. Then she noticed Reid standing apart. "What about you, Reid? How do you like your chances?"

"Aye! Aye!" a dozen people yelled and Fergus slapped Reid on the shoulder. "Take her, lad! Teach her a lesson for us."

Everyone laughed including Reid. He almost accepted....and then he glanced over at Betty watching the whole exchange. All the color had drained from her face and he changed his mind.

He never got a chance to pull out. Jaimee followed his gaze and her expression changed when she saw Betty.

Jaimee waved Betty into the circle. "Come on, Betty! Come spar with me."

Betty's eyes glazed for a second. She stared like she didn't see Jaimee at all....and then Betty burst into a huge grin. "All right. You're on."

The hall erupted in even more laughter, cheering, and elbowing as everyone shoved to get a spot where they could see the match.

Jaimee went over to Boyd and handed him her dirk. She kicked off her shoes and socks and stripped off her jacket. She started rolling up her sleeves.

"Scratch her eyes out, lass!" someone yelled.

"Pull her hair!" another called.

Everyone laughed. No one knew or cared which lass did the scratching or the hair-pulling. Betty crossed the floor, but when it came to getting inside the circle, she couldn't get through with so many men standing around.

She came over to Reid and his chest tightened when she stood close to him preparing for the match. A surge of protective emotion gripped him. He didn't want her to get hurt, but more than that, he felt incredibly proud of her for accepting Jaimee's challenge in front of all these strangers.

He shouldn't feel proud of her when she wasn't his yet. He didn't know if she ever would be, but he couldn't help but congratulate her inwardly. She took a giant stride toward earning his Clan's respect by agreeing to this.

The assembled Clansmen went wild when she pulled off her jacket and handed it to Reid just as though he might be her lieutenant or something. He took her dirk and saber, too. He couldn't be prouder to hold her belongings for her.

He didn't even care if she won this match. She had already won just by stepping into the ring.

She rolled up her sleeves while she and Jaimee circled each other. They eyed each other dangerously and Reid started to seriously wonder if Jaimee might not have finally met her match.

Jaimee stopped grinning and all her features went hard and mean. Reid's heart raced watching the two women square off. Betty didn't look big enough or strong enough to take Jaimee. No one knew better than Reid what Jaimee was capable of.

Betty pulled the tie on her hair, wound her hair tighter, and retied it. Then she flexed her knees, extended her arms in front of her, and braced herself for anything. She was ready.

A hush fell over the hall as the two women sized each other up. Reid couldn't breathe. Tension gripped him. He wanted Betty to win, but at the same time, he wanted to see once and for all which of these women was stronger and more skilled.

He had come to believe no one could be stronger or more skilled than Jaimee and he knew he wasn't the only one. Now all of Clan Buchanan was about to find out if that was true.

What would Clan Buchanan be without that belief in her? Would the whole Clan come apart at the seams?

The two women woke him from his thoughts when they both moved in at once. Jaimee tried to grab Betty and Betty kicked her hard in the sternum. She sent Jaimee backstepping to keep her balance, but Jaimee reacted just as fast.

She charged Betty, made another grab for Betty's head, and when Betty blocked her, Jaimee ducked and hooked Betty around the middle instead. In a split second, Jaimee yanked Betty off the floor, reared back, and slammed Betty down on the hard stone floor.

The whole assembly groaned as one and then the fight exploded into one of the most intense brawls Reid had ever seen. Betty took the hit with no trouble at all. She landed across her shoulders and tried to throw Jaimee, but Jaimee had already consolidated her hold on Betty.

Betty strapped her legs around Jaimee trying to grapple her friend off. She crushed Jaimee between her knees and Betty started punching for all she was worth. She landed a dozen blows on Jaimee's sides and then started on Jaimee's head.

Jaimee had to duck under Betty's arm to protect herself and Betty took advantage of that position. She threaded one arm under Jaimee's armpit and ripped Jaimee off. Betty jerked sideways, overturned Jaimee, and reversed their positions in no time.

Betty scrambled on top and straddled Jaimee's chest swinging her fists like anything. Reid gaped at the pair in slack-jawed shock, but he was the only one who did. All the other Clansmen bellowed themselves hoarse cheering Betty on.

Jaimee bucked her hips to throw Betty off balance, but Betty had positioned herself too well. She landed four punches from right and left slamming Jaimee's head back and forth.

Jaimee shot out one arm and blocked the next punch. She reared off the floor and nailed a vicious punch into Betty's nose. Betty hesitated only a second and wound up for another assault when Jaimee made her move.

In the split second when Betty let her guard down, Jaimee wrenched onto her side, grabbed Betty's leg, and pulled her knee off the floor. Almost faster than Reid could see, Jaimee slithered out from under Betty, flung one leg up, and knocked Betty over.

The two women grappled and tussled on the floor for a minute. They got so tangled up with each other that Reid couldn't see anymore what either of them was doing. They each tried to pull some complicated maneuvers on each other, only to get thwarted by the other's defenses.

All at once, Jamiee gave an almighty heave and hurled Betty off. Betty tumbled several feet across the floor, rolled to her feet, and spun around to face Jaimee also on her feet.

The two women confronted each other one more time. Both of them had become disheveled, dirty, and bloodied in the scuffle. They glared at each other baring their bloody teeth and snarling like animals. Their eyes blazed with insane menace as they prepared to re-engage.

The noise in the hall rose beyond anything Reid had ever heard—maybe because this was the first time his Clansmen had ever held one of these training sessions indoors. They usually trained in the courtyard.

He glanced around and found Colton at his side. Colton beamed at the two women, clapped, and put his fingers in his mouth to whistle over the noise. The female archers had gravitated to the hall from all over the fortress. They surrounded the men and joined in applauding the two women.

Jaimee sprang forward, feinted, and then dodged the opposite way. Betty reacted to each feint....and then, for no particular reason, she suddenly realized what was going on. Her eyes darted to the spectators.

She stared at them clapping, pumping their fists at her, and yelling their heads off. Her expression changed....and then she just stopped. She let her arms fall and she walked out of the circle.

She shoved between Colton and Reid and stalked away. The Clansmen mobbed Jaimee congratulating her and laughing over the match. Colton's face shone with a light Reid hadn't seen in a long time—or at least since he first met Jaimee.

Colton shot Reid a brilliant grin and then Colton strode into the crowd to congratulate Jaimee, too. Only Reid remained outside. He couldn't stay here. He turned away to follow Betty.

Chapter 6

Betty rested her elbows on a high parapet, leaned over the side, and looked down at the rugged mountain landscape far below her. She didn't really have any idea how she found this part of Icemeet. She wasn't sure she could find her way back if she tried, but she couldn't go back to the great hall with all the Buchanans in there.

This parapet stuck out of the fortress wall six floors up. It looked out at the cliff face behind Icemeet. She couldn't see the battle or the dragons on the other side—or even if the dragons were still there.

Everything sounded quiet over there, but that could be deceiving. The Creightons might be camped right outside the destroyed courtyard to make sure no one went in or out.

What was she doing up here, anyway? Whatever brought her to this fortress seemed so far away from the mission that Liam had sent her here to accomplish. She had lost her mission, her friends, and all sense of where she was or what she was doing or even *who* she was.

She seemed to have gotten swept up in this war. Now she was here in the heart of Clan Buchanan.

Footsteps brought her back to reality and she stiffened when Reid walked out onto the parapet. "There ye are, lass. I've been searching high and low for ye."

"Don't ask me to go back down there. I'm not going back."

"No one said ought about ye going back. What's amiss, anyway? Ye conducted yerself so well down there."

She spun around and stared at him. "I did not!"

"Och, lassie! They're all down there wondering why ye didnae stick around for them to congratulate ye. They're delighted. We all are."

She glanced up into his pale blue eyes and immediately looked away. "I don't want anyone to be delighted with me. I forfeited the match."

"Not a bit of it, lass." He stepped up to the parapet and looked over. "Ye were magnificent. They're all saying so. Ye should hear Colton down there. None of the lads could land so many blows on Jaimee. She winnae live that fight down in a hurry."

She couldn't hold his gaze. "I don't want to talk about it."

"What do ye want to talk about, then?"

Her head snapped around without her meaning to. She wound up gazing into his eyes again. She tried to resist his pull on her, but it had been becoming more and more impossible ever since she and Echo came through the portal.

Betty felt drawn to Reid from the beginning. She found it so easy to talk to him. Nearly everything they did they wound up doing together.

She felt herself getting closer to him—too close. She couldn't let that happen. She would leave this time period and go back to the present. She couldn't start something with a man she barely knew three hundred years in the past.

What would she go back to? She couldn't go back to Ironforge—not with only three members of the Last Division remaining. She didn't even know where Echo was or if Echo was still alive.

Betty had nothing left—nothing but Reid—but she couldn't think that way.

Jaimee was still here, but for how long? Jaimee wouldn't leave the Buchanans. The last shred of doubt about that evaporated when she saw how involved Jaimee was in this Clan's fate and future.

"Listen to me, lassie." Reid's voice murmured in her ear like the subtle voice of her own thoughts. "If ye dinnae fancy taking part in this war, I can arrange with Colton to send you through to Stronghold. Ye can stay there until we find Liam to send ye back to yer own world."

"What?!" she cried. "No! I want to. That's what I'm here for. I don't want to leave! Are you crazy?"

He only shrugged. "I'm going back down to the hall to train with the lads and to help Colton and Jaimee rearm for the new moon assault. Ye can step aside. No one will think less of ye—not after that match. The choice is all yers.... or ye can come with me. No one will ask ye to do ought ye dinnae want to. Ye're good enough as ye are. Ye dinnae need to train."

She made a face. "Tell Jaimee that."

"I dinnae have to tell her. Ye've just now told her yer own self."

She cringed. She didn't want anyone complimenting her on running away from a fair fight. She especially didn't want Reid complimenting her, now that she realized how much it meant to her.

She couldn't pin so much of her happiness and excitement on winning his good opinion. He was just a guy—a nice guy, a stunningly handsome man, a kind and attentive and courteous guy....

She tried to shake those thoughts out of her head, but his presence at her side sent her spiraling into confusion. What the hell was she doing here, anyway?

"Ye cannae stay out here, lassie," he almost whispered. "It isnae safe. If ye dinnae want to see the others, I can show ye a place ye can stay on yer own until ye're ready to come out."

She shuddered. "No. I want to do this. I have to do this."

He frowned down at her like he wanted to ask if she was sure about this. She couldn't stand that. She shouldn't have come up here to feel sorry for herself. She should have handled this better.

Why did the Buchanans disturb her so much? She couldn't put her finger on it.

"Lassie...." he began again. "I ken ye dinnae understand our ways...."

"It isn't that. It's just...." She looked over her shoulder, but there was nothing there. "I've never done that in such a public way. No one has ever stood around and cheered like that."

He burst out laughing. "It takes some getting used to. I'll give ye that."

"You?! You couldn't have to get used to that. You're all used to it."

"We arenae born used to it, lassie. We grow up watching from the sidelines. Even after years when we begin doing it ourselves, it doesnae start that way." He jerked his chin toward the doorway leading back into Icemeet. "Och, no! I dinnae think so."

"How does it happen?"

"Lads start sparring with their friends when they're young, but they dinnae do it in crowds. We do it in twos and threes here and there—never like *that*. I tell ye, lassie, it took me many years to get up the nerve to go in for me first match."

She blinked at him. "That's amazing!"

"It wasnae amazing at all, I can tell ye. It was humiliating."

She laughed in spite of herself. She couldn't help it. She never felt such relief. "Wow. I had no idea."

"The lads are all delighted with yer match, lass. Take me word on it. Jaimee can skin any man down there with the possible exception of Colton. Ye did very well."

"Yeah." She passed her hand across her forehead and then laughed nervously. "I kind of amazed myself by holding her off the way I did."

He chuckled. "Ye see? Ye can hold yer own." He nodded toward the door. "Come downstairs. Ye dinnae have to do ought, but I cannae leave ye here. Colton would have me head on a dish."

She beamed up at him. "Thank you for telling me. You really made me feel better."

"Of course, lassie. If ye need me, I'm just here."

He turned away and led her inside, but his last words burned her guts. *If ye need me, I'm just here.*

She followed him back inside and they returned to the great hall. The noise got louder as they got nearer, but it didn't rise to a thunderous tumult the way it did before.

He grinned at her and shot forward to stride into the hall. She suffered another squirm of adrenaline when she saw that grin. He was excited. He loved this. He was in his element in ways she'd never seen him before.

He never let his inhibitions weaken in the forest. This was the first time she'd seen him totally unguarded.

She crept closer to the threshold and halted there. She couldn't go any further.

He went over to one of three large squares that had formed while she was gone. Forty men assembled in each square with two men training in each one. They wrestled as men in one square, as cats in the second, and they practiced with their weapons in the third square.

Betty froze and her blood ran cold when Jaimee stepped into the second square. She was still barefoot with her sleeves rolled up and a young Highlander stepped out to meet her.

He couldn't have been more than seventeen, but he and Jaimee smirked at each other like they had known each other all their lives.

The boy wore no shirt, no socks, and no shoes like all his Clansmen. As soon as he stepped out, he pulled his tartan down to his waist and tucked it into his belt. He faced Jaimee bare-chested, but no one seemed to care.

Betty stared in stomach-turning horror as the young man shifted. He left the ground in a kind of tornado of fur and claws. One minute, he stood there as a young man where everyone could see him.

The next minute, he plastered himself to Jaimee's head with all four limbs wrapped around her skull. He hit her so hard and so fast that she crashed down on the ground fighting to tear the cat off.

The tiger screeched in a spine-chilling yowl that set Betty's hair on end. Jaimee whipped back and forth on the floor trying everything to dislodge the cat, but she still couldn't manage it.

The cat twisted his back end around, released one hind foot, and kicked out. He ripped Jaimee's shirt down the sleeve and left a bloody gash all the way to the wrist.

She bellowed in fury, floundered onto her knees, and finally headbutted the cat into the floor. Betty heard someone yelling, "Hang onto her, Fletcher!" That must be the boy's name. Fletcher Buchanan.

Jaimee finally slammed her own head into the floor hard enough to dislodge him, but he immediately launched himself at her again. She held him at arm's length with the cat whipping back and forth in her hands.

He broke free and made another bloodthirsty lunge for her face. She coiled her arms and hurled him across the floor. He landed on his feet across the square with his Clansmen hooting and whistling as loudly as ever.

Jaimee crouched to ready herself again and none too soon. Fletcher rocketed off the floor, soared straight into her, and toppled her, but she didn't give him a chance to latch onto her this time.

She rolled backward on her shoulder and launched him behind her. She put a lot more strength into this throw and he slammed into his Clansmen's shins.

He shot away with a vicious shriek, and when he flew in to attack her, she bolted upright and punched him square in the nose.

The cat didn't have a chance to get his feet under him this time. He smashed down on his back twenty feet away. Jaimee got to her feet first while he was still trying to straighten his legs.

He pushed himself licking blood off his nose. He shifted and ran his wrist across his upper lip, but he didn't try to attack her again.

The Clansmen behind him stepped in, clapped him on the shoulders, and pulled him outward to join their circle. They left Jaimee standing there alone, but not for long.

The Highlanders on her side surrounded her and congratulated her. They had to pull her away to make her stop glaring at Fletcher like she still thought he might come after her.

The next minute, the spell broke and she started laughing. Her comrades put ointment on her arm and the tension dissolved.

Betty couldn't relax, especially not when the next two combatants stepped out of the square. Reid stretched his shoulders and cracked his knuckles. His Clansmen massaged his neck and shook him to prepare him for the coming fight, but he barely heard or felt them.

His eyes flashed in ways Betty was starting to recognize. When he came face to face with an enemy, he became hard and ruthless just like the rest of his Clan.

His challenger stepped out on the other side of the square and the whole crowd erupted when Colton faced off against his brother. The Buchanans in the other two squares broke up to come and watch.

Colton pulled off his tartan and started unbuttoning his spotless jacket while he glared at Reid across the square. Reid smiled and blushed—once. Then he became even colder and more dangerously determined than before.

Colton handed his jacket to someone and then pulled off his shirt. He was much bulkier than Reid and just as chiseled. He looked like a tank and all his civility and refinement evaporated when he took his shirt off.

He kicked away his socks and shoes, put his tartan back on his shoulder, and faced his brother barefoot and bare-chested just like the others. That undefinable wild ferocity seeped from his very pores as he stepped into the ring.

Reid paced back and forth on the other side. He kept shooting menacing glances across the square while Colton limbered up.

Jaimee stood with the rest of the Clansmen yelling at both brothers. Betty couldn't hear a word over the noise. She knit her fingers together in anxious tension and she realized she was shaking.

Colton looked big enough to break Reid in half, but something in Reid's bearing told her that he wouldn't go down easily. He wouldn't face his brother in an open fight if he didn't think he stood a decent chance of winning.

How many times had these men confronted each other? Was one of the boys Reid fought in childhood his own brother? Why would it be any other way? They must have fought dozens of times—maybe even hundreds of times.

Clansmen on both sides jostled the brothers, rubbed their backs and necks, and yelled last-minute instructions into their ears. Reid nodded to someone near him and then both sides pushed the brothers toward each other.

Betty couldn't watch this, but she couldn't tear herself away, either. She said she wanted to fight this war. She was on the Buchanan side, so she had to see what it was really all about.

Neither brother shifted right away. They didn't circle, either. They advanced to within inches of each other and Colton started talking to Reid in a clenched undertone. No one could hear him but Reid.

Reid nodded a few times and then sniffed. Finally, Colton finished and Reid said something back. The two brothers back-stepped twice and then lunged for each other.

Chapter 7

Reid and Colton caught each other grappling, hooking each other's ankles, and trying to punch each other in the face. They blocked each other with such precision that Betty fought the urge to punch and kick, too.

Reid held his own against his brother's bulk. Colton tried more than once to throw his weight against Reid and topple his brother, but Reid proved more flexible and more agile.

He deflected each of these attempts and even managed to turn them to his advantage. Was this what his comrades had been telling him or did Reid already know? If these two brothers had fought each other often, Reid must know all his brother's weaknesses—and vice versa.

They wrestled back and forth for what seemed like hours. Both brothers planted their muscular legs and dug their bare toes into the floor. They leaned into each other marshaling all their strength to unseat each other.

Colton made one more surge to overthrow Reid, and this time, Reid let Colton come. Reid didn't try to resist or deflect Colton's weight. Reid reared back taking Colton with him.

Reid's knees buckled just as though Colton had thrown him, but instead of falling, Reid hurled himself into a backward roll. He didn't guide his brother's weight past himself, either.

Reid grabbed Colton around the shoulders and smashed Colton onto his back with ground-shaking force. The hall descended into another deafening roar with everyone cheering on their favorite.

Betty felt sick and her knees almost buckled completely when Reid shifted. He sprang off the floor just as fast as Fletcher, whirled around, and landed on top of Colton. Reid attacked so fast that he took Colton by surprise.

Colton's eyes popped when he saw the tiger soaring toward his face. Colton shifted in a blink and squirmed out of the way. Reid landed on the floor, and in a split second, two tigers met in a rolling, tumbling, flailing ball of fur and claws.

They cartwhipped sideways so fast that the assembled Highlanders had to scurry out of their path. The square dissolved with the Buchanans following the fight across the hall.

Jaimee moved with the others and yelled as loudly as anyone. Betty didn't have to guess too hard who Jaimee was rooting for.

The two tigers thrashed, slashed, and clawed at each other much faster and much more ferociously than any of the others Betty had seen so far. They scratched, bit, and mauled each other so violently that she didn't see how either brother could survive.

They got so wrapped up with each other that she couldn't tell which brother was which. Each one sank his teeth into his brother multiple times. Blood soaked their fur and they left bloody patches on the floor every time they rolled to a new spot.

She didn't see what caused the end of the fight or even if one brother bested the other. For some reason she didn't recognize, the two tigers separated by flying apart. It looked as though some invisible force yanked them apart and flung them away from each other.

Both tigers landed on opposite sides of the hall. Their fur dripped blood and both were limping. They eyed each other from a distance and one of them sneezed blood out of his nose.

The other flicked a shredded ear...and then they both shifted. They didn't have a chance to get near each other before the assembled Highlanders swarmed them even more enthusiastically. The hall disintegrated into such an uproar that no one even pretended to train anymore. This was nothing but a free-for-all.

Some of Reid's relatives tended to his wounds, but most just pounded him, rumpled his blood-stained hair, and yelled at him. He grinned back at them much more broadly than he should have considering how injured he was.

The other group did the same thing to Colton. These men were supposed to be at war, but no one seemed too concerned about two of their best fighters getting injured on the eve of their most important battle.

The brothers finally worked their way toward each other. They exchanged a few words and then embraced in front of everyone. They clasped each other with genuine affection while their Clansmen smiled at them and patted their arms and backs.

Reid and Colton pushed each other apart and Colton's face pinched when he patted his brother's cheek. They looked into each other's eyes with a deep gaze of obvious affection. What must it be like to feel that way about one's own sibling?

Betty didn't have that with any of her family. Did she make a mistake by staying at Ironforge for so long?

The two brothers finally broke apart. The crowd swallowed Colton and Reid elbowed his way toward the exit where Betty stood quaking.

Reid still limped and he held one arm across his stomach. Blood saturated his tartan and the sticky brown ointment smeared on dozens of gashes covering his chest, arms, back, and neck.

He had been the cat with the shredded ear and blood soaked one half of his head. So much gore surrounded his ear that Betty couldn't even see it. Blood dripped from his hair, but his eyes sparkled with a light she hadn't seen before. He had never looked like this, not even when he laughed.

This gleam wasn't mirth or even happiness. It came from somewhere much deeper. It was more like pure wildness finally let out of its cage, but it left him calm and centered in curious ways. He didn't have to hide his true nature here. Not even those times when she saw him shift in the forest came close to fully embodying his true innermost being.

He hobbled over to her and those eyes, the eyes of untamed primal purity, met hers. "Och, lassie! I've neglected ye. Let's go on with our tour and I'll show ye where ye can spend the night."

"Are you sure you're up to it? You should get those taken care of."

He chuckled. "Aye. I will. Come along. I'll show ye where to go and then I can get cleaned up."

She didn't know what he meant, but anything was better than standing here watching him drip blood on the floor.

She cast one backward glance into the hall before she followed him to the stairs. All the other Buchanans had surrounded Colton. Betty couldn't see Jaimee at all in the throng. None of them seemed all that concerned about Reid's condition. Should Betty do.... something?

He reached the stairs first and paused there to wait for her almost as though she was the one *he* should be taking care of. He didn't really plan to give her a tour now, did he?

He took a long time dragging himself upstairs. He moved more and more slowly and winced a lot more as they got nearer to the top. She was just starting to worry about him when he stepped out on the landing, paused again, and finally sighed.

"Och, lassie!" he panted. "That was a hard fight. I havenae had one like that in a long time."

"So.... who won?"

He bit back laughter. "Let's be diplomatic and say it's an ongoing matter between Colton and me."

"How often have you guys fought like that?"

"Like that? Never. No, never like that. We havenae ever gone as far as that before."

"Good," she murmured. "I hope you won't let it go any further."

He only chuckled. "He doesnae dare."

She studied him. He really was much more relaxed and confident than she'd ever seen him. That fight did something for him. Was it the same for Colton? Maybe these rough, rugged mountain people needed to fight like this. Maybe they needed to test their own strength and tenacity against each other.

He set off down the corridor on the third floor. Several rooms stood open on either side and Betty stole peeks inside. They were all bedrooms and they were all empty.

Reid stopped at a closed door and threw it open. "Ye can stay in here, lass."

She looked in on a beautiful room decorated with heavy, expensive, elaborately carved furniture, luxurious furnishings, a massive canopy bed with heavy velvet curtains, and a breathtaking view across the Boundless.

"What is this?" she asked.

"It's a guest room. Jaimee stayed here when she first arrived. Ye can stay in here. Ye'll be comfortable." He jerked his thumb down the landing. "I'm going down to the barracks where all the single men stay. Colton and Jaimee's room is just over there in case ye need ought. Dinnae hesitate to come and find me if ye need me. That's what I'm here for." He waited and watched her gazing into the room. "Arenae ye happy with the room, lass? I can find ye another if ye...."

"No! It's great. It's too good."

He frowned. "Would ye rather go downstairs with the archers? They'll take ye in if ye prefer."

She turned bright red. "No. That won't be necessary. I'll stay here."

"What's on yer mind, lassie? Arenae ye tired and all?"

"It isn't that." She looked down the corridor toward where he said Jaimee and Colton's room was. Why did it bother her that Jaimee and Colton shared a room? They were married, weren't they?

"If ye dinnae want to talk to me, I'll be off to the barracks. Jaimee will thrash me for getting blood on the floor."

She jolted out of her trance and shook her head. "I'm sorry. I just...I don't know what's wrong with me."

"Perhaps it has some-ought to do with traveling three hundred years back in time, seeing dragons and Highland tigers for the first time, nearly getting burned to a cinder by dragons, and landing in a fortress surrounded by strangers."

She tried to smile at him, but his words wrung her heart. "I don't know where I belong. Jaimee is so close to your people. I don't know if I could ever be that close to you when you're...."

She couldn't say it. She didn't know what the Buchanans were. She knew they were tigers....and that he was a tiger. She just never saw it on display with such unashamed savagery and blatant violence.

The Buchanans being tigers was one thing. This man—this kind, courteous, protective, handsome man—he was a tiger, too. He was a tiger to the bottommost corner of his soul. That fight downstairs proved it.

He was more tiger than man. He vibrated with it. It infiltrated every hair on his head and every lash on his eyes. It was the sum total of his nature.

How could she be this attracted to a man who was so.... inhuman? He looked as appealing as any man she'd ever met, but that on its own didn't explain how she felt about him.

She liked his cat nature when they were out in the forest. She found it charming and fascinating to think that he wasn't human. Now it took on a whole new meaning. He was beyond wild. He was an animal.

He stood there looking at her so intently. What did he see in her? Did he see her as weak and alien because she was human?

She couldn't meet those eyes so she gazed into the guest room, but she still couldn't enter it. She lingered between one decision and another.

She finally heaved a sigh and forced herself to face him. "I guess I'll see you in the morning if the Creightons don't get us first. I hope you feel better." She looked directly into his eyes. Then she could break away and shut the door on all these feelings churning in her soul.

She didn't break away. His eyes held her with a magnetic pull. Without warning, he took a step toward her, cupped her cheek, and kissed her.

She froze hardly daring to breathe. Was he really kissing her? She'd wondered on their journey here if he might be thinking about it. She had almost convinced herself that he would never do it.

Now his lips compressed hers with so much softness that she didn't know what to do. She explored the sensation of her mouth touching his. His warmth flooded her face. Was she kissing him back...or did she just imagine it?

He pulled back and looked her in the eye. "Reid...."

"Dinnae say ought, lassie," he breathed. "Just let me stand here and dream about yer lips."

She blushed and looked down at the floor. "I really like you, but...."

"Dinnae say 'but', lass, and dinnae say whatever ye were about to say after that. Ye like me. That's enough."

"Is it, really? I don't feel attached to your Clan the way Jaimee does, and with the assault coming up, I'll be leaving Icemeet soon anyway."

"I ken all that, lass," he murmured. "Ye arenae telling me ought I dinnae already ken."

"Then you know there can never be anything between us. We could never have a future. I would have to leave sometime....and I know what you're going to say. You're going to say Jaimee did it so I can do it, too."

"I wasnae about to say anything of the kind, lassie," he murmured in a heartbreaking undertone. "Just tell me ye feel the same way without all that."

"Tell you that I feel what way?"

Before she could stop him, he stepped in and kissed her again. This time, he opened his mouth and devoured her tongue and all. He cradled the back of her head and steered her mouth into his.

She felt herself melting, dissolving, sinking under a tide of sensation and emotion. What was he doing to her? She swam in that kiss. She drowned in that kiss. She might die in it.

Her mind reeled so wildly that she almost fell over when he released her. He took his hand off the back of her head and straightened up. He left her dizzy and struggling to drag her eyes into focus.

When she did, she gazed deep into those eyes that seemed to see everything no matter how deeply it might lie buried in her being.

"Ye dinnae have to say it, lass," he breathed. "Ye've given me yer answer."

Chapter 8

Betty shifted her weight from one foot to the other trying to figure out what the heck just happened. Reid kissed her, but that wasn't nearly as confusing as her own response.

She shouldn't have kissed him back, but how could she not? How could she let him believe anything could happen between them when it was so obviously impossible?

He walked away down the landing and headed for the stairs as slowly and painfully as he climbed up them.

She turned to enter the guest room, but when she saw how nice it was, she couldn't go in there. The rest of the Buchanans wouldn't be living like this.... except maybe Colton and Jaimee.

Betty walked off in the opposite direction, only to run into another enormous bank of windows at the end of the corridor. The windows looked out over a different stretch of the mountains that she didn't recognize.

She couldn't stand still. She had to keep moving before all these confused ideas and emotions caught up with her. She went back the way she came. Reid was gone by the time she reached the landing.

The noise coming from the hall wasn't as loud as before. A few guys still sparred in there while others stood around talking, but most had wandered off. Betty secretly felt relieved to see that Jaimee and Colton were gone, too.

Betty didn't want to talk to anyone she knew. She didn't want to think. Where did this whole mission go wrong? Did Liam know when he sent Echo and Betty back in time that the mission had disintegrated into such a chaotic mess?

How in God's name was anyone supposed to put Duncan on the throne? How was he supposed to marry a woman who didn't exist?

Betty left the great hall. She couldn't go into the dining hall, either. No one had cleaned it up since all the maids and servants had evacuated to Stronghold. No one at Stronghold would be living in luxury, either.

She was just thinking about trying to find some out of the way place to curl up for the night when she spotted the apartment where the wounded had been. She had made her way all the way down to the keep without realizing where she was. The apartment would be deserted, too. That would be perfect. No one would ever find her there.

She pushed the door open and froze when she saw Colton and Jaimee inside. They stood aside against one wall—or Colton stood against the wall. He rested his broad back on it and he had his arms around Jaimee.

They smothered each other in kisses and anyone could see how deeply in love with each other they were. She wrapped her arms around his neck and crushed her body against him. He raked his fingernails up her back, gripped the back of her neck, and her hair spilled over both of them while they kissed. Betty could even hear them both breathing heavily.

Colton straightened up and his coal-black eyes smoldered with seething passion when he trailed his fingertips down her cheek to straighten her hair. She let her hand drag across his face and then dove in to kiss him again.

Betty stood rooted to the spot. She had never seen anyone kiss like that—ever. She never would have believed Snowflake would be capable of kissing someone like that.

All at once, Colton's eyes snapped to the door and he looked right at Betty. Then Jaimee followed his gaze and turned around. Both of them stared at her, but not as much as Betty stared at them. Should she run away?

Colton cracked a grin, whispered something to Jaimee, and pushed himself off the wall. He squeezed Jaimee's hand, strode to the door, and pulled it the rest of the way open. He ducked around Betty, murmured, "Lassie," and walked away.

Betty couldn't speak. She couldn't turn away. Her insides writhed with a combination of shame and terror. Would Jaimee do something awful to her for walking in on them? How could Betty know that they were down here doing *that*?

Run away. Run away now. Betty couldn't move. Jaimee straightened up, shook her hair out of her eyes, and stalked over to Betty. Jaimee squared her shoulders with more than enough of her old military stiffness. "I'm sorry you had to see that. We came down here because we thought no one else would come down here. We obviously made a mistake."

"I...uh...." Betty looked over her shoulder at nothing. "Don't you guys have a room upstairs?"

Jaimee burst out laughing. "Of course we do...and everyone in Icemeet knows that. If anyone wants to find us, that's exactly where they go to look for us. Hence...." She waved at the apartment, which was deserted. "This is the first time we've been alone in weeks."

"I'm really sorry. I'm a tool." Betty shuffled her feet some more. "I'll just go back upstairs...."

"Actually, I'm glad you're here. I want to talk to you."

Betty froze. "Am I in trouble, Lieutenant?"

Jaimee cracked another grin and then got serious. "Not like that. I'm not your lieutenant, but I am Colton's wife, which means Reid is my brother-in-law."

Betty's jaw dropped. "Reid! What about him?"

"Oh, come on, Betty! Do you think I'm blind? Anyone can see what's going on between you two."

"Is that why you've been so mad at me—because of Reid?"

Jaimee pursed her lips and her grin vanished. "I haven't been mad at you. I've been worried about you....and Reid."

"Why would you be worried about *me*? We're safe in here...for now, at least."

"The Highland tigers of Clan Buchanan mate for life. Did you know that?"

Betty opened her mouth and shut it again trying to figure out what this was all about. "Uh...yeah. I know."

"Then you know that, if you ever do it with Reid, you'll be mated for life. *You* might be able to go back to Ironforge and the modern era and everything you had back home, but he wouldn't. He would never be able to move on. His life would be over. He would never be able to be happy or at peace and he would never be able to get with anyone else as long as you're still alive. He might not even be able to if you *weren't* alive. Do you understand all that?"

Betty gulped. She did know that, but she hadn't given herself a chance to grasp the full import of it until now.

This was just another reason nothing could ever happen between her and Reid. She squared her shoulders and faced Jaimee. "Don't worry. Nothing is going on between me and Reid."

"Are you sure about that? I might not have known these guys for very long, but I know him well enough to know that *he* thinks something is going on between you. I would bet any amount of money on it. Are you sure you made it absolutely clear to him that you didn't want to take it any further?"

Betty squirmed. Jaimee's cross-examination left her more uncertain than before. "Yeah. I told him just now."

Jaimee nodded at something past Betty's shoulder. "Come with me for a minute. I want to show you something."

She swiveled around Betty, stepped out into the corridor, and waited for Betty to join her. "Where are we going?" Betty asked once they started walking.

"You'll see. I'm really glad you're here. Icemeet gets lonely when there's only one of me around." Jaimee shot Betty another quick grin. "You really made an impression on the guys earlier."

"Not really," Betty muttered. "I forfeited our match."

"Things don't work that way here. The fights never go all the way or someone would get killed. They almost always end with one or both walking away or just stopping." Jaimee bestowed the warmest smile on Betty that Betty could ever remember from her commanding officer. "You never fought like that at Ironforge. You really put your all into it. I was really worried."

"You—worried?" Betty snorted. "You're messing with me."

"You would have had me if you hadn't walked away. You should stop doubting yourself."

Betty didn't answer. She fell back into dark thoughts. She didn't see where Jaimee was leading her until Jaimee left the stairs and stepped out onto the parapet where Betty had been just a little while ago.

"What are we doing here?" Betty asked. "Reid said it wasn't safe to be outside."

"It isn't, but we aren't going to stay long. I brought you here because I want to show you something."

"What is it?"

Jaimee pointed up at the mountain cliffs nearby. "That."

Betty strained her eyes to see. The sun was going down and delicate colored light beamed from the clouds racing across the darkening sky.

A flutter of movement drew her gaze to something high on the mountain's jagged shoulder. Betty looked more closely and saw a woman standing up there. She wore a long dress that flapped in the wind. That movement had caught Betty's attention in the first place.

The wind blew the woman's long auburn hair back from her chiseled face. She gazed across the landscape toward Kald and the dusky light made her look indescribably sad.

"What is she doing up there?" Betty whispered. "She can't stay up there! If it isn't safe for us, it can't be safe for her." Betty glanced toward the estuary. "Any of the Creightons could see her." Betty frowned looking more closely at the woman's features. She looked familiar. "She's a Buchanan, isn't she?"

"That's Edeena Buchanan. She's Colton's sister—Reid and Duncan's sister."

"What is she doing there? Why isn't she inside? She should be at Stronghold, shouldn't she?"

"She isn't going anywhere. She's looking for Liam."

"Liam!" Betty exclaimed. "You mean...Liam Barnett—the same Liam Barnett who...."

Jaimee nodded. "The very same. He and Lily captured Edeena on their first trip to Kald. Liam cast a mate-bonding spell on Edeena to get her to give them information ....and to stop her from killing them both. He didn't know at the time that it would be permanent."

"So.... they're mated for life? He can't undo it?"

"He's tried several times. In fact, he says the spell should have worn off by now. He didn't know when he did it that the tigers mate for life. Now the spell is gone and the bond is still there. Liam isn't here and she can't stop thinking about him. She spends all her time searching for him or up on those rocks waiting for him to come back. She'll probably stay there forever unless he does come back for some reason, but I don't think he will."

Betty's shoulders slumped. "Oh. I understand."

"That's what will happen to Reid if you let him bond with you and then you walk away. You only just met him. I've known him longer than you have and I know these Buchanans about as well as anyone from outside their Clan can ever know them. I love Reid like he was my own brother. I'm begging you, as your friend and as his sister-in-law.... if you aren't serious enough to stay here with him for life, just leave him alone. It's the kindest thing you can do for him."

Chapter 9

Reid stamped his foot on the wooden floor. "How's the leg now, laddie?" Fergus asked.

"It's right as rain. Thanks."

Fergus jutted his chin at Reid's tartan. "Ye'll want to change out of that."

Reid looked down at his tartan. It was in a sorry state, stained with blood and mud, and torn in more places than one, but that was nothing compared to how *he* looked.

The ointment had killed the pain of his many cuts and scratches. It had also repaired most of the damage to his leg and arm. He felt good enough, but he looked like he just crawled out of the sewer.

How had he been walking around with Betty like this? No wonder she pushed him away.

He nodded, took a clean tartan out of the barracks cupboard, and went into the kitchen. It was empty. All the cooks, maids, and servants were gone, but he didn't care about that.

He went into the stable yard behind the kitchen. It wasn't a stable since the Buchanans didn't have horses, but the Clan had called it that for as long as Reid could remember.

He went to the water pump, stripped off everything, and started pumping. He scrubbed every inch of himself, washed his hair, and dried himself on a towel from the kitchen before he buckled on his clean kilt.

He went back to the barracks and opened another cupboard. No one had opened it since his father's funeral. He took out a clean shirt, a black jacket with gold buttons, a pair of clean socks, and a pair of shoes.

"What in the name of thunder are ye doing?" Fergus snapped when Reid pulled on the shirt.

"I'm getting dressed as ye say." Reid tucked his shirt into his belt, buttoned up the jacket, and arranged his tartan back on his shoulder before he sat down to put on his socks and shoes. He should have done it the other way around, but he would do it better next time.

"What in God's name is the matter with ye?" Fergus gasped when Reid straightened up and started tidying his hair.

"A man has got to grow up someday, lad." Reid tugged his jacket into place and checked every detail of his appearance. He walked out of the guard room and left Fergus sitting there with his mouth open.

Reid didn't care what his Clansmen thought about his appearance. He needed to clean himself up before Betty saw him again.

He went to the dining hall. He didn't know what he would do when he got there, but he needed to do something to occupy himself. He couldn't sleep.

He needed to think about Betty. He was more convinced than ever that she was the one. She was the woman he would mate with and eventually marry. She might not be ready, but he sure was.

That kiss they shared outside her room left him in no doubt that she felt the same way he did. She only just arrived at Icemeet today. She needed time.

He didn't want to take time. He wanted to storm up to her room right now and seal the bond with her. Every minute before that happened tormented him with agony and anticipation. He wouldn't feel this way if she wasn't his destined mate, the other half of his soul.

He had an inkling when he first met her in the forest, but now he was sure. Now he knew what Colton went through when he first met Jaimee. So many couples had gotten together in Reid's life and they all followed the same pattern.

Most of them knew within seconds of meeting that the other person was their destined mate. These women from the future were different only because they were fully human. They didn't understand about mate-bonding, but they would learn. Jaimee learned and now Betty would learn.

Reid tried to remember how long it had taken for Jaimee and Colton to finally figure it out—or for Jaimee to figure it out.

Reid considered going to find Colton, but then Reid passed the dining hall. He didn't expect to see anyone in there, but he did see a whole bunch of food, plates, crumbs, and hastily stripped bones lying all over the tables.

No one else would come along and clean it up, so he started. He gathered all the plates and carried them to the kitchen. Someone would have to clean them all, now that the cooks weren't around to do it.

It was too late at night to do them now. Reid would start tomorrow if the Creightons didn't attack first.

He returned to the hall and was just collecting the rest of the bread when Betty marched in.

She crossed the threshold before she saw him and froze. She stared at him in shock, opened her mouth, and then her eyes traced down to his clothes. "Um...."

"That bad, lass?" Reid teased.

She blinked and then blushed. "Tell me you didn't do that for me."

"Would it be so bad if I did?"

"I thought I told you...." She wouldn't look at him and her cheeks flamed.

"Aye. Ye told me.... but dinnae ye worry yer head on it. I didnae dress this way for ye."

"You didn't?" His stomach tightened when her face fell. She cared!

"Och, no!" he exclaimed. "I dressed this way to clean the hall. I couldnae do it the way I was."

She gaped at him and then burst into musical laughter. Her eyes screwed up at the corners when she smiled and she picked up a platter with some bones on it. "Do you want some help?"

"Ye dinnae need to do that, lassie. Ye're our honored guest."

"Do you send all your honored guests out to die on the battlefield? I'm here to fight with your Clan. All your people have been evacuated and I just ate this food. I think I can help you clean up."

He didn't know what to say so he didn't say anything. She tipped the bones onto another meat platter and then added all the others to the same dish. She combined them and stacked the empty platters together with the bones on top.

"Where do I take this?" she asked.

"I'll show ye."

He led her into the kitchen. She put the stack of empty platters and scraped bones on the table. It was the only place left to put it.

She nodded to the dishes. "I could get started washing those."

"Not tonight, lass. We can do it tomorrow."

"Really. I don't mind," she insisted.

"The fire's gone out and it would take hours to heat the water. Ye're up too late as it is. I couldnae ask ye to do that."

She blinked at the dying embers, the big empty cauldron hanging on its hook, and then at the worktables all around the kitchen. "Oh. I see."

"Ye see what?"

"Where I come from, we have.... Never mind. It's complicated."

"Explain it to me. I want to understand all about yer world."

She blushed and flapped her hands. Then she made a face. "It would take me years to explain ALL about it, but where I come from, we have pipes that bring hot water into the kitchen. We have....um.... we have built-in heaters that heat the water. We don't have to heat it over a fire."

He furrowed his brow at her. "How is that possible, lassie?"

"It's complicated. Just.... you don't want to know about my world. Believe me."

"I do." He sat down at the kitchen table, rested his elbow on it, and looked up at her. "Tell me more."

She laughed nervously and blushed even darker. "I can't. You think it would take hours to wash those dishes? It would take me years to tell you even a small part and you still wouldn't understand it. It's complicated. You wouldn't be able to understand it."

"Try me." He squared his shoulders. "Now ye've brought me a challenge. I cannae let it pass."

She burst out laughing again. God, she was so beautiful! "You want a challenge? Okay. Try this. We have vehicles that fly high up in the sky and can travel around the world in hours."

He blinked. He wasn't sure he had heard her properly.

"We have machines that allow people on opposite sides of the world to talk to each other and send messages that travel instantaneously to the other side of the world. Are you with me so far?"

He blinked again. He wasn't hearing this.

She laughed at his reaction. "Okay. Forget the challenge. Come on. Let's get the rest of the dishes."

She left the kitchen while he still sat there stunned. Vehicles that could fly around the world in hours? Machines that allowed people to talk across the world? Was she mad?

She couldn't be. He only had to ask Jaimee to confirm Betty's story. Betty must know that. She wouldn't blatantly lie if the lie could be so easily disproven.

He got up and went back into the dining hall. She had finished collecting the last dishes. Now she was brushing all the crumbs into a pile with a rag she had found somewhere.

"Lassie...." he began. "Are ye fooling with me?"

She didn't laugh anymore and she wouldn't look at him. "I wouldn't do that. You wanted to know so I told you. Just forget it, okay? What my world is like doesn't matter. We have more important things to worry about here."

He finally snapped out of it long enough to realize that she was almost finished collecting the crumbs. He went back to the kitchen and came back with the broom. He helped her clear the tables and the floor. Then he dumped everything out in the stable yard.

He put the broom away, and when he returned, he found her waiting for him outside the kitchen. "Look. I'm sorry if I made you uncomfortable. I shouldn't have told you about my world."

"Not a bit of it, lass," he countered. "I asked ye. I insisted."

"Well, let's just call it a day. I'm going to bed. I'll see you tomorrow. Thank you for bringing me here. I really appreciate it."

She started to walk away. "Lassie!" he called after her.

She turned around and her face shone with that pearlescent light of hers. "Yeah?"

"How would ye like me to bring *ye* a challenge?"

Now it was her turn to blink. "What do you mean?"

"Come back to the hall."

"What do you mean?" Her eyes darted into the dining hall that they just cleaned. "We're already here."

"The great hall, lass." He nodded behind him.

He went over to the great hall, strode in, and started unbuttoning his jacket.

She tiptoed to the threshold, but she didn't come inside. "What are you doing?"

"Spar with me, lass. Ye've sparred with Jaimee and ye've seen the rest of us doing it. Come on. I challenge ye."

"You.... want to spar with *me*?" She snorted and looked over her shoulder toward the stairs. "Haven't you been injured enough today?"

He laughed out loud. She made him so happy. "Apparently not. Come along. We've never sparred—just ye and me."

Her eyes widened. "You're serious!"

"Aye." He pulled off his jacket and then his shirt.

He got another thrill when her eyes ranged over his chest. Cuts and scratches criss-crossed his body, but she wasn't looking at that.

She was taller than Echo by several inches but not as tall as Jaimee. Betty was curvier than Jaimee but not as curvy as Echo. She was also more muscular than either of them.

She stood back in the doorway and watched him kick off his shoes and pull off his socks. He finally straightened up in front of her wearing only his kilt and tartan. "Well? Are ye coming or not? Are ye really going to back down on a challenge?"

"How do I know you won't shift in the middle of the fight?"

"Och, I plan to, lassie! If ye're to take part in this war, ye'd best get used to it."

Chapter 10

Betty inched her way into the great hall. Reid didn't smirk anymore. She couldn't remember now if he ever did.

He sidestepped to give her space. Was she really going to do this? Was she going to fight one of those tigers? She'd seen enough to know what to expect and she wasn't looking forward to it.

The worst part was that Reid was right. She couldn't back down from a challenge. He really had her number.

She circled him measuring him down to the inch. She would have hesitated to engage with him even as a man. He was bigger, heavier, and stronger, but that wasn't the most intimidating part of this.

A mixture of excitement, fear, and shame struggled for control of her feelings. Should she walk away from touching a man—from getting physically intimate with a man—with him?

He wouldn't be a man. He would be one of those deadly cats. She'd seen so many people get injured fighting them. She didn't want that to happen to her.

He was right about another thing, though. She chose to get involved in this war. She could have stepped aside, but she chose to stay.

She couldn't go another day without facing her fear. Jaimee fought the Highland tigers. Elliot did it. All the Buchanans did it.

Now it was her turn. She didn't take off her shoes the way Jaimee did. Betty would face this in her usual way. Changing anything now would only court disaster.

She confronted him and they both deepened their stance. She couldn't know the moment when he would shift. She just had to take it as it came. At least she'd seen Jaimee fighting Fletcher so Betty wasn't completely in the dark.

The trick was to prevent Reid from latching on....and then blows. She had to land as many blows as possible while holding him off so his claws wouldn't latch. He could only hurt her if his claws and teeth got within range.

They both circled to the left, but he still didn't shift. He waited for her to make the first move. Her nerves threatened to snap if he didn't do something. He was messing with her head.

She rushed him and feinted. He swept his arms at her head, but when she dodged out of his reach, he stayed where he was. He didn't follow up.

She couldn't wait any longer or she would lose her nerve to go through with this. She had to go on the offensive.

She feinted again and he did the same thing. He tried to grab her and she dove under his arms. She landed a crushing sucker punch to his kidneys and then somersaulted past him onto the floor.

She rolled past his leg, twisted around, and caught his ankle. She toppled him and he fell right into her trap by shifting. He was too big and too heavy in his human form for him to do much. If he hadn't shifted and stayed human, he would have beaten her for certain.

The cat exploded out of him and spun around to pounce on her. He could move so much faster than she could, but that only played into her hands.

The instant she saw him shift, her adrenaline spiked off the charts. This wasn't a man. This wasn't the nice, friendly guy she'd spent so much time with in the forest.

This was a demon straight out of Hell. She had to kill him rather than let him get near her.

She snatched the cat out of thin air, swung him by his leg, and slammed him down on the floor with all her strength. He gave a piercing yowl that set every nerve on end.

He reacted instantly by contorting back in her direction, but she still held onto his leg. She locked her elbow to hold him away from her face and body.

Her brain switched into battle mode and she forgot all about him being a man. She had to kill this creature. She thought fast and remembered Jaimee hitting her own head against the floor.

She seized the cat's fur with her other hand to consolidate her grip on him. He writhed and yanked and hissed and clawed at her wrist. He fought back so ferociously that she had to strain every muscle just to keep her hold on him.

He jerked back and forth trying to fight his way nearer. She dropped on her knees and pounded his body on the floor again and again, but his body only seemed to bounce under the impact. His bones flexed with every strike.

He screeched louder and that sound triggered her into a panic. She felt her fingers weakening. She had to do something.

She glanced around and that moment of inattention gave him all the time he needed to break her grip. He gave an almighty twist, tore himself free, and hit the ground at her feet.

She dove for him, but he was too fast. He skidded between her ankles and sprang off the floor onto her back.

All his claws dug into her clothes and stabbed her in a dozen places. He kicked and clawed climbing up her shirt toward her head.

She spun this way trying to reach him and dislodge him, but he stuck tight. She had to do something drastic.

She gave two more hard jerks to either side, but when that didn't work, she exploded out of herself. She jumped into the air, arched backward, and body-slammed him onto the floor.

He grunted under her weight and another eruption of adrenaline carried her through the next part of her move. She contorted onto her side, seized his hind leg again, and gave him a massive heave.

She ripped him out from under her and flung him away with all her strength. Desperation and panic clouded her judgment so much that she threw him much harder than she intended.

He struck the far wall and hit the floor. He didn't have time to get his feet under him and he sprawled on his side. He wriggled to his feet in a split second and turned to find her standing up.

She stared into his haunting yellow eyes....and stopped. Was this monster really Reid? Would she ever be able to look at him the same way again? How could she kiss this fiend? How could she even think about liking him? What on earth was wrong with her?

She whirled away and charged out of the hall. She didn't even wait long enough to see him shift. She had to get as far away from him as she could before she did something really bad—like maybe kill him. She *would* kill him if she stayed in the same room with him for a second longer.

She went up to the guest room, shut herself in, and collapsed on the bed panting hard. What the hell just happened? She fought one of those cats. Did she win? Did *he* win because she walked away?

Jaimee said these fights usually ended when someone walked away first. The Buchanans did it that way so no one would get killed. Wasn't that what Betty did?

She couldn't decipher her own feelings. Her heart hammered a mile a minute and her palms sweated. She had to calm down. She had to think, but her eyes kept racing around the room searching for anything that might come after her.

How could she stay in this fortress with dozens of those cats? Jaimee was the only other human being here. Betty couldn't go to Stronghold, either. The place would be absolutely crawling with Buchanans. What in God's name had she gotten herself into?

One thing she knew. She would never get close to Reid Buchanan again. She would never kiss him and she sure as heck would never let him touch her. She would avoid him like the plague. When this was all over, she would hightail it back to Ironforge where she never had to see him or any of his Clansmen ever again.

Chapter 11

B etty glanced out the high window at the mountains towering over Icemeet. A thin sliver of a moon hung over the tallest peak. "I still can't believe we're doing this tomorrow."

"I can't, either." Jaimee picked up a saber, checked the blade, and set it down on one of the many piles she had been sorting. "I sure hope someone is out there helping us or we're finished."

"We're finished either way." Betty sat down and picked up the saber that Jaimee just checked. Betty started running a honing stone down the blade to sharpen it. "Are you sure the Creightons can't get through to Stronghold if anything happens to us?"

"The dragons have already destroyed the only public entrance. The Creightons won't know we evacuated at all unless they find another way to get inside the fortress."

"Unless the Laird uses magic, you mean," Betty corrected.

"We have wizards, too. They'll stop the Laird from using magic against Stronghold. Besides, it's too far up in the mountains for the Creighton army to mount any kind of assault. The people at Stronghold will be fine. We're the ones in danger."

"Are you sure about that?" Betty asked. "It seems like a mighty big risk to take."

"The Buchanans have fallen back to Stronghold for centuries. The Creightons have never been able to take it before."

Betty didn't answer and concentrated on her sharpening. She had been getting progressively more nervous as the new moon approached. Now only tonight remained. The Buchanan fighting force would assault the beach and invade Kald tomorrow morning—if they made it that far.

Jaimee put the last saber on the pile to be sharpened and she loaded the old, broken weapons into her arms. "I'm taking these downstairs. I'll be back."

Betty tried to make her voice deep and booming while she affected a thick Austrian accent. "I'll be back!"

Jaimee laughed. "We could use a few terminators about now, couldn't we?"

She left and Betty chuckled to herself. At least someone around here understood corny jokes like that from the modern era. The Buchanans would think she was crazy if she said that to anyone else.

She went on with the sharpening and then Jaimee came back to help her. Colton showed up an hour later. "How're the numbers looking, lassies?"

"We have plenty of weapons," Jaimee told him, "more than we can reasonably carry. We should send these through to Stronghold. They won't do anyone any good here."

"We cannae do that now. There isnae time. We'll stow them here for the next round. Put them in Father's apartment. It's deep enough in the mountain that the weapons will still be there when we come back."

"I'll do it. I need to move around anyway." Betty got to her feet and started collecting the rest of the blades that she and Jaimee had already finished. "My feet are falling asleep."

She headed out of the room and Jaimee called after her, "I wish I could."

Betty chuckled and took her pile of weapons down to Neill Buchanan's old apartment. In the few days she had been inside Icemeet, she had learned her way around and a few details about who lived where.

This apartment was deeper inside the fortress than any other living area. It would be the first place the Buchanans returned to when they came back from Stronghold—if they ever came back.

She put the weapons in a corner with the few scanty supplies the defenders still had. The evacuees had taken almost everything else. The defenders had been living on very little food since then and no other comforts.

She went back out to the great hall, only to find it empty. Jaimee and Colton were gone. Ewan, Fergus, and Fletcher had been working with Boyd to revive a few broken siege machines. They had already been broken and on the ground when Elliot destroyed all the Clan's other defenses.

Now even the men were gone. Betty looked everywhere, but she couldn't find anyone. Where did they go?

She wasn't sure what to do until she heard banging in the kitchen. She stuck her head in. The noise was definitely coming from here, but she still didn't see anything. This was really odd.

She followed the sound to a huge pantry between the kitchen and the stable yard. She went into the kitchen and approached the pantry.

She stopped dead in her tracks when she saw Reid in there. He wore his usual shirt, jacket, socks, and shoes. He wore them all the time now and he kept his hair neat all the time, too. He looked so different from the disheveled wild man she met in the forest, but none of his friends or relatives mentioned it.

He was in the process of organizing a bunch of items on the pantry shelves, pulling out pots and pans, stacking them on the floor, and moving them from one pile to another. He looked up when Betty walked in and his face went through a rapid series of expressions one right after the other.

"Ye've been avoiding me, lassie."

She realized a fraction of a second too late that her own face had been going through a similar flurry of twitches while she tried to figure out which would be the most appropriate expression to show him at this moment.

Then she compressed her lips in annoyance, more at herself for getting flustered than at anything else. "Of course I've been avoiding you. Can you blame me after what happened?"

He straightened up and took a few steps forward. "What happened?"

She instinctively drew back to keep more space between herself and him. She didn't want him getting too close.

He pulled up short and raised his eyebrows. "Are ye scared of me, lass? Is that it? Did fighting me as a tiger scare you that much? I wouldnae have done it if I had kenned it would do that. I didnae mean to scare ye. I only meant...."

"I wasn't scared," she blurted out. "I mean...."

She passed her hand across her eyes and shuddered involuntarily. She shouldn't be getting this unnerved by being near him.

"If I scared ye, lassie, I didnae mean to." He took another step, and this time, she managed to stay where she was.

"You didn't scare me. I mean...." She heard herself babbling. "You *did* scare me, but.... well, I scared myself more than anything. It's no big deal...."

He lowered his voice to nothing. "I'm sorry about the other bit as well, lass. I cannae stop thinking about ye. I cannae help but feel that ye're me own mate..."

"I'm not, okay?" Did she scream those words or did she just feel like it? She fought her voice under control. "Look. I'm really sorry, but I can't let anything happen between us. I really like you and I don't want to hurt you, but I can't stay here."

"Is it this Last Division all ye lasses belong to? Is that it?"

She gulped. She couldn't even fall back on that excuse to get her out of this. "I wish I could say it was."

"What is it, then? Tell me the truth. I need to ken."

He halted a few feet away from the threshold where she stood. No one could say he was threatening her, but the energy radiating off him burned her skin.... or did she just imagine that, too?

It pounded into her very being. It blasted past her skin into the deepest parts of her. It kept her tense and aching for.... something.

He stood there waiting for her to speak. The longer the silence went on, the stronger that feeling got—that feeling that he was burning her with his unstoppable presence.

He took one last step, but she couldn't move. He held her spellbound. How?

"Ye feel the same as me. Is that it?" He barely whispered. "Ye feel this. Say ye do."

Those words slashed at her body and eyes and mind. She couldn't get them out of her head no matter how hard she pushed them away.

She wasn't scared of him. She might have been triggered by fear during their fight, but not since. That wasn't why she had been avoiding him.

She couldn't stand this, but not because she wanted to get away from him. Every shred of rational brainpower she still had commanded her to run from him, to get as far away from him as she could before she did something.... something she couldn't go back on.

She couldn't look at him. That would be too much. She didn't know what would happen or even who she would be if she looked at him, but she couldn't leave, either. This power held her in place.

"Lassie...." he breathed and his hand appeared on the side of her face.

He tipped her head up and she plunged body and soul into his eyes. She drowned in those eyes. She drowned in the feeling that she couldn't break away even if she tried. She didn't want to try. She wanted to die in that bottomless tide of meaning too deep to even understand.

Irresistible gravity pulled their mouths together, and before she knew what she was doing, she succumbed to the undertow melting her mind and heart into him. Their faces merged into a seamless lava flow of heat and overwhelming passion. Then their brains merged and she understood everything there was to know about him.

He was right. They were made for each other. She didn't understand how. She kept telling herself it couldn't be.

Her body and heart and being understood at a deeper level. They understood in the bottommost roots of existence where being didn't exist anymore.

Her body melted into his. His arms surrounded her and her arms laced around his neck. She couldn't survive any distance between them. She had to go into him and beyond him to something bigger and still more powerful.

He backstepped into the pantry pulling her out of sight of the kitchen. She saw what he was trying to do. Her rational mind told her to stop this before it went too far. She couldn't do this, but she found it impossible to stop herself.

He bumped into one of the shelves, pivoted around, and crushed her against them. His weight compressed all the air out of her lungs and she gasped in ecstasy. She never experienced the volcanic rising madness of needing anything as badly as she needed him.

Her body exploded in a frenzy, but she needed something so much stronger and so much bigger than just relief from the pressure. Only one thing would satisfy this longing. She needed all of him and she needed to know that he had all of her.

How did this happen? How did coming to Icemeet change so many things for her?

He flexed his knees and drilled his hard body up into her. She felt him trying to drive her legs apart and her lust spiked off the charts. Her whole body craved him.

He tore off her mouth with a cruel, ripping bite. He grabbed her by the chin and steered her lips to his with rough, commanding force. He demanded that she respond, and when he pushed her back against her will, his features smoldered with barely suppressed fury.

Those eyes locked her in place once and for all. Was she really going to do this?

He jammed his hips into her even harder and sweet, aching need scorched her insides. He directed her to respond with the slightest movement.

"Now tell me, lassie," he growled through his teeth. "Tell me why ye've avoided me these past few days. Dinnae tell me ye really mean to go back home and leave this."

He gave her one more pointed shove. Her spine and shoulders dug into the shelves. It hurt in the most delicious way. Could she really do it *here*—like a sex-crazed teenager? That thought only made her more excited.

He stiffened and frowned even more deeply. "Ye cannae go back, lassie. Ye must stay. I cannae live without ye."

"I......" She looked down at his mouth and the cloud hanging over her mind evaporated. She could think now even as their bodies continued to move together. The torturous waves of heat wouldn't stop. "I have to. I'm sorry. I never should have let this happen."

"Why do ye have to? The Last Division is all here. Ye havenae ought to go back to."

"I have family back there. My parents live in Lansing, Michigan, and I have a sister in Chicago and a brother in Los Angeles. They both have children. I'm an aunt. I know what you're going to say. The Last Division swore off love and family and society and all that. I know all that. I haven't seen my family in years, but all this time, I've known that they were still there if I ever wanted to see them. I've always known while I was with the Last Division that my family would welcome me back someday. I would have to completely give up the possibility of ever seeing them again if I stayed here. Don't ask me to give that up. I would never ask you to give up your Clan for me. You can't ask me to do it."

She blurted it all out as quickly as she could. She gasped for breath as soon as she finished and waited for lightning to strike.

He didn't answer for a minute. He studied her with that same simmering frown and she waited for the explosion of anger to follow. How could he not be angry?

She shouldn't have kissed him the first time and now this time was so much worse. She said she didn't want to hurt him, but she knowingly led him on.

Maybe she *should* go to Stronghold after all. She should tell Jaimee.... but Betty couldn't do that. Jaimee would be furious when she found out about this.

Besides, the Buchanans needed Betty. They needed everyone they could get who knew how to fight. How could Betty go back on that now?

Reid still didn't move so Betty had to make the first move. She weaseled out from under him and took a few steps toward the pantry threshold before she dared to look back.

He still stood there frowning at her. Was he mad or was he just thinking? She couldn't deal with him being mad at her—not over this.

She breathed one last, "I'm sorry," and hurried away.

Chapter 12

"**A**re we really going over there?" Fergus asked.

Jaimee puffed out her cheeks in a heavy sigh. "It's suicide. We'll never make it off the beach."

"We winnae ever make it *to* the beach," Colton countered. "We winnae ever make it off this mountain. I'd lay any odds none of us ever sets foot in the bloody water."

Reid eyed the situation down the mountain and agreed with his brother. Creighton forces carpeted the beach on the Kald side. They covered every inch of gravel between the estuary and the city wall.

Another force just as big blockaded the Buchanan bank of the river. They only looked thinner because they had more space over here.

The Creighton army blanketed the mountain halfway up. They had pitched their camps farther down, but not because they wanted to leave the Buchanans any breathing room.

The Creightons occupied the gentler slopes. The ground was too steep up here or they would have camped right outside of Icemeet.

"What's the plan?" Betty asked.

"Plan?" Colton repeated. "Och, there isnae any plan, lassie! The plan is to go out there and get ourselves killed. That's the only plan."

She laughed, but she was the only one who did. "I meant what to do we do when we get into Kald—*if* we get into Kald."

"If we get into Kald, we converge on Tyrekirk," Jaimee replied.

"We winnae get anywhere near the place," Fergus countered. "It's surrounded by spells and enchantments."

"Connell will undo them for us," she replied.

Connell snorted. He stood behind Colton, but everyone in their party could see the herculean task ahead of them. "I winnae be able to undo them, lassie. The Laird is too powerful."

"Why are we going over there to get ourselves killed, then?" Betty asked.

"We're doing this to keep as much of the Creighton force occupied as we can," Jaimee replied. "We're giving cover to the rebels and to whoever Grant and Lily have working for them. We're doing our part to hold this side. That's all we have to do."

"And stay alive," Reid added.

Now she laughed and some of the tension went out of the group. Reid kept surveying the battlefield. It looked as hopeless as everyone said, but his mind kept going back to Betty. Not even the prospect of this suicide mission could make him stop thinking about her.

He didn't blame her for walking away from him. He also didn't blame her for avoiding him after their meeting in the pantry.

She was right. He would never leave his Clan and he would never ask her to abandon her family. That didn't make this any easier for him.

Her presence at Icemeet had become a torture for him and everyone seemed to realize it. Even Colton and Jaimee treated him differently. They spoke to him more softly. Colton treated Reid more deferentially and gave his orders much more gently. Everyone treated Reid like a patient in a terminal decline—which he supposed he was.

If he could only find a way for Betty to leave Icemeet, maybe he could start feeling normal again. It might take him years, but he would recover. He couldn't do that as long as she was around.

Even now, he became painfully aware of her presence at the far end of the line. At least a dozen people separated him from her. Their bodies should have protected him from her presence, but instead, they only made him more aware of her than ever.

He wanted to launch this assault. He needed to do something to take his mind off of her. Maybe he could get himself killed and end this nightmare.

"We dinnae even ken if the rebels or Grant will uphold their sides of the bargain," Connell pointed out.

"We have to go," Reid murmured under his breath. "If they came out and we stayed behind, we'd be to blame for them getting hurt or killed. We cannae let that happen. If any of them risks ought—ought at all—we have to do this. Grant and Elliot have already risked their lives for us many times. We owe it to them to handle this side. I dinnae ken about the rest of ye, but I'm going out there alone if I have to. I winnae stay behind while they take all the risk."

No one said anything, but Reid felt the change sweep through the assembled Highlanders at his words. Everyone stood up a little straighter and narrowed their eyes at the Creightons down on the planes.

Reid's resolve hardened the way it always did before a battle. These bastards made a big mistake setting foot on Buchanan land—on his land. They deserved to die for that and he would send them where they belonged. Dragons wouldn't stop him. Nothing would stop him.

The Creightons had already done enough damage to Icemeet. He wouldn't give them one more inch—not as long as he still had life in his body to stop them.

Every minute he spent in battle with them here was another minute they would stay away from Stronghold. That was reason enough to go through with this even if it meant certain death.

The unmistakable sound of metal scraping metal rang down the line as the Buchanans unsheathed their blades. That sound set Reid's blood on fire. It was now or never.

Reid drew his saber. He hefted it in his hand and tightened his grip on the handle. He measured the battle lines one more time.

"Let's go," Colton ordered.

The Buchanans started marching down the hill. No one ran—not yet. Colton, Jaimee, Reid, Fergus, Connell, and Boyd went first. They climbed down the rubble piles that now formed Icemeet's outer rim.

In a few seconds, hundreds more Highlanders streamed down the hill behind them. The Buchanans started to spread out as soon as they reached the ground. They stretched into a long, sloppy line. No one tried to keep to any kind of formation. It would only fall apart as soon as they engaged with the enemy.

The Creightons encamped nearest to Icemeet noticed them. Soldiers came out of their tents and grabbed their weapons to face off against the Buchanans.

Reid's pulse quickened and he walked faster. His Clansmen did the same. The Buchanan flank started to sweep forward moving faster and faster.

Reid didn't know who started running first. Without warning, a furious roar ripped out of the ranks to his left and the sound triggered a chain reaction through the Buchanan line.

Voices took up the call. It set Reid off and he bellowed at his enemies. Then everyone burst into a run charging full tilt down the mountain.

The Buchanans swept into the Creighton encampments before the Creightons fully prepared themselves for the assault. The Buchanans met them hacking men still scrambling to get out of their tents.

Reid plunged into the assault and lost all sense of where he was or who he was fighting. He slashed, stabbed, and ran on carving his way closer to the Boundless. Nothing mattered but getting across.

The Buchanans surged onto the planes sweeping the Creightons before them. The Buchanans left a trail of bodies in their wake and the few survivors started to fall back.

The noise of screams and clashing arms woke the Creightons on the Kald side. They raced to arm themselves and orders called up and down the beach. Reid caught glimpses of soldiers forming lines over there. They drew their weapons and prepared themselves to defend the beach.

He pushed harder when he saw the estuary in sight. The Creightons retreated a little more and he splashed into the water. The Buchanans had reclaimed the planes on their side. Just a little further and the Buchanans would be able to cross. They would fight their way onto the Kald side of the estuary for the first time in centuries.

He threw himself at the enemy with all his strength. He fought like a maniac and felt himself giving way to animal madness. Blood lust and murderous rage consumed him. He would kill anyone who stood in his way.

He faced five Creighton soldiers all attacking him at once, but he didn't care. He blocked two of them, caught their sabers on his blade, and hurled them off.

One of them stumbled backward a few feet and toppled into his comrades on the other side. The second one fell into the water and Reid attacked even more ferociously. He stepped into the water. He was standing in the Boundless.

The cold sensation of the water around his knees sparked an even more explosive reaction in him. Buchanans fought at his sides on the right and the left. They were doing it. They were pushing the Creightons back to Kald.

He spun around to face the other three soldiers blocking his path....and then he felt it. Some forgotten instinct told him to look over his shoulder.

Betty fought only a few yards away. He had been so looking forward to the battle taking her farther away from him. Now he saw that he had somehow worked his way right over to her side.

She hacked and chopped with her saber in one hand and a dirk in the other. She whirled and danced from one foot to the other with a dancer's grace. Not even Jaimee fought like that.

She did much more stabbing with her dirk than she did hacking and chopping with her saber. She hardly used the saber at all. It must be too heavy for her.

She seemed to come to this conclusion at the same instant. She fought a cluster of soldiers back to buy herself some time. Then she looked around, spotted a dead soldier on the ground, and sidestepped over to him.

Reid's heart seized when he realized she was coming closer to him. She blocked another strike with her saber, ducked, and picked up a dirk. In a flash, she dropped her saber and fought on with two dirks.

She moved much more quickly now. She stabbed, impaled, and sliced in a tempest whirlwind that mesmerized Reid, but he couldn't stand here admiring her technique when he had his own battle to fight.

He made a snap decision—or rather his gut made the decision for him. He migrated sideways to get nearer to her.

He took a position right next to her and now he could move forward much better. He didn't have to worry about where she was or what she was doing. She was right next to him.

He turned sideways now that he didn't have to defend his left side. She was there and she held that part of the battle against all comers.

One step at a time, they fought their way across the Boundless. The retreating Creighton forces merged with the soldiers already guarding the beach. They bolstered the ranks so the job of getting onto the beach became even more daunting.

Reid gritted his teeth for the last desperate push. The Buchanan line extended all the way down the Boundless in both directions.

A guttural bellow of primal rage echoed across the landscape. Reid knew that sound. It was Colton calling everyone forward.

Reid lunged for his enemies and the Buchanans charged onto the beach. The Creightons met them full on, but now the Buchanans had to fight uphill with the Creightons defending the high ground.

Betty attacked with all her might, but too many Creightons stood against the assault. Reid saw soldiers hacking at her with their sabers and protective fury overflowed all sense of proportion. They were attacking his mate. They were trying to kill her.

He roared in a rage and flung himself even harder at his enemies, but the Buchanans couldn't get onto the beach. The Creightons surged and his foot plunged into the water. The Buchanans started to fall back to their own side.

Reid glanced around one more time and saw a mob of soldiers forcing the Buchanans back. Ten of them rushed Betty. She raised her dirks above her head to block them, but there were too many of them.

Reid reacted without thinking. He spun around and thrust his saber between her dirks. All three weapons met to form a tent and the enemy sabers smashed down on them.

Betty's head snapped around and she stared up into his eyes. That look gave him superhuman strength. No one was going to touch her as long as he was around.

The next instant, the Creightons stormed into the Boundless. They swept the Buchanans back to their own side, but so many soldiers rushed into the estuary at once that they surrounded Reid and Betty. They got trapped and surrounded by enemy soldiers.

She whirled the other way to defend herself and Reid did the same thing. They turned back to back and her body touched his. They merged into one being the way they did in the pantry. She really was his destined mate. He didn't just imagine it.

They became a single being with four arms instead of two. They held the soldiers at bay, but Reid and Betty couldn't move, not even to retreat to their own territory.

Reid slashed everyone who came near him. He forgot all about getting onto the beach. He even forgot about defending his homeland. He had to fight tooth and nail just to stop the soldiers from cutting him down.

He whirled from one side to the other fighting anyone who came near him. He felt Betty moving against his back. She was still there. She was still alive and on her feet.

He should be the one defending her. He *was* the one defending her. He guarded her back. She was safe from one direction at least as long as he stayed upright to guard her. He couldn't let her down.

He whirled the other way searching for his next attacker when he noticed something strange. All the Creightons were rushing him from his right—from the Buchanan side.

The Creightons charged into the water and ran out.... on the Kald side. His rage-fueled brain took a second to realize the truth. The Creightons were falling back. They abandoned Buchanan country to return to Kald.

Reid searched the battle for Colton.... or anybody. The Creightons raced past him all trying to run back toward Kald. Why?

Then he saw it. A dozen dragons launched from Tyrekirk's highest turrets. They spread their wings and stooped toward the Boundless. They separated to put more distance between each other.

The Creightons kept flooding back to Kald. They left the beach exposed. Nothing stopped the Buchanans from advancing.... except the dragons.

"Hold yer ground!" Colton bellowed. "It's a trap!"

Reid turned just enough to growl over his shoulder. "Are ye all right, lassie?"

"Yeah!" she panted. "You?"

"Aye. Come. We must retreat before they...."

"Come on!" A shrill female voice yelled over the battlefield. "Come on! You can make it! Forward!"

Reid didn't recognize that voice. He looked up the Buchanan line to see if Jaimee or anyone else from his Clan was giving that order.

Jaimee, Colton, and the others stood stock still glaring across the Boundless. None of them moved a muscle.

Reid turned back to Betty. He didn't want to unstick his back from hers. He didn't trust to separate from her even one inch.

Then he saw what everyone else was staring at. A woman in black leather clothes charged down the beach toward the Buchanan line. She was armed with a saber and dirk, but she was totally alone.

She forced her way through the retreating soldiers and ran over to Colton and Jaimee. It was Lily Barnett—Lily Ritchie Armstrong.

She waved the Buchanans forward. "Come on! Let's go! Grant ordered the soldiers to fall back. You can make it. It's all clear!"

"I dinnae think so, lassie," Colton countered. "They'll mow us down."

He pointed up at the dragons stooping closer by the second. They lowered their heads and narrowed their eyes at the Buchanans as the dragons prepared to unleash their fire on their enemies.

Reid started to take hold of Betty's elbow. He moved in front of her to protect her from the dragons when, without warning, one of them pulled out of line.

A giant black monster four times the size of the other dragons peeled away, flexed his massive wings, and picked up speed. He whizzed in front of them, pulled around in a steep curve, and came back at the Creighton dragons from the Buchanan side.

"Come on!" Lily yelled. "Come now before he....!"

Grant unleashed a devastating breath of fire on the Creighton dragons. Three of them screeched as the flames engulfed them. The others all rounded on Grant. They spat fire back at him, but they couldn't overcome his power.

Lily charged into the Boundless, waded across the estuary, and grabbed Jaimee. "Come on! You have to come now!"

She pulled Jaimee toward Kald. Jaimee and Colton snapped out of their shock and Colton raised his saber. "Forward, lads!"

The Buchanans stormed the beach roaring in triumph, but the Creightons were all long gone. Reid turned to check on Betty again. Their eyes met and then they both joined the assault.

Lily led the way to an open gate in the city wall. The Creighton soldiers ran ahead all going in the same direction.

"Follow me!" Lily called. "I'll take you to Tyrekirk."

She darted up the street following the soldiers. Jaimee and Colton set off after her followed by the rest of their Clansmen.

Reid glanced at Betty at the same moment she glanced at him. They really were about to enter Kald and make their way to Tyrekirk. Reid still didn't want to believe it.

Betty started forward and Reid set off after her when a dragon's shriek made him turn back. Eight Creighton dragons surrounded Grant, but he still held his own. He battered them with his wings and incinerated them with his fiery breath.

Reid almost turned away for the second time when another five dragons came pelting out of Tyrekirk. They swarmed in to surround Grant, but at the last second, he contorted out of the ball of his attackers and let loose a colossal inferno that enveloped all five.

They twisted and seethed as the flames crackled around them. The others hesitated to reengage with him and he rounded on them swelling himself up to a gargantuan size.

He spread his wings and arched back his neck to finish them off when a mystical net of golden sparks drifted out of nowhere. It came from so high above Tyrekirk that Reid couldn't see where it came from.

He stuck his head out through the city walls and squinted upward at a skeletal old man standing on the castle's high turrets.

The net drifted toward Grant and he panicked. He whirled away and extended his wings to save himself, but he was too late. The net that seemed so vaporous and fragile swept forward at impossible speed, surrounded him, and he imploded in midair.

A piercing scream raised every hair on Reid's scalp. "GRANT! GRANT!!"

Lily slammed into Reid's shoulder, knocked him out of the way, and rushed down the beach toward the estuary. Reid stared in horror as the giant dragon collapsed smaller and smaller. He changed into a man and smashed down on the planes on the Buchanan side.

Lily reached the estuary, splashed across, and rushed over to him, but now nothing protected her from the surviving dragons. They tilted on their leathery wings and glared down at her bending over Grant's broken body.

Something else brushed against Reid and he looked down to find Betty at his side. They both looked down the beach at Grant and Lily on the ground. Nothing could save them.

The dragons angled downward and tucked their wings to divebomb the pair. The dragons coordinated their flight and Reid saw in a heartbeat what they were about to do. They lined up so they could each take turns bombarding Lily with fire.

She heard them coming and looked up. She went very still and crouched lower bracing herself for the end, but she didn't leave Grant. She leaned over to cover him with her own body.

A wrenching sensation in Reid's middle told him a split second too late that Betty had left his side. He yelled out, "No, lassie!" but she was already running down the beach toward the Boundless.

She ran across it heading for Grant and Lily, but the dragons were too intent on their target to notice one woman coming from behind them.

The first dragon swooped low over the plane coming closer and closer, faster and faster. He picked up speed and opened his mouth.

Betty pumped her legs running for all she was worth. Her hands raised her two dirks. She couldn't possibly defend herself against dragon fire with those.

Reid's throat tightened. This was not the way he wanted to free himself from the bond between him and Betty. He couldn't stand here and watch her die, but he couldn't move. All his strength and energy had drained out of him.

The dragon arched its neck back, lunged forward, and a wicked spurt of flame shot from his mouth. It billowed at Lily, and at the last second, Betty skidded between Lily and the dragon. Betty pivoted onto her knees and crossed her dirks in front of her.

Reid winced as the dragon's fire struck her crossed dirks, but he couldn't look away. His whole life hung in the balance of this one instant.

He stared in blank disbelief as the fire hit the point where her blades crossed. A blinding flash of light exploded outward and then imploded just as fast.

The dragon whooshed past and the others fell in line to follow him...except that Betty wasn't there anymore. She, Lily, and Grant had completely vanished.

Chapter 13

Colton stepped in front of Reid and broke his line of sight, but Reid didn't see his brother. Reid kept seeing that flash over and over. She couldn't be gone, just like that. Betty couldn't be gone.

"Laddie! Come along! We must go!" Colton searched Reid's stunned face. Then Colton poked his head through the gate and scanned up and down the Boundless. "Where's yer lassie?"

Reid couldn't answer. Not even Colton revealing that he already knew about Betty could bring Reid back from this.

She was gone. What happened at the moment when the dragon fire touched her blades? Did she do it or did the dragon do it? Was she dead?

Some part of his innermost being told him that she was still alive.... somewhere—but where? She could be in another country. She could be back in her own time for all he knew.

Colton rotated in front of Reid again. He raised his voice to a commanding snap. "Laddie! Reid!"

Colton grabbed him and shook him. Reid barely felt it.

Jaimee came over to them. "What's going on?" She looked out at the estuary. The dragons were retreating. "Where's Betty?"

Reid opened his mouth, but no sound came out. He couldn't get his voice to work.

"Reid!" Jaimee snapped. "Where's Betty? Did Lily come this way? We were going to follow her to Tyrekirk and then she ran back here."

He gulped. He couldn't leave Jaimee in the dark about her two friends. "She.... uhh...."

Colton and Jaimee watched him waiting for him to say something. What could he tell them?

"What happened to her? "Colton asked. "Did she fall in the assault?"

"No, she...." Reid's eyes flickered back to the spot where Betty, Lily, and Grant disappeared. "She vanished."

"She what?" Jaimee gasped. "How?"

"I dinnae ken." He waved toward the plane as though that could somehow explain this. "She.... ran in front of the dragons. She was trying to protect Grant and Lily."

Jaimee turned white as a sheet. "Did the dragons hit her?"

"They...." Reid glanced over at Jaimee and he knew he had to tell her. He couldn't keep this to himself. "They hit her with their fire. She crossed her dirks...and then some sort of magic transported her away. Dinnae ask me how or where it took her for I dinnae ken. The spell took her, Lily, and Grant."

"Grant was in the air," Colton countered. "He was miles away."

Reid shook his head. He felt numb. He had to gulp again to unstick his throat. "He fell.... The Laird took him down...."

Jaimee covered her eyes. "Jesus, no!"

"He fell.... over there...." Reid pointed. "Lily ran out to defend him and the dragons went after her....and then Betty...."

Saying her name hurt. She was gone. She wasn't here and now this torn, bleeding place in his heart would keep bleeding and bleeding and bleeding for the rest of his life. He would spend his days up on the rocks with Edeena, watching and waiting for Betty to return.

He would rather die right now, but he had to keep living. He had to keep surviving this torture on the slim chance that he might see her again. Nothing else kept him alive.

Colton compressed his lips and nodded. "It's obvious what's happened."

"It is?" Jaimee asked. "How do you figure?"

"Dinnae ye see, lassie? Betty's magic must have transported them away."

She gaped at him in stupid disbelief. "Betty's.... what? Betty doesn't have magic. Magic doesn't exist in our world."

"We both ken that isnae true, lassie. How do ye suppose Liam brought ye here in the first place? Liam's a wizard and he comes from yer world. Of course it exists in yer world. It must. Betty must have had magic all this time and didnae ken it."

"That's impossible!" she countered. "I've lived with her for years. Why didn't it show itself before now?"

"I lived with Duncan for more than twenty years and he didnae ever show it. It can come to the surface anytime. Perhaps living in a world that says magic doesnae exist made her suppress it. How should I ken?"

"So what are we supposed to do about it?" she asked. "How do we find her?"

"It doesnae matter." The words came from somewhere else. Reid heard his own voice saying them, but they didn't feel real.

"How can you say that?" Jaimee demanded. "You care about Betty more than any of us. Of course it matters."

"No, lassie," Reid murmured. "The same thing happened when Duncan disappeared. She could have sent herself anywhere, especially since she didnae even ken she was magic. We wouldnae even ken where to begin to look. She would have no control over where she went. We planned this assault and now we're in Kald. We'll go on with the offensive."

"Are ye sure, lad?" Colton asked. "We can go on and ye can go find her."

"No." Reid let out another shuddering breath and straightened up. His mind was starting to clear. "We're going on—all of us."

"All right, lad." Colton gripped Reid's shoulder and his brother's firm hand brought Reid the rest of the way out of his stupor. "Let's go."

Jaimee turned away, too, but not before giving Reid a strange look. Her features pinched with almost as much pain as he felt—almost, but not quite. Both she and Colton knew now, but that didn't bring Betty back.

They headed back toward the east, back toward Tyrekirk, but now they no longer had Lily leading them—not that it mattered.

In a matter of seconds, it became clear exactly where the trio should be going. The Buchanans charged through the streets of Kald hunting every Creighton soldier they could lay their hands on.

Cats and men fought all over the place. Everywhere Reid turned, he saw the Highland tigers pulling men down and mauling them in the streets before running on to find more victims elsewhere.

Reid, Colton, and Jaimee just had to follow the trail of mayhem, bodies, and the deafening noise of battle. They overtook Fergus, Boyd, and Callum hacking their way through a contingent of soldiers. The fight blocked a narrow street that looked like it ended in a massive wall.

The Creightons held their ground, but the Buchanans slowly and steadily pushed them back. Colton and Reid lent their sabers to the effort and the end of the alley came in sight.

"It's Tyrekirk!" Colton yelled to his brother. "It's the castle wall!"

"It cannae be this easy," Reid replied.

"It winnae be. The Laird kens about Grant now. The Laird kens Grant called the retreat. If he brings dragons...."

At that moment, the soldiers turned tail and ran straight toward the wall behind them. They didn't wait for the Buchanans to turn the tide. Fergus and Boyd charged forward to finish them off.

Fergus overtook two soldiers who stumbled and fell behind. He raised his saber on high to hack them to death when, with no warning at all, they ran through a magical field at the end of the alley.

It was invisible until the moment the two soldiers ran straight through it. A giant blue-pink dome of shimmering energy flashed into sight for a split second and stayed visible after that.

The next second, Fergus collided with the field and it whiplashed back at him. It smacked him off his feet and flung him back across the alley. He hit a wall and Colton ran over to pick him up.

Reid, Jaimee, and the others pulled up where the dome had been a moment before. Reid put out his hand to touch it, it sparked into view once and snapped his hand away.

"Look," Jaimee murmured.

He followed her gaze to the left and his scalp prickled. A dozen Highland tigers had gotten trapped inside the dome somehow. Battalions of Creighton soldiers went after them and hunted the cats down with murderous precision.

They hacked the cats to death one after another. The cats tried to fight back, but the Creightons outnumbered them by the dozen. The cats turned to flee, only to run into the dome again.

The dome became solid enough when any Buchanan tried to get through it, but it didn't affect the Creightons at all.

"Bastard!" Colton snarled. "This is the Laird's work."

"Let's skirt around to the north," Jaimee suggested. "Let's see if we can find another way in."

Reid didn't hold out much hope for getting through this field, but the Buchanans were out of any other options without Grant and Lily's help.

Colton led the way back down the same alley. The trio returned to the street that brought them here, but when they reached the end, Colton dodged out of sight and pushed Reid and Jaimee behind a corner.

They peeked out and watched a cluster of Buchanans defending themselves against the Creighton army. Creighton patrols drove the Buchanans back one painstaking step at a time across a square where four streets met.

The Creightons drew level with the trio's hiding place before a bright green dragon strutted into view. The Laird's dragons were much smaller than Grant and Elliot, but they were plenty big enough to do all the damage they wanted to.

The dragon's long, serpentine neck bobbed back and forth while he eyed the battle. His tail lashed and he flexed his wings menacingly.

The Buchanans retreated from him, but he kept advancing until he cornered them against a building. They couldn't reach any of the available streets that might give them a way out.

The dragon arched his spine, spread his wings, and gave a deafening shriek of deadly triumph. Then he dropped his head low to the ground and coiled back his neck.

Reid saw the dragon about to unleash fire on the Buchanans. He couldn't stand by and watch this. He stepped forward, but Colton grabbed his arm. "No, lad...."

Reid yanked his arm away and rushed forward with a roar of his own. He raised his saber and charged straight into the Creighton platoon from the side.

He dropped one soldier and slashed two others before anyone could react. Reid forced his way deeper into the platoon fighting anyone who raised a weapon.

He didn't know what he would do once he got there, but his attack worked. The dragon glanced over at him. The cornered Buchanans remained frozen to the spot until Jaimee darted out and waved them forward. "Come on! Run!"

The dragon whipped around to glare at her and spotted the Buchanans making a break for it. He took one step forward to track them down when Colton waded into the fight.

He leveled a bunch of soldiers who had pivoted to encircle Reid. Colton cleaved four men to the ground, seized Reid's collar, and hauled him out of the fray.

The two brothers fought side by side as they retreated back the way they came. They entered another narrow side street before they earned themselves enough breathing space to flee.

Colton skidded around a different corner and dragged Reid in behind him. Both brothers sealed their backs to the wall while they caught their breath. "Did ye.... see them...." Colton gasped. "Did ye see.... them following us....?"

"I didnae see," Reid choked back. "Jaimee must have gone on with the others."

"That was a stupid thing to do, lad," Colton snapped. "Ye shouldnae have done that."

"So I should have stood by and watched the dragon torch our lads without doing ought to help them? I wouldnae have believed I would ever hear ye say that."

Colton brought his face within inches of Reid's and snarled through gritted teeth. "Ye may have lost yer lassie for the moment, lad, but that doesnae give ye any right to throw yer life away. I understand how ye feel. Believe me. I understand. I've felt it many times, but Betty is still out there. She's still alive and ye must be the same way when ye see her again. Is that clear?"

Reid looked down so he wouldn't see his brother glaring at him. "Perfectly clear."

Colton squeezed Reid's shoulder. "We'll find her. She's here somewhere."

Reid swallowed hard. He didn't want to think or talk about Betty, but he had to. He wished he could feel as confident as Colton sounded that Betty was still here somewhere, somewhere he might find her and....

"Her mission is here," Colton went on. "Her friends are here and ye're here. Her magic wouldnae send her anywhere else. It would keep her here but out of danger. She's either in Kald or in Icemeet or the forest beyond. I'd bet anything on it, but if I had to say...." He shot Reid a strange look. "I'd say she's here. She'll be near ye, but out of sight somewhere. We'll find her."

Reid gulped again. He seemed to be doing that a lot more now than he ever remembered doing before. Colton was right. He had to hold on. If Betty was alive anywhere, in this time or another, he had to take care of himself so he would be there when he found her again—*when* he found her, not if.

Colton tugged his sleeve. "Come along. Let's go see if we can find Jaimee."

Reid followed his brother without saying anything. Now he felt terrible for feeling sorry for himself. Jaimee could be anywhere. She could be in danger. Colton said he felt the same way about being separated from her, but he didn't fall apart.

Of course he didn't. Colton didn't have to worry about Jaimee being his mate. They were already married.

Reid struggled to pull his head back to the present, and a second later, they entered a different street and ran into Jaimee leading the same Buchanans that Reid just saved from the dragon.

His Clansmen surrounded him all hugging him and clapping him on the back and talking fast. "Did ye see ought?" Colton asked Jaimee.

"Just more soldiers and dragons working their way through the city. A few of our Clansmen took shelter in random buildings, but we couldn't get to them."

A shadow passed overhead and Colton squinted up at the sky. "More dragons are coming out from Tyrekirk. We need to get under cover. We winnae be able to make much headway with them around and Grant gone."

"What about the tunnel from Tyrekirk that Lily and Grant used to get us out of the castle?" Jaimee asked. "We could take it back inside and strike from within."

Colton grimaced at her. "Do ye think ye could find that tunnel again—assuming the dragons and the soldiers didnae ambush us on the way? Do ye have any notion where that tunnel is in this city?"

She looked around in all directions and blinked. "Well.... no."

"Neither do I." Another crash of arms interrupted their conversation and Colton pulled her out of sight. "We cannae get near the castle with that dome in the way. We must work our way to the west. Maybe we can find some shelter in this place."

Chapter 14

Betty opened her eyes, but she didn't recognize where she was. A few frightened people peeked out of their windows in nearby houses and buildings. Streets crisscrossed the area and went off in all directions.

All those streets were paved with cobblestones and the few men she could see were all wearing kilts, but none of them wore either Buchanan or Creighton tartan.

The only other kilt she had seen since she came to this country was Elliot Ritchie's tartan and none of these people were wearing that, either. Where in the name of thunder was she?

The last thing she saw before this happened was Reid's face staring at her. He looked like he didn't recognize her....and then he was gone. No, that wasn't right. She was the one who was gone. She went somewhere else. She was on the banks of the Boundless. Then she was here. How did that happen?

She started to stand up when a choking noise distracted her. She looked down at Lily bending over Grant.

Betty's stomach turned when she saw him. Blood covered his face and body. He lay curled on his side on the hard paving stones. One of his legs had been hopelessly shattered. The foot pointed in the wrong direction and part of his thigh had also twisted the other way.

He made a pathetic groaning noise in his throat, tried to sit up, and failed. Lily frantically worked to rip off her own jacket, tear a strip of linen from the bottom of her shirt, and press it to a bloody tear on his stomach.

"Lassie...." he husked.

"Quiet!" Lily roared. Then she looked up and her fierce, battle-frenzied eyes skipped around the neighborhood. "We have to get you off the streets. If anyone sees you out here in Armstrong tartan, you'd be dead in seconds."

"I cannae go anywhere like this." He winced again. "Ye must...."

"Shut up!" she shrieked. "Get up! Help me, Betty! Come on!"

Betty couldn't stop looking at the surroundings. "Where are we?"

"We're in Kald," Lily replied. "Get over here, Betty! Now!"

Betty stumbled over to them. She hesitated to touch Grant, but when Lily tried to pick him up, his blood made her hands slip against his skin. He collapsed back on the ground whining in pain.

Betty got her elbow under his other arm and the two women heaved him onto his one good leg. He trembled all over and his head started to loll as soon as they stood him up.

Betty tried to ignore the noises he was making. What if he died? What would the Buchanans do then? What would happen to all their efforts to launch this campaign?

Betty glanced over at Lily. Lily compressed her lips and glared around her with so much fury and determination that Betty understood exactly what Lily was going through. How could Grant survive his injuries out here without any medical help?

Both women strapped Grant's arms over their shoulders. He kept groaning and whimpering every time they took a step and jostled his ruined leg.

"Where are we going?" Betty asked.

"I know somewhere we can go to hide," Lily replied. "We were out here before when Liam brought me through the portal."

Betty didn't ask any more questions. She didn't want to know the details. Lily turned a corner, but since Betty didn't know ahead of time that Lily was going to turn there, they ended up yanking Grant in different directions.

He made an even more wretched sobbing noise. This couldn't go on.

Betty was just about to say something when an explosion went off a block away. Betty and Lily both looked that way and Lily whispered. "Damn it! Come on! This way!"

She staggered into an alley, followed it to its end, and veered hard into a different street. She crossed it and wedged Grant into a dim doorway that led to some stairs.

Lily lowered him to the ground and took a fresh grip on her weapons. "Stay here," she whispered to Grant.

"Lassie...."

Lily only tightened her lips and clamped one hand on Betty's wrist. She dragged Betty back into the street and Lily aimed her dirk back in the direction they had just come. "Look!"

The two women stood guard in front of the stairs as the noise built to an epic pitch. Betty's blood pounded in her ears. She didn't know what to expect and then she saw it.

A mob of people passed beyond the last alley that Lily took to get here. These people wore a strange mixture of tartans. They didn't seem to belong to a single Clan, but they all fought together as if they did.

They fought tooth and nail against a squad of Creighton soldiers who drove them across another square at the alley's far end. The battle paused there where Betty could see everything and then she stared in stark horror as a billowing jet of fire struck the townsfolk.

Screams echoed off the walls as their bodies shriveled in the flames. Blast after blast lit the defenders on fire and the rest bolted into the slums.

Lily whirled away. "Come on!" she hissed, but Betty couldn't move. She stared with her jaw on the ground as a bright green and yellow dragon stalked into the square flattening anyone who stood before him. Charred remains of bodies littered his path and his feet thumped the cobblestones as he advanced.

Lily charged back to Betty's side. "Come on! You have to come now before he sees you!"

She grabbed Betty, but before either woman could move, the dragon looked in their direction and stared right at them.

Lily went nuts. "Come on!" She yanked Betty nearly off her feet and hauled her back to Grant.

The two women picked him up and stumbled on through more streets that Betty didn't recognize. Betty didn't dare to ask where Lily was taking Grant.

She finally entered another dark doorway, and this time, she panted, "Up! Climb! Hurry!"

Betty cracked her spine pulling Grant's weight up a flight of stairs. They had to climb five floors before they reached the roof.

Lily put Grant down and knelt next to him again. She tried to clean him up while her eyes kept darting around in all directions. "We can't stay here," she panted. "The dragons can see us from the air."

Betty knelt down next to Grant, too. God, he looked awful! "Can you shift and heal yourself?"

"What?" Lily gasped. "Heal himself—how?"

Betty shrugged. "Elliot was injured the first time he shifted, and when he shifted back, he was fine."

Grant tried to chuckle and wound up choking. "Good for Elliot. I wish I could see him again...."

"Shut up!" Lily snarled. "You're gonna be just fine."

He started to smile at her and winced.

"He did get hit by Duncan's magic," Betty recalled. "That's what made him shift. We weren't sure if Elliot had healing powers or if Duncan's magic did it. Duncan was out of control at the time."

Lily gave her a dirty look. "Well, it was probably that, then. None of the Creighton dragons have healing powers. We would know if they did."

"Sorry," Betty mumbled. "I was just trying to help."

"That doesn't help us get out of here," Lily snapped. "The Laird's magic will track us down if the dragons don't find us first. Grant can't shift without triggering the Laird's tracking spells."

"Ye cannae use yer magic, either, lassie," Grant added.

Betty took a second to figure out who he was talking to. She gasped and looked over at Lily. Lily had magic?

Grant wasn't looking at Lily, though. He was looking at Betty.

She frowned. "What do you mean? I don't have any magic."

"How do you think we got here?" Lily asked. "You sent us here when that dragon tried to burn you."

Betty's jaw dropped. "I did not! I do NOT have magic."

"It can lie dormant for years," Grant went on. "Just look at Duncan."

"I don't want to look at Duncan!" Betty shot to her feet, but she couldn't exactly walk away from these two. "I....do.... not.... have.... magic!"

"Yer life was in danger. It happened like that for me the first time I shifted. Ye were scared for yer life and ye...."

"I DID NOT USE MAGIC!!" she screeched. She couldn't stand the way Lily and Grant were both looking at her.

She whirled away and strode to the other side of the roof. She would have walked away from them completely, but she had nowhere else to go.

She stopped and looked out over Kald, but the view only made her feel worse. Ice-cold water flooded her veins. It chilled her from the inside.

This couldn't be happening. She didn't have any magic. She couldn't. That was impossible.

A small voice in the center of her being told her something else. What if it was true? How did she get herself, Lily, and Grant away from the Boundless?

She replayed that moment over and over in her mind, but each time made the small voice stronger and louder. That flash blinded her....and then she was here—miles from where she started.

What if....?

She tried to shake that voice out of her head....out of her heart and being, but it wouldn't go away. Could she really be magic?

That would be her worst nightmare. The Last Division falling apart was bad enough. If she had magic, she might not be able to go back to her old life at all.

What would her family say? How would she function in modern society?

Lily muttered under her breath behind Betty's back. "To hell with it. Betty can heal you and then we'll move you before they get here."

"Ye cannae, lassie." Grant's voice sounded raspier and softer. He sounded like he might be fading out. "The wizards would be here in seconds."

Lily's voice cracked and ended in a sob. "You can't give up! We have to do something!"

Betty couldn't stand that. She turned around and walked back over to them. Grant lay flat on his back with his eyes half-closed. Was he dying?

She jolted to high alert when she heard footsteps coming up the stairs. She spun around and her hands flew to her weapons. She brandished both her dirks as a young man in Creighton tartan stepped out onto the roof.

"Stay back!" Betty ordered. "Come one step closer and I'll kill you!"

The young man raised both hands where she could see them. "I'm a friend, lassie. I'm here to help ye...."

"Get back!" She stabbed her dirk at him to make him stop where he was. "Don't come any closer."

He opened his mouth to say something when Lily charged past Betty. Lily raced to the young man's side and grabbed his arm. "Tristan! Thank God you're here."

She towed the young man over to Grant and they both knelt down next to him. Betty stared at them while Tristan did something to Grant's leg.

"Where have you been?" Lily gasped under her breath. "Did you make it out of the castle all right? We were worried about you. We thought you might have fallen to the Laird."

"I managed to evade him just long enough to get down into the tunnels. Then he overcame me spells, but I suppose all his wizards and guards were already outside by then. I escaped into the neighborhoods." Tristan turned back to Grant. "Is it better now?"

Grant relaxed back on the roof and shut his eyes. "Aye. I cannae tell ye how grateful I am, laddie. I didnae think I'd see ye again."

Betty snuck up behind them to see what Tristan was doing.

Ripples of light and sparkling energy flowed up and down Grant's leg. They enveloped his body and healed all his injuries. His leg straightened out and became whole.

"What are you doing?" she asked.

"Tristan is a wizard," Lily replied. "He's using healing spells to fix Grant's leg."

"Ye dinnae have any internal organ damage," Tristan remarked. "Ye'll be able to move as soon as I finish."

"Thank ye, lad," Grant replied. "Ye're worth yer weight in gold."

Tristan chuckled and Betty backed away feeling sick. She didn't want to be anywhere near a wizard. She didn't want to have anything to do with magic or for anyone to think she had it.

Tristan didn't notice her. "Ye'll have to leave straight away. The dragons are all hunting ye and the Laird will have locator spells out for anyone using magic. They'll be here soon enough."

"Thank you," Lily replied. "We'll leave now. You should come with us, Tristan."

"I cannae. I must go a different way. If we got ambushed and I used magic to defend meself, I might attract them to ye." He turned back to Grant. Grant looked fine now and Tristan grabbed his hand to pull Grant to his feet. "How is it now?"

Grant put his weight on his leg and then stamped his foot. "It's grand. Ye're a miracle worker."

"Hardly. Dinnae shift whatever ye do. Understand? Yer grandfather will be looking out for ye and Elliot to show yerselves."

"I sincerely hope Elliot isnae anywhere near this town." Grant grabbed Tristan, pulled him into a hug, and pushed him away. "Thank ye, lad. Now be off."

"Aye. I'm going." Tristan turned away and saw Betty standing off to one side. She gaped at him in horror. How could anyone talk so lightly about doing magic and casting spells? He acted like doing magic was the most normal thing in the world.

Tristan smiled at her, but that smile only made her feel worse. She wanted to run from him and kill him all at the same time even as she sensed that he was a friend. He had been telling the truth about that and now he basically saved Grant's life. Tristan had to be a friend.

He took a step toward her and held out his hand. "It's a pleasure to make yer acquaintance, lassie. I'm Tristan Brodie. I've met yer friends Jaimee and Echo and they...."

He broke off when Betty recoiled from his hand like it might harm her. He held it out to her and then let it fall. She saw her own behavior insulting him, but she couldn't stop herself. She couldn't go near any wizard. Forget about touching him.

Lily came over to Tristan's side and murmured in his ear. "What should we do about Betty's magic?"

Grant advanced, too, and all three of them studied Betty like a rat in a lab. She opened her mouth to say.... something. What could she say?

"She cannae use her magic," Grant observed. "She doesnae even ken how she transported us away from the battle in the first place."

"That means naught," Tristan replied. "She's used it once. It could break out at any moment. Ye'll just have to keep going and hope for the best. If she uses it again, perhaps she'll learn more quickly how to use it to yer advantage." Tristan turned away. "I must be off. I'll do me best to keep track of ye, but I cannae promise ought."

Grant clapped him on the shoulder. "Ye mind yerself, lad. Dinnae do ought to put yerself in danger."

Tristan headed for the stairs and Grant followed him for a few steps. "Come along, ye lassies. We must move before they come for us."

He paused on the threshold and turned to look back. Betty stood rooted to the spot. This couldn't be happening. She couldn't have any magic. She couldn't be the one responsible for putting Grant and Lily in danger, not to mention whatever else she might do with magic she had no idea how to use.

She tried to shake that thought out of her head. She didn't have any magic. She couldn't. It was impossible.

Lily stood there considering Betty for a long time. What was Lily thinking? Was she thinking what a freak Betty was? Did Lily want to ditch Betty because Betty was too abnormal to be her friend anymore?

That couldn't be right. Lily was more than happy to welcome Tristan. Then again, Tristan knew how to use his power to help people. Betty was a liability to everyone, especially to herself.

Lily walked up to her and narrowed her eyes with that harsh determined glare she got when she had to do something unpleasant or dangerous. Betty gulped. This wasn't going to end well.

Lily pursed her lips and then murmured, "Let's go, Betty."

Lily turned to walk away, but Betty didn't move. She didn't understand what Lily meant until Lily halted, came back, took Betty by the arm, and propelled her toward the stairs.

Lily said again, "Let's go," in a more commanding tone and Betty snapped out of her trance. They were taking her with them. Maybe she wasn't as much of a timebomb waiting to go off as she thought.

Chapter 15

Reid darted out from behind a corner, scanned an intersection ahead, and pulled back to hide in an alley with Colton and Jaimee.

"What do ye see out there, laddie?" Colton whispered.

Reid counted on his fingers. "Three water troughs, four rain barrels, seven doors leading to businesses, five apartment houses...."

"Dinnae give me yer cheek. I meant soldiers, ye droog!" Colton slapped his brother's shoulder. "This isnae any time for jokes."

"I didnae see any soldiers nor any dragons, but that doesnae mean ought. They could be anywhere, and with the Creighton wizards helping out, the enemy might appear at any time. Our mission is Tyrekirk, We must find Connell to help us break through that field."

Colton turned to Fergus. "Did ye see Connell anywhere in this?"

Fergus shook his head. "Not since we entered the city. I dinnae ken where he is."

Colton turned back to Reid. "What's yer next idea?

Reid smirked and Jaimee interrupted. "We can't keep running and hiding or we'll be out here all night."

"We cannae get near the castle without magic," Colton pointed out. "This wasnae the best thought-out plan I've heard of."

"But we already knew that, right?" Jaimee reminded him. "We came here to unseat the Laird and we can't do that without a wizard. Even if we had a wizard, he or she might not be strong enough to defeat the Laird."

"Can ye kindly tell me something that *will* work?" Colton replied. "I dinnae want to hear ought anymore about what winnae work."

She chuckled and exchanged a knowing glance with Reid. Good old Colton. He never changed.

He shoved Reid out of the way and took his own look into the intersection. "All the squares in this town are the same. How do these people tell one from the next?"

Jaimee pointed behind herself. About thirty Buchanans stood over there. "The castle is to the east and Icemeet is to the north. What more do we need to know?"

Colton gave her a contemptuous look and stepped out into the open. "Come along, ye lot. I've had enough of scurrying about in alleys with the rats."

He advanced and the other Highlanders surrounded him. They all carried their weapons drawn and kept glancing into every side street, open doorway, and window just to make sure no one attacked.

Reid stayed at Colton's side. Whatever the Buchanans did to help this assault, Reid didn't want to be anywhere but right at the front. He wanted to be the first to see an opportunity to bring down the Laird and to act on it when the time came.

The party turned a different corner, but everything stayed quiet. They proceeded for four more blocks before Jaimee gasped under her breath. "Can you believe people actually live like this?"

Reid turned to see what she was looking at. An entire large apartment building had been blasted to smithereens. Most of it was still standing, but the whole front wall had calved off into a giant pile of broken bricks and rubble in front of the building.

Reid looked in on bedrooms, school rooms, washrooms, and dining rooms filling the whole building. Most of the beds, tables, and other furnishings had been burned beyond repair. The building and those surrounding it showed the unmistakable black scorch marks of dragon fire.

At least fifty children sat lined up in the gutter outside. Some of the older ones hugged and tried to comfort the younger ones who were crying. At least a third of these children had been injured in the attack that ruined the building.

Ten women hustled up and down the line of children trying to take care of everyone at once. A few of the women had to clamber over the giant pile of bricks to get into the building. They brought out supplies and food, but they couldn't take care of everyone fast enough.

Reid, Colton, and Jaimee stood there watching for what seemed like a long time. Reid saw in a flash that this building must have been an orphanage. Now all these people were out on the street with nowhere to go.

He scanned the neighborhood with new eyes and saw the same evidence everywhere. Poverty, despair, and oppression hung heavy over Kald.

"So much for the Laird's benevolent mercy," Colton snarled.

"All the more reason to get rid of him," Jaimee muttered. "Come on. Let's get out of here."

The Buchanans continued through the neighborhood heading east. Reid still couldn't think what they would do when they got to Tyrekirk.

He heard voices yelling before the party came to the next crossing. Colton held out his arm to keep everyone behind him. The Buchanans slowed when they saw Creighton soldiers in the square, but the soldiers didn't see the invaders watching them.

The soldiers stood around another building. Reid couldn't tell what this one was from the outside, but it didn't look dangerous. The neighborhood looked residential from what he could tell.

The soldiers surrounded the building while two dragons flanked it on two sides, flexed their wings, and bombarded the building with fire. Women and children tried to flee through the doors and some through the windows.

The soldiers charged the fleeing civilians and hacked at them with raised sabers. The residents had to retreat back inside the building to save their own lives. A few made it out through other doors, but plenty of screams still echoed from inside.

Jaimee stepped forward and started to raise her own weapon, but Colton held her back. She struggled to break his grip and the movement caught the soldiers' attention.

One of them glanced over his shoulder and Colton pushed Reid and Jaimee away, but it was too late.

Half the soldiers separated from their comrades, turned around, and came after the Buchanans. Colton picked up the pace as the soldiers dashed across the square to intercept the fugitives.

Reid spun around. "Run!" The Highlanders took off, but not fast enough.

They dashed into another square and down another street. The way ahead looked all clear until they entered the third square and tried to bolt when a completely different mob of soldiers materialized out of nowhere. They blinked into existence right in front of the alley that the Buchanans were going to use to escape.

Reid, Boyd, and Fletcher were running so fast that they nearly collided with the soldiers. Reid barely got his weapon up in time to stop four soldiers from chopping his head off.

Fletcher didn't get there in time. Two soldiers attacked him and knocked him flat on his back. They pounced to finish him off and Reid sprang sideways to defend his cousin.

Reid got into a brutal sword fight against at least ten soldiers. Boyd worked his way over to Reid's elbow and they fought side by side.

Reid heard weapons clanging behind him, but he couldn't turn around to make sure his Clansmen were still alive. The soldiers outnumbered him and forced him and Boyd to retreat.

The two men held their ground just long enough for Fletcher to scramble to his feet. The three of them did their best to hold the enemy off, but it was no good.

A rough hand seized Reid's jacket and yanked him backward. He stumbled and prepared himself to kill someone for attacking him before he realized that Colton was pulling him away from the fight.

Reid whirled backward and his stomach dropped when he saw what Colton was doing. All the soldiers the Buchanans had seen a few minutes ago showed up from a different direction. They blocked the Buchanans into this square and the same two dragons landed not far away.

The dragons stalked closer and arched their heads downward to breathe fire on the helpless Buchanans. Reid held up his weapons, but they wouldn't save him from this.

Colton towed him in line with Jaimee and the rest. The Buchanans packed more tightly together, but soldiers surrounded them on every side. The Buchanans ended up retreating into a wall. Now nothing stood between them and the dragons while the soldiers prevented the Highlanders from escaping.

Reid's gaze darted everywhere searching for some way out. There had to be a way, but he couldn't see a single inch of space to get out of here. There was only one option and that was straight through the dragons.

He tore out of Colton's grip and leapt in front of his Clansmen. He heard Jaimee yell out, "No...!" but he didn't care.

He jumped forward and rushed the nearest dragon. He raised his saber to slash its head off when, without warning, his dirk and saber both vanished. He looked right and left trying to find them, but they were gone.

The rest of his Clansmen all blinked down at their empty hands and then at each other. They were all unarmed. This had to be some magic trick, but knowing that didn't help anyone.

Colton and Jaimee pulled Reid back into line and the dragons kept advancing. The whole Clan would fall in a second and Reid couldn't do a thing to stop it. It couldn't end like this.

A howling shriek set his hair on end. He barely registered another group of people surging into the square from his right. They flooded out of an alley and overran the soldiers in a heartbeat.

He had half a second to see that most of them were wearing Brodie tartan. The rest wore a random collection of dozens of tartans, but that hardly mattered now.

A grizzled old man wearing a black patch over one eye let out a bellow that shook the earth. He dodged a dozen soldiers, took a skipping step, and hurled a massive spear at one of the dragons.

The creature had been so intent on torching the Buchanans that it didn't see the newcomers until it was too late. The spear impaled the dragon through the thickest part of his neck where it met his shoulders.

The dragon screamed out a deafening death call, reared on his hind legs, and flailed his wings. He rose higher and higher and then crashed down on the cobblestones.

The sight triggered an insane reaction in Reid's being. He roared and shot forward in a blind fury. He shifted and called out to his Clansmen to follow him. They might not have dirks and sabers anymore, but they had other weapons just as deadly.

He streaked past the dead dragon. The other one unloaded its fire on the Buchanans, but none of them was there anymore. They all shifted and launched into the battle flying at top speed.... all except Jaimee.

She dove and rolled across the cobblestones to dodge the dragon's fiery breath. Reid lost sight of her in the mayhem. He was too out of his mind with bloodlust to see or care what any of his Clansmen were doing.

He soared for the nearest soldier, slashed and sliced, and sprang on to the next. Bodies fell behind him and their dying screams played sweet music in his ears.

He spotted three soldiers fighting the Brodies and Reid landed on one soldier's shoulder. Reid twisted his body around the soldier's neck and ripped out the man's throat.

Reid sprang clear before the man even realized what happened. Reid landed on his next victim only to realize a second later that this man was wearing Brodie tartan.

Reid struggled to pull his mind back from the crazed frenzy of killing. He cast a glance around the square searching for anyone wearing Creighton colors.

Cats and people swarmed the last remaining dragon. Cats hung from its neck hanging on with their claws and fangs. They shredded its scales while these new fighters hacked and stabbed the creature to death.

Two cats scrambled onto the dragon's back and Reid recognized Colton and Boyd. They anchored their claws into the creature's scales and climbed up the dragon's neck while the monster flailed and thrashed in all directions.

The two cats finally gained the top of the dragon's head and went to work on its face and eyes. The dragon erupted in pain and terror. It thrashed even harder to fling Colton off.

The cat managed to sink his claws into the creature's face. Colton held on against the dragon's furious convulsions and Colton's weight dragged the dragon's head to the ground. Boyd rode him down and the surrounding Brodies mobbed the stricken dragon by the dozen.

They put it out of its misery and the townsfolk drove the remaining soldiers out of the square.

Reid trotted over to his brother and Boyd. They touched noses, but Reid's blood was still on fire from so much adrenaline and noise. He didn't want to shift back yet, not when more soldiers might ambush them at any second.

More tigers assembled from all over the square and Jaimee walked over to join them. None of the other Buchanans shifted back into men, either.

Reid checked the surroundings to make sure all the Creightons were gone....and then he spotted the old man with the eye patch. He and his people stood across the square, but they weren't celebrating their victory.

Jaimee glanced behind her to see what Reid was looking at and then all the Buchanans saw the same thing. No one had to explain to anyone what these townspeople were thinking. They eyed the tigers with obvious suspicion and none of the townspeople had lowered their weapons.

They lined up across the square in a battle formation. The old man came to the front and bared his teeth at the Buchanans.

"Stay here," Jaimee murmured. "I'll go talk to him."

She took one step and pulled up short when the old man and all his comrades advanced as one. Reid didn't realize until now how many townsfolk had come out to fight the Creightons.

Nearly fifty Brodies and at least as many others formed ranks to confront the Buchanans. If this escalated into a battle, it would likely turn into just as big a bloodbath as the one that just ended.

Reid couldn't let that happen. He shifted and Colton shifted a second later. Both men stepped forward to flank Jaimee.

The old man wrinkled his nose and snarled at all three of them. "Ye're Buchanans."

"That's right," Colton replied in his coolest tone. "And who might ye be?"

"Me name's Clyde McKay and this is me own territory. Ye're trespassing....and ye dinnae belong on this side of the water. State yer business. Ye're stirring up trouble, I'll wager."

Colton dipped his eyes once to the man's filthy tartan. So much grime and soot caked his kilt that Reid couldn't even make out which Clan it was from. "Would ye stand there and have me believe ye're leading these Brodies in battle?" Colton snorted. "I winnae believe that if I live a hundred years. *Ye* state yer own business and why ye're carrying weapons against the Creightons."

The old man opened his mouth, probably to demand to know why the Buchanans were carrying weapons against the Creightons, but he was at least smart enough not to ask that. He didn't have to ask.

Colton didn't give him a chance to say anything. He turned to some of the assembled Brodies. "Why are ye lads following this dobber? Dinnae ye have yer own leaders who ken how to wash?"

"Ye mind yer tongue, laddie," the old man snarled.

Colton dropped his voice to a deadly undertone. "Ye winnae call me a laddie. I'm Colton Buchanan, Chief of Clan Buchanan and ye lads will put down yer blades if ye dinnae fancy yer chances against the lot of us."

Reid stiffened. His eye flicked from one man to another in the opposite ranks. The Brodies were certainly sturdier and better armed than the other townspeople. The Brodies also carried themselves much more determinedly. Their eyes flashed with fire like the real fighters that they were.

None of the townsfolk backed down an inch. The Brodies didn't look at all fazed by the idea of fighting the Highland tigers. Reid was just preparing himself to shift back into a tiger when Jaimee spoke up.

"You're all against the Creightons and the Laird and so are we. We organized an offensive to try to take Tyrekirk and hopefully unseat the Laird. We planned our assault with two other armies to strike on the new moon and we had help getting this far. Join us and we'll all stand a much better chance of overthrowing the Creightons once and for all."

Clyde whipped around fast and stared at her. "Ye talk like that lassie. She talked with that foreign tongue of yers and she spoke of an assault on the new moon."

Jaimee gasped out loud and her eyes popped. "Who was she? What did she look like?"

"She was smallish," one of the Brodies chimed in. "Much shorter than ye with long black hair and...."

"She looked like a pixie," another Brodie added. "Beautiful and smallish like a child—a pixie child."

"Echo!" Jaimee whispered. Then she spoke in a fast rush. "Where is she? Is she here? Did she tell you where she was going?"

"She went off with that dragon," the first Brodie growled. "The Laird's wizards came after her. They would have killed her, but that dragon came and took her off."

"Which dragon?" Reid asked. "What did he look like?"

"Huge, he was," the second Brodie replied. "Huge and black and.... a bit of gold to him, too."

"That's Elliot," Reid remarked. "They're together, at least."

"That lassie was the one who told us about the assault. We didnae ken *this* was what it was all about." Clyde waved at the Buchanans and the dead dragon and soldiers lying all over the square.

"Help us," Jaimee urged. "Please."

"Why, where's yer two armies and all that?" Clyde sneered.

"We got as far as Tyrekirk. The Laird has a magical dome around the castle to stop anyone from getting in."

Clyde bared his ugly teeth again. That must have been his version of a smile. "Aye. He does that, but we have wizards of our own. Come along and we'll see what we can do."

Colton, Reid, and Jaimee exchanged glances. Reid didn't want to follow anyone but Colton, but with all the Buchanans unarmed, what choice did they have?

Clyde noticed the glance and called over his shoulder. "Dinnae ye bother about ought. I have a hundred fighters waiting to take up the call as soon as they hear that revolution is afoot. We'll take ye where ye can find new blades and then we'll go take the castle."

Chapter 16

Lily, Grant, and Betty hurried through the city streets trying to put as much distance as possible between themselves and the rooftop hideout where Tristan had healed Grant's injuries.

"There has to be somewhere we can go where the Laird can't find you," Betty remarked.

"There isnae," Grant paused at a corner just long enough to make sure no soldiers, dragons, or wizards came out to track him. "I must return to the castle. I can call back the soldiers...."

"Forget it," Lily snapped. "You aren't going anywhere near the castle."

"Then I'm no good to this offensive," he countered. "I'm meant to be the third prong of the attack. Ye and I were meant to help get the Buchanans across the Boundless and then get them inside Tyrekirk. What happened to that?"

"Then we'll find the Buchanans and...."

"No way," Betty interrupted. "Not a chance. The Buchanans will kill you on sight."

"Colton won't," Lily pointed out. "He knows we're on his side and so does Jaimee."

"And so does Reid," Betty finished. "So how are you going to tell which Buchanans are which? If Colton and Reid are with their Clansmen, you wouldn't be able to get to them before the other Buchanans kill you first." Betty turned to Grant. "You're running around in Armstrong tartan. That's the only excuse anyone needs to get rid of you."

"So what other option is there?" Lily asked.

"If we see any Buchanans, you two will have to hide. I'll do my best to talk to them, and once I explain the situation, I'll come and get you. Until then, you just have to stay out of sight."

Lily pursed her lips and sighed. "I guess that will just have to be good enough."

"Now if I only knew where to find them..." Betty scanned the neighborhood. She still had absolutely no idea where she was.

"The Buchanans came over to Kald to break into Tyrekirk," Grant pointed out. "They'll go there so we can find them there."

"This better not be your subtle way of getting back inside the castle," Lily growled.

He only smiled at her. "If it is, ye'll be there to crack me head open to stop me, I'm sure."

She bit back a smirk and the three of them headed off toward the west. Betty kept an eye out for the Buchanans. She had to find a way to reconnect with them. She didn't want anyone to think she was on the Laird's side.

Where were Colton, Reid, and Jaimee right now? Betty suffered another wave of nausea when she thought about the look on Reid's face when she used magic. So much for that. He would never want to have anything to do with her after that—not that it would have been possible anyway.

Tramping feet and the rattle of weapons startled her back to the present. She, Grant, and Lily hustled into a nearby alley and held their breath as another bunch of soldiers trooped past.

"They're heading west," Grant whispered. "They're going out into the city."

"What for?" Betty asked. "Aren't they worried about guarding the castle?"

"The Laird's magic should stop anyone from getting in," Lily replied.

Betty turned away with a pained grimace. Why did every other sentence seem to include a magic reference now?

The three friends walked for a long time until Grant led the way into another random alley. All these streets and alleys looked the same to Betty, but he knew exactly where he was going.

He nodded toward a stone wall at the end. "There's the castle. We can get in through the laundry chute."

"What about the field?" A crash interrupted Lily and the three of them peeked out at a bunch of soldiers fighting kilted townspeople.

"The Brodies are rising up!" Grant hissed. "It was only a matter of time."

"Could they be trying to help the offensive?" Betty asked.

"How would they have found out about it?" Lily countered.

"Clan Brodie has been opposed to the Laird for generations," Grant replied. "He's tried a hundred times to drive them out of Kald, but they're just too bloody tough."

"I'll say!" Betty watched a mob of ferocious Brodies driving the soldiers into a different street. "They don't seem to be having too much trouble about it."

"They're heading for the castle. They must be trying to get inside, too. Let's follow them." Lily took one step to leave the alley. She didn't show herself in the open, but one of the Brodies must have seen her.

A man glanced over, raised his saber on high, and roared out for all to hear, "Creighton bastard!" He charged the trio with a bunch of his Clansmen right behind him.

"I told you so!" Lily cried and bolted.

The three friends raced down the alley where another street offered them a way out. Now they had no choice but to run away from Tyrekirk. This was getting them nowhere.

Grant grabbed Lily's hand to make sure they stayed together. Betty dashed into the square and saw at a glance that there was no one around. The three friends had a straight run to....

They burst into the square and Grant lunged for some nameless street leading God only knew where when a hair-raising shriek made Betty's skin crawl. She had heard that sound way too many times not to recognize it.

Another flood of soldiers erupted into the square with dozens of Highland tigers at their heels. The soldiers poured from four different streets all running for their lives toward Tyrekirk.

The tigers dashed after them on their springy, silent paws. They overtook the soldiers easily, sailed onto the fleeing soldiers' backs and heads, and brought them to the ground. The cats had no trouble dispatching their enemies and running on to catch anyone who escaped.

Armed men burst into the open to help the cats mow down every Creighton they could catch. In a split second, the battle flooded the square. Cats and men surrounded Grant, Lily, and Betty.

The same raging cry flew from mouth to mouth. "Creighton bastard! Die, Creighton scum!"

More townsfolk veered out of line to come after Grant. They boxed Grant and Lily in with two dozen fighters surrounding the couple and then, as if out of Betty's worst nightmare, the cats came after Grant and Lily, too.

Betty dove in trying to carve her way to her two friends. She had to stop the Buchanans from attacking Grant. She had to stop anyone from attacking Grant. If he shifted into a dragon, he could burn the whole Clan to ash right here in front of her. She couldn't let that happen.

She slashed and stabbed her dirks back and forth. She started out trying to target only the townsfolk, but they fought back and she lost track of who was fighting whom.

Grant and Lily both drew their weapons to defend themselves. Betty slashed her way into the mob from their side. She saw Grant and Lily fighting the townsfolk, Grant and Lily fighting Buchanans, Highland tigers fighting soldiers, and soldiers fighting townsfolk.

The whole square dissolved into chaos with everyone fighting everyone else. Betty faced off against so many attackers that she couldn't count them. Her fevered brain spotted weapons flashing and she blocked, parried, and retaliated without ever seeing who was holding them.

She whirled through the mayhem trying to get.... somewhere. She didn't even know where Grant and Lily were anymore or if they were still alive at all. So many bodies and weapons surrounded Betty that she couldn't think. She just had to keep herself alive long enough to....

A screech set her nerves on fire. She had a fraction of a second to see a Highland tiger soaring toward her head. She stabbed out with her dirks, but the cat saw and contorted around them.

The tiger whipped his body around her arms and sank his claws into her skin. All the insanity of her fight against Reid came back in a split second. This creature was trying to kill her. Who he was didn't matter anymore.

She dropped the dirk out of her left hand, seized the tiger by the fur, and ripped him off, claws and all. His claws raked her skin, but the pain only ignited an even more furious response from her.

She hauled back her arm and slammed him down on the cobblestones with all her might. She bared her teeth in a primal snarl of deadly fury, pinned him down, and raised her dirk to drive it into his body.

She locked her eyes on the tiger just long enough to check her aim. She tensed every muscle to stab the blade down...but it wasn't a tiger. A man stretched out on the paving stones under her hand. His eyes drilled up into hers. It was Reid.

"Lassie...." he panted. "Dinnae kill me! It's me! It's Reid."

She could see perfectly well who it was, but she couldn't force her muscles to relax. Her hand pressed down on his bare chest. He wasn't wearing his shirt and jacket anymore. His feet and legs were bare and sweat drenched his hair, face, and body.

A layer of sweat sealed her hand to his chest right above his heart. His heart pounded through his sternum and that drumming rhythm vibrated into her through her arm.

She felt herself holding him down on the ground, but she couldn't move to take her hand away. She no longer had any desire to kill him, but she couldn't lower her dirk. Would she ever be able to turn off this raving, murderous frenzy?

A familiar bellow made Betty look up. Everything changed in a split second when she spotted Colton and Jaimee trying to fight their way to Grant and Lily.

Grant and Lily stood shoulder to shoulder against a nearby building. They faced outward in both directions struggling to hold the combined townsfolk and Buchanan fighting force at bay.

"Get back, ye bastards!" Colton roared. "Get back before I tear ye apart meself!"

He kicked a few tigers out of his way and plunged into the crowd of townsfolk throwing elbows, grabbing heads, and smashing them onto his knees.

Jaimee had armed herself with a saber and dirk that Betty had never seen before. Betty thought she recognized the Creighton crest on Jaimee's weapons.

Jaimee chopped her saber at everyone within range and fought her way through the crowd right behind Colton. They started to get near Grant and Lily only for both armies to turn on Colton and Jaimee, too.

"Traitors!" a few of the townsfolk yelled out. "Turncoats!"

Betty sprang to her feet to rush over to help them. She barely hesitated long enough to extend her hand to Reid and help him up.

The situation threatened to disintegrate again with more and more townsfolk turning on Colton. The standoff would blow up any second now.

Betty shoved her way into the crowd, too, but she didn't get there quickly enough. Two townsfolk raised their sabers to cut Colton down.

Jaimee leapt in front of him and blocked their strokes and Reid and Betty reached them a second later. The four friends rotated in line in front of Grant and Lily. "Listen here, ye lot!" Colton roared. "Ye Buchanans, ye listen to me if ye ever hope to go home to Icemeet."

The townspeople's grumbling disturbed what would have been a tense silence, but at least no one attacked trying to kill the four friends.

"How do ye think we got across the Boundless?" Colton thundered. "Do ye think it was an accident that the Creighton army retreated before us and left the beach clear? Do ye think the gates opened by themselves to let us in? This man called the army back and opened the gate for us. Without him, we'd be out on the planes right now getting our arses fried by those dragons. Didnae ye see him fighting his own to protect us?"

All the grumbling died to a whisper and then a breath, but Betty didn't relax an inch. Her wild eyes darted over the crowd searching for the one person who would make the first move.

If the townspeople or even the Buchanans turned against Colton now to get to Grant, then Reid, Betty, Jaimee, and Colton fighting together wouldn't be able to stop anyone. The four of them would be the first to go down.

Plenty of people glared at Grant and more than a few glared at Colton for standing up for him.

"Who do ye think ye'll elect as Clan Chief once ye've killed me and Reid into the bargain?" Colton bellowed. "Ye—Callum! Ye—Dougal! Do ye fancy yerself as Clan Chief once all Neill Buchanan's sons are gone? Is that it? Do ye plan to stand by and watch this riffraff cut me down? Huh? I'm unarmed. Is that the honor of Clan Brodie now—cutting down unarmed men? Ye're all cowards!"

"Those three are armed," someone grumbled from the left.

Colton whirled in that direction and bared his teeth even more dangerously. Betty sent up a secret prayer of relief that Colton wasn't looking at her like that. "Who said that? Which one of ye coward scum said that? Ye'd face off a hundred-strong army against two unarmed men and three lassies half yer size? Is that yer honor? Is that what Clan Brodie is worth now? Is that the mettle of men who'll free this city from the Laird? I dinnae think so. Ye take that radge hackit back to the slums where ye belong....and ye Buchanans pack yer tadgers off to the forest for ye winnae set foot inside Icemeet again as long as I'm alive."

An old man with a disgusting kilt and a black patch over one eye shouldered his way through the crowd. "Ye'd stand with one of *them* against us? Ye deserve to die in the streets like a dog."

Colton didn't back down at all. In fact, he swelled up his shoulders until he looked twice as big. "If it's war ye want between yer kind and ours, we'll take ye to the cleaners. Then ye can kiss yer glorious revolution goodbye for ye winnae get any help from us or ours ever again."

A deadly silence fell over the square. No one moved or breathed. Everyone stayed perfectly still watching and waiting for someone to twitch the wrong way. Then the square would explode into the biggest killing spree in history.

The old man finally humphed and waved to the townsfolk. "Put yer blades down, lads."

No one moved, but the old man pretended not to notice. He turned back to Colton. "None of us can get inside the castle with the Laird's protection in the way. Do ye have any wizards with ye?"

Colton scowled at him for a second. Was Colton going to let this slide or not?

He finally cleared his throat and waved at something behind the old man's shoulder. "Connell's here. He's the best we've got."

The old man nodded and turned to Reid. "Ye're his brother, then?"

"Aye." Reid stuck out his hand. "Reid Buchanan."

The old man shook Reid's hand and a shiver went through the assembly. People started to relax.

The old man turned to Betty. "And ye're another of these lassies from somewhere else, I suppose. Me name's Clyde McKay."

"He knows Echo," Jaimee chimed in. "She told him about the offensive and asked him to bring these people to join us."

Betty didn't move. She wasn't ready to start trusting this man. She jumped out of her skin when Reid elbowed her. She glanced over at him and he jutted his chin at Clyde's hand.

She pulled her head out of the clouds and shook it. She mumbled. "It's very nice to meet you," and that was it. The standoff came to an end.

Clyde curled his lip at Grant. "Ye dinnae have any wizards with ye, do ye?"

"I did, but he's gone now. I wish I did, but as ye can see, it's just the two of us."

"Ye said ye had wizards of yer own," Colton cut in. "What happened to that?"

"Aye," Clyde muttered. "I was just asking. The more we have, the better our chances. Where's yer laddie?"

Colton's eyes flashed one more time. He gave Reid a pointed nod and then Colton pushed his way into the crowd.

It took him longer than it should have to work his way all the way across the square. Every Buchanan and Brodie seemed to decide to stand before him and meet his gaze.

He didn't miss a single man. He stood up even straighter and didn't hesitate to confront anyone who wanted to confront him. He held their gaze as long as necessary before each person moved out of his way.

Another male voice drifted out of the crowd from the very back. "Get out of the way, ye glaikit coward bastards! Get the devil out of me way before I crack yer heads, the lot of ye!"

Connell finally shoved enough of his Clansmen aside to reach Colton. "Sorry, lad!" Connell panted. "I had the deuce of wizards back there. I got here as soon as I could. Where do ye want me?"

"Come on with me, man." Colton shot one last menacing glance around at his Clansmen, the Brodies, and all the other townsfolk who stood silently watching.

Colton hooked his arm around Connell's shoulders and steered him forward to face Clyde.

"This is me cousin, Connell," Colton told Clyde. "If he cannae do it, it cannae be done."

"We'll see about that," Clyde growled back. "Ye lot follow me. We'll meet up with our own lads and see what's what."

Clyde turned back to the mob and started motioning everyone away. "On ye go, lads. We're going back to the hotel."

"Hold it." Reid stepped forward to stop him. "We cannae go to any hotel. We must return to Tyrekirk and try this magic of yers on the field. The longer we delay, the stronger position the Laird will be in to stop us."

"We cannae take down the field with one wizard. We've tried it a hundred times already." Clyde turned to Connell. "Did ye try to get through the field, lad?"

"Aye. I saw our Clansmen trapped inside, but I couldnae break the spell. It's stronger than any I've seen."

"It's the Laird's. Ye see?" Clyde said to Colton. "We need more than one and that means meeting up with our own lads. They'll meet us back at our own place. It isnae any hotel. I can promise ye that." He waved the Brodies away. "Ye lot go on back to yer own territory. We'll send ye a messenger when it's time to kill a few more Creightons."

Grant spoke up for the first time. "If it's wizards ye need, perhaps Betty can take down the field."

"Yeah! That's an idea," Lily exclaimed. "Try it, Betty."

Betty shook her head and tried to back away, but she only wound up bumping into a bunch of Buchanans standing behind her. "Naw! I couldn't do that. I don't really have magic."

"You could combine your magic with Connell's," Jaimee pointed out. "You wouldn't have to do it alone."

"No!" she snapped much louder than she meant to. Her own voice sounded unnaturally loud in the much larger silence. "I told you! I don't have any magic."

"Leave her be," Reid chimed in. "She doesnae want to do it and I dinnae think there's a man here that would have her do it against her will."

Those words rang out even louder. His voice echoed back, reverberated in her ears, and made her even more uncomfortable. She didn't want anyone talking about her having magic, but Reid talking about it felt like the lowest blow yet.

"The sun will be going down soon at any rate," he went on in a much softer tone. "It winnae be safe on the streets with the dragons prowling about. We can fall back to this hotel and find these wizards ye mentioned. We'll decide what to do and then we'll do it come the morning."

So many Highlanders jammed the square that it took a long time for everyone to get out of the area. The Brodies left first. The Buchanans had to clear the back of the square to let the Brodies through and then Clyde took his people off.

Colton leaned in close to Grant and Lily. "Ye two stick close to me and Jaimee. Dinnae let yerselves get separated from us for any reason. I dinnae like to think about a blade in need of a home finding its way to either of ye before the sun rises."

"Dinnae ye worry yerself on that," Grant murmured back. "I dinnae plan to be alone with any of these people tonight—not even yer own."

Colton only nodded. He, Jaimee, Reid, and Betty hung back while Fergus, Callum, and Boyd led the Buchanans off to follow Clyde's people to whatever hiding place they had lined up for the night.

Chapter 17

Clyde and his men led the way around one of the few undamaged buildings still left standing in Kald. The townsfolk entered the kitchen yard behind the hotel, but there was no one around. The building looked abandoned.

Clyde walked into a doorway and down some stairs to the basement. The rest of his gang went with him and Reid heard what sounded like hundreds of voices down there.

The first Buchanans disappeared along with Betty, Jaimee, Lily, and Grant. Reid picked up his pace to catch up with them. He didn't want any of them in Clyde's hideout without being on hand to keep an eye on them.

He ducked his head to step into the stairway when Colton caught his arm. "Laddie ....One moment, lad."

"What's up?" Reid asked.

Colton pulled him aside and lowered his voice. "Listen, lad. We winnae be able to keep these bastards in sight at all times. Once we get down there, ye go straight to Grant and Lily. Ye keep them in yer sight while I get word to Fergus and the others. We'll divide up the men we ken are with us and we'll post watches to stand guard.... but we'll do it softly. Let these fools think we're making friends, but dinnae let yer guard down even for a moment. Are we clear?"

"Of course. I planned to."

"Good lad." Colton pushed him toward the stairs. "On ye go."

Reid trotted down the stairs and entered a much bigger underground space than he expected. A lot more people crowded the basement than had been out on the streets. Clyde had been telling the truth about having a hundred more men just waiting to join the rebellion.

Talk bubbled from all sides. Clyde and his men stood around a table going over maps of the city. Reid didn't know or care what they were discussing. He looked around for Betty.

He didn't see her, but he did see Jaimee and Lily standing in a corner with their backs to him. Grant stood to one side listening to them.

Reid went over to them and his temper flared when he realized that Lily and Jaimee had cornered Betty against one wall.

"I told you I can't do anything!" she insisted. "It was a one-time fluke. I don't even know if I could do it again."

"You have magic," Jaimee countered. "You wouldn't have been able to do it once if you didn't already have it. You just need to learn how to use it."

"I can't!" Her voice started to rise to a shriek. "I told you!"

"Do you really want to stand aside and watch more Buchanans die?" Lily asked. "If you made the three of us disappear like that, you could give us a decent advantage over the Laird. Only another wizard can defeat him and...."

"I'M NOT A WIZARD!!" Betty bellowed. "How many times do I have to tell you?"

"You heard what Clyde said," Jaimee added. "The more wizards we get working together to take down that dome, the more likely it will be that we'll succeed."

"Well, maybe there's another way to get past the dome." Betty pointed at Lily. "You said there were tunnels leading underground into the castle."

"Yeah, but we don't even know where they are," Jaimee countered. "We would never be able to find them."

"I bet Clyde knows where they are," Betty argued.

"I ken where they are," Grant chimed in from the side.

"There you go," Betty returned. "Maybe the dome doesn't extend down that far."

"The Laird's magic *does* extend down that far," Lily told her. "He would still be able to detect us even if the dome wasn't there."

Reid stepped forward. He had to nudge Lily and Jaimee out of the way and he planted himself at Betty's side. "What's this all about?"

"We were just trying to convince Betty to use her magic to help the other wizards," Jaimee replied. "We need every wizard we can get."

"I....am.... not.... a.... wizard," Betty snarled. "How many times do I have to say it?"

"If she doesnae want to use magic, that's her own business," Reid returned.

"How are we supposed to get into the castle, then?" Lily asked. "We need to take down that dome."

"Ye've just heard her. Why should she use magic when she's already come up with another way to get past the dome?"

"We don't know if that will work," Jaimee pointed out. "The dome could be down in the tunnels, too."

"Even if the dome isn't there, his locator spells will be," Betty countered. "If I did any magic there—and I'm not saying I could—it could tip him off even if it happened accidentally. You saw what happened with Tristan."

Jaimee's eyes popped. "You know about Tristan?"

"Why dinnae ye go and ask Clyde to check if the dome is blocking the tunnels?" Reid suggested. "Then we'll all ken if this plan will work or not."

"Okay," Jaimee replied. "Go ahead."

"I winnae go anywhere. I'm under orders to guard ye lot in case it all goes wrong in this cludgie."

Grant laughed "I'd go meself, but I dinnae suppose Clyde and his lads would appreciate me joining their conference."

Reid looked around and spotted Boyd nearby. Reid grabbed him, relayed the message, and sent Boyd off to talk to Clyde about the dome and the tunnels.

Reid turned back to the others. "Are ye satisfied now?"

Lily and Jaimee eyed him. Then Jaimee glanced over at Betty. Betty didn't exactly cower before her two friends, but she stood just a few inches closer to Reid. Reid didn't like this at all.

He didn't outright glare at Jaimee. He couldn't do that, but he mentally projected at her a powerful urge for her to go away and leave him and Betty alone. Jaimee had been doing the same thing to him ever since she married Colton and he learned to follow her directives in that regard.

Now he did the same thing back to her and she must have gotten the message. She touched Lily's shoulder. "Come on, Lily. Let's see if these guys have somewhere we can spend the night."

She gave Grant a look, too, and the three of them wandered off somewhere. Reid made sure there were plenty of trustworthy Buchanans around before he turned his attention to Betty. "Are ye all right, lassie? Dinnae let them under yer skin."

She caught his eye and immediately looked away. "Thanks for sticking up for me. I feel like...."

She didn't finish, but she didn't have to. "Dinnae think ought about it a moment longer. It's naught."

"How can you say that? What if they're right and I'm......?"

"It's naught if ye are or ye arenae. Ye're here to fight a war. I dinnae care how ye fight it so long as ye're all right."

She gulped and her face wrenched. This was really getting to her. "It isn't nothing to everyone else. They make it out like we can't win if I don't."

"It's naught to me, lassie."

She finally looked up at him and held his gaze. When she gulped again, she didn't look away. "You don't understand. I only came up with this plan because I'm too scared to...."

Reid would have given anything to put his arms around her right now, but he didn't. "Ye cannae even say the words, lass. That's all the reason I need to ken ye winnae do this. I winnae allow it."

She blushed, tried to look away, and then smiled up at him. "Thanks. I really appreciate it."

"Think naught about it again, lassie. It doesnae exist. It never happened. It's naught."

She flashed a brilliant smile and his heart flipped. He half-hoped she would start laughing. She really needed it right now, but at that moment, Jaimee came back with Boyd, Grant, and Lily.

"Good news," Jaimee announced. "Clyde sent scouts down to the tunnels and the dome isn't there. We can get into the castle that way after all."

"Ye see?" Reid replied. "Betty was right."

"He's willing to go along with your plan to use the tunnels, but he still wants to get as many wizards together as he can."

"Go ahead," Betty snapped. "No one is stopping him."

"Oh, come on, Betty," Lily chided. "You obviously have some incredible power. You might even be more powerful than Tristan."

"You know what? Forget it." Betty threw up her hands and spun away in the opposite direction. "Do whatever you want to do as long as it doesn't include me."

She elbowed her way through the crowd and vanished toward the stairs.

Reid rounded on Jaimee and Lily. "What the devil is wrong with ye lasses? Cannae ye see how distressed she is over this? She's meant to be yer friend, but ye dinnae treat her as one."

"We're at war," Lily told him. "Why shouldn't we use every resource at our disposal?"

"She isnae any resource for ye to dispose of and I cannae believe I even have to tell ye this! She's yer friend and she just saved yer blimmin' life! Doesnae that count for ought with ye at all? I dinnae understand yer thinking, lassie. I really dinnae. She's proved her worth a hundred times whether she has magic or not. I dinnae care if we win the war at all if we mean to throw our own people to the wolves over some mite of nonsense as petty as this. That isnae any victory I care to take part in and I cannae believe that ye would."

He stormed off fuming mad. Why should he have to correct these people on how to treat each other? Didn't they understand what was important anymore?

Chapter 18

Betty climbed the stairs and paused in the kitchen yard behind the hotel, but she only paused for a second. She couldn't stay here. She wanted to get as far away as possible from anyone who knew she had....

She swallowed hard. She couldn't say it. She couldn't think it. She strode out of the yard into a dingy alley behind the hotel. It looked deserted, but that could change at a moment's notice.

She shouldn't be out here. It wasn't safe, but she couldn't go back inside.

She set off down the street. It ended at another intersection and she looked out at another square surrounded by buildings. Women moved around their homes doing their evening chores, but Betty felt the tension and fear hanging over the city.

The women cast glances around and a weighty silence muffled all sound. The few people outdoors spoke in whispers and murmurs. Then they hurried back inside, shut their doors, and didn't return.

They left the square yawning and empty. Betty couldn't stay here. This area was much more exposed than the hotel kitchen yard and the alley behind it.

She retreated back in that direction, but an impassable barrier separated her from everyone downstairs. She couldn't face them.

Jaimee and Lily were right. She should use this power to help the Buchanans. What did she come to Scotland for if not to bring this war to a successful conclusion? What was she waiting for—a sign from on high?

She reached the wall surrounding the kitchen yard and slumped down next to it. She could hear voices coming from downstairs. The people sounded happy down there, but she could never take part in that happiness. She would always be an outsider. She would be Other for the rest of her life. She would be a freak and an outcast.

She sighed and rested her head back against the wall. The sun had gone down long ago. The sky in the west still glowed with color, but the stars were starting to come out in the east.

A silver moon hung over the mountains to the north. That moon would go down behind the mountains of Icemeet. Was Edeena still standing up there watching and aching for Liam?

Thinking about Edeena stabbed at Betty's heart. Would Betty ever go back to Icemeet? She liked it there. It gave her one moment of safety and welcome in this dangerous country. She felt comfortable and at ease inside the fortress walls. Now she might never be able to go back there.... just like she might never be able to go back to her own world.

She remembered feeling anxious and awkward at Icemeet, but only because of the weird dynamic between herself and Reid. Icemeet would have been wonderful without that. Betty could understand now why Jaimee decided to stay there.

Footsteps coming up the stairs made her stiffen. She relaxed when Reid stepped out of the yard. He glanced up and down the alley and came over to where she was sitting.

He slid down the wall to sit next to her. "Dinnae ye bother yerself about those lassies. I've just set them straight."

"You.... what do you mean—you set them straight?"

"I told them to leave ye be. They winnae make any of their demands on ye again."

She jerked around to stare at him. "What did you say?"

"I told them to leave ye be about the whole magic business. I told them ye've the brains and skill to fight this war on yer own merits. Ye dinnae need any magic to be the best of us."

She looked away and went back to staring at the moon. She should thank him again for defending her, but no words seemed to encompass the magnitude of what he had done.

She should have been able to rely on Lily and Jaimee to cover her that way. She never would have dreamed a few days ago that her own friends would push her so far that she needed a total stranger to stick up for her.

She'd known the other members of the Last Division for years. They had stood by each other through the worst. She'd only known Reid for a matter of days. Now their positions in her life had completely flipped.

"It's a beautiful evening," he remarked. "Icemeet looks a mite different from this side, dinnae ye think so, lass?"

She stole a sidelong glance at his profile and he looked over and smiled at her. She hardly dared to believe what she was seeing and hearing.

He really didn't care. He smiled and relaxed against the wall like they were just two friends enjoying the evening. He would really drop the whole subject of magic and everything.

He must have really meant what he said. Her having magic meant nothing to him.

"Do you think....?" She broke off again. How should she put this?

"Do ye want to ken what I think, lassie? I think, when it comes to fighting the Laird's men and even the Laird himself, ye're worth more without any magic at all. Ye've shown us all that enough times. I dinnae mind anymore.... Well, I winnae tell ye a lie and say I've completely given up hope of making ye mine, but even without that, ye're worth more with us than otherwise."

She winced and looked away, but that left her nothing to look at but the moon. That moon told her so many secrets. It brought her face to face with the reality of her predicament. It brought her face to face with Icemeet and all its hidden meanings.

"It probably doesn't matter anymore anyway," she muttered.

"What doesnae matter, lass?"

"I probably couldn't go home anyway—not like this. I could never live like this back home. I couldn't be around my family. Something might happen. I mean, I'd be going back to the same version of America that I came from—presuming Liam actually sent me to the same version of it. He came from there which means there are wizards there and everything...."

He frowned at her with his head on the side. "What are ye telling me, lassie?"

"I just don't care anymore." She let out one last shaky breath and her resolve crumbled. She didn't think about it first. She leaned sideways and rested her head on his shoulder. "I can't go home. I might as well stay here."

He didn't speak. He rested his cheek against her head so effortlessly—almost as if he expected this. He didn't sing and dance or even hesitate.

His solid presence felt so right—so easy. Everything that happened since she got here had been so easy because he was with her. The only hard parts had come from trying to hold him at a distance.

Now those barriers dissolved and left her with nothing—nothing but him and his Clan—the Clan she had already begun to think of as her own.

He turned his head sideways and kissed her hair. "I couldnae think or even function without ye, lassie. I was sick with worry when ye disappeared."

She gulped. Why should she hold anything back from him? She couldn't see or even think of any reason not to let this happen. "Getting separated from you....and then almost killing you in the battle.... I never want to go through that again. I never want to wonder where you are."

"Lassie!" he breathed and he put his arm around her shoulder.

She let her weight fall into his. It all happened so easily. Only holding herself off made it hard. She just couldn't summon the energy to keep fighting what was meant to be.

She settled against his shoulder and all her fears evaporated. This was where she belonged, right here in his arms. He didn't care if she had magic or not. He didn't care if she ever used it.

Warm certainty spread through her. They would win this war together, with magic or without it. That moon over the mountains meant something so different, now that she was with him.

She would never end up like Edeena because she had Reid. Knowing they belonged together gave her so much peace and happiness that she didn't know what to do with it.

He brought his other hand over to her face, cupped her chin, and turned her around so she looked right up into his eyes. She felt herself plunging into the depths of his being. She recognized that sensation, but she didn't try to fight it anymore.

He lifted her lips to his mouth and the kiss swept her away as never before. It consumed her being and burned away all trace of her old self. She didn't have to hide or protect herself anymore.

That feeling of being totally exposed with no protection or hiding place in this tempest—it should have scared her. It should have triggered a reaction of trying to protect herself and stop the storm from raging. It would annihilate everything she knew...about everything.

It didn't scare her. It felt good and she embraced it with all her heart. She didn't want to go back to her old life. She wanted this, even if it meant being magic.

He leaned back, and when he smiled at her, sunshine poured from his face. It flooded her being and made her so indescribably happy. That happiness almost hurt. She wanted to cry from the excruciating happiness of being here with him.

Then she remembered and frowned.

He noticed and a cloud crossed his features. "What's bothering ye, lass?"

She puffed out her cheeks and leaned back against the wall, but that moon comforted her. She didn't fall back into the same funk. "It's all this magic stuff."

"Put it out of yer mind, lassie. It's naught."

"But what if it isn't? What if they're right and I could.... what if I could turn the tide?"

"If it bothers ye that much...."

"Wait a minute. What if this.... this whole thing about me having magic.... what if I could be the lynchpin to putting Duncan on the throne? What if I'm......?" Her hand flew to her head and she gasped in shock at the thoughts going through her mind. "Oh, my God! What if I'm the wizard who's supposed to defeat the Laird?"

"That isnae possible, lassie. Ye're a raw novice. Wizards take decades to learn their craft. Ye've worked magic once in yer life. Ye couldnae defeat the Laird. Ye heard Clyde. All his wizards tried to take down that field and that's naught compared to what the Laird can do."

"But what if I could? What if I trained and learned how to use this magic?" She turned to face him and she couldn't look away from his eyes. "What if this is the reason Liam sent me back in time in the first place?" He started to shake his head. "If it's even possible, I can't turn my back on that. I can't let any more innocent people get hurt and die if there's something I can do about it."

"What do ye plan to do, lass? Dinnae do ought to put yerself in danger...."

"I'm going to be in danger either way. We both will. We're at war. You said yourself I've proven myself in combat. What difference does it make if I use one weapon or another...except that these weapons are a lot stronger?"

He hugged her closer. "Only tell me what ye want me to do and I'll help ye. I dinnae ken what I'll do, but I can try."

"So...how do I do this? How do I learn how to use the power?"

He snorted with laughter. "Ye're asking the wrong man there, lass. I dinnae ken ought about magic at all. Ye must ask another wizard. Ask Connell. He can tell ye."

She nodded and went back to staring at the moon. "I guess I'll have to."

"Dinnae do ought tonight, lassie. It's already late and we'll be lucky to find a bed in that basement. Leave it to the morning."

She opened her mouth to say that it couldn't wait until morning and he read her mind.

"There isnae any time for ye to get good enough to do any good in the assault, but that doesnae matter. Ye're good enough as if ye had no power at all. Ye'll go out as ye are and that's all there is to it."

Those words tore down the rest of her defenses. She leaned in and kissed him. That kiss went on and on until the end of time. She never wanted it to end. She wanted it to lead her to all the bliss and passion waiting for her on the other side of this.

The other end of this was Icemeet. She would go back there with Reid when this was all over. She never had to leave it again. The thought gave her another rush of elation. She could live with that.

His other hand glided past her cheek and his fingers buried themselves in her hair. He pulled her close and her breath hitched when he dragged his fingertips down her neck. Her body quivered for him to touch her all over and claim her as his own. She wanted him to. She wanted to surrender everything she was on the altar of spending the rest of her life with him.

She wanted to give him a harbor from the terrible fate that destroyed Edeena and those like her. She wanted to be the bulwark that made his life a blessing instead of a curse.

A loud burst of sound startled her out of her skin. She and Reid spun around in time to see a flash of light. It erupted fifteen feet off the ground and spat out a young man. He crashed down on the cobblestones and struggled to twist himself onto his knees.

Betty tore out of Reid's arms and sprang to her feet. "Tristan! Oh, my God!"

She rushed over to him and tried to pick him up. Black and blue bruises covered his face and neck. His lip had been squashed and he looked like he had a broken nose.

He tried to stand up and stumbled. "Lassie.... where is he? Where is he, lass?"

"Who—you mean Grant?"

He nodded. "Where is he, lassie?"

"Do ye ken this man, lass?" Reid asked.

"Yeah. He's a wizard. He's a friend of Grant's." She heaved Tristan to his feet. "Come on, Tristan. I'll take you to him. He's right here."

Chapter 19

Reid followed Betty back into the basement and this wizard that interrupted his moment with Betty staggered down the stairs. When they got there, they found the underground chamber deserted.

"Where is everybody?" Betty muttered.

"I hear voices down here." Reid stepped around them and turned into a side passage leading under the hotel.

Doorways lined the corridor on all sides and he saw Buchanans in several of the rooms. Most were bedding down in bunks and berths with seven or eight to a room. The place looked comfortable enough and his Clansmen relaxed much more now than they did when they first encountered these rebels.

Reid was just making up his mind to go into one of the rooms and ask where Colton and Jaimee were when he spotted her farther away. He strode over to her. "Where are Grant and Lily, lassie?"

"I'll show you. Clyde assigned us all places to stay. As soon as you see Colton, I'll show you and Betty where to...." Jaimee spotted Betty and Jaimee's eyes fell out of their sockets. "Tristan!"

"Lassie...." He choked. "Where is he?"

"He means Grant," Betty explained.

"This way." Jaimee set off down the corridor at a brisk pace. Reid fell back to wait for Betty and Tristan.

Jaimee finally waved into one of the rooms. It had a single large bed and an armchair. Lily sat on the edge of the bed and Grant sat in the chair.

He jumped to his feet when Betty lurched into the room. "Tristan!"

"I've been.... searching everywhere for ye.... lad...." Betty tried to lower Tristan onto the bed and he toppled. "Thank God ye're all right."

"What happened, Tristan?" Lily asked.

"Wizards.... the Laird...." Tristan twisted over and looked straight up at Betty. "Help me, lass. I cannae use me own magic on meself."

Betty stiffened and Reid stepped over next to her. No one was going to pressure her into doing anything as long as he was around.

She melted a second later. "I.... I don't know how. I would, but I don't know how."

"Don't worry about it," Jaimee called from the doorway. "I'll go get Connell."

She left and her footsteps faded. Grant drew Tristan's attention away from Betty. "Tell us what happened, lad. Did they ambush ye?"

"They didnae have to." Tristan coughed and hugged his arms over his stomach. He didn't look hurt badly enough to be acting like this. The Laird's wizards must have injured him internally. "I saw them coming all right, but there were too many of them....and then the Laird...."

"You fought the Laird?" Lily gasped. "Jesus!"

"It wasnae him in person. He sent out a shade of himself to occupy me while the wizards finished me off. I barely got away."

Just then, Jaimee came back with Connell. Betty backed away, but not far enough away that she couldn't see what was going on.

Connell approached the bed and passed his hand a few inches over Tristan's body. Different colored sparks danced between his palm and Tristan's jacket. "Och! This is no good," Connell muttered. "They've done some serious damage here."

"You can heal him, can't you?" Lily asked.

"Och, aye." Connell cocked his head and looked up at the window. Then he lowered his palm to rest on Tristan's chest. "Off ye go to sleep, laddie."

Tristan sank back on the bed and shut his eyes with a cracked sigh. "Thank ye, lad. I dinnae ken how to thank ye."

Connell chuckled and then went quiet. Reid didn't see anything happen until all the bruises started to fade from Tristan's face. His nose repaired itself and his lips returned to their original shape.

"How are you doing this?" Betty whispered, but Connell didn't hear her.

He shut his eyes and bowed his head. He stood there quietly for a minute. Reid couldn't see any other change in Tristan, but that was all an illusion.

Connell snapped awake and looked down at Tristan. Connell removed his hand, but Tristan didn't move. "He's asleep now."

"Thank you so much, Connell," Lily murmured.

"We must move him somewhere he can sleep," Grant decided. "It must be somewhere quiet—somewhere no one will disturb him until morning."

"I'll take him." Connell stepped away from the bed and waved his hands over Tristan's body. Threads of light surrounded the young wizard and lifted him up. Tristan floated off the mattress toward the door. "Show me where to take him, lassie."

Jaimee led him back into the corridor and Tristan sailed out of the room. "That was amazing!" Betty breathed. "Are you saying I could do something like that?"

"Do you remember how much worse Grant was on the rooftop?" Lily asked. "Now do you realize how much we need you?"

Betty's features drained of all color. Reid couldn't stand that. He put his arm around her shoulders. "Whatever Betty does, she'll do it in the morning."

He steered her away, but once they got into the corridor, he realized he didn't know where to take her. They had to wait until Jaimee came back for them.

"That was incredible!" Betty murmured again. "What was I thinking not to try it?"

"Ye were thinking ye might still be able to go home to yer family," Reid told her. "There isnae ought wrong with that. No one wants to be a wizard."

"They don't? Is it like that for everyone?"

"Not everyone. The ones that develop young grow up kenning their wizards. They dinnae ken any other way.... like Connell. It comes naturally to him. It always has. It's easy for him and he had other Clan wizards to teach him all his life."

"Wow! I can't even imagine what that would be like."

"And then there's the ones that *dinnae* develop young.... like Duncan...."

She jolted as though she'd been stabbed. Her face twisted in pain at that name. "Don't say that."

"I'm only trying to tell ye, lassie, that ye're all right the way ye are. Dinnae try to fight it if ye can help it. Fighting what ye are will only hurt ye in the end."

"Why did you say it didn't matter, then? Why did you tell me I didn't have to use it if I didn't want to?"

He shrugged. "I dinnae care for ought but that ye're happy and content. If I'd told ye to use it or go insane like Duncan, ye'd have fought it even more."

"You're right. I would have."

"Either way, ye're as excellent as ye ever were without it. I dinnae need magic to ken I want ye for meself."

She looked up at him with eyes so moist with emotion that he couldn't keep his hands off her. He put his arms around her and kissed her right there in the corridor. He didn't care if any of his Clansmen saw him with her. They would all find out pretty soon anyway.

He recognized Jaimee's footsteps coming back and he pulled away. He let go of Betty and they both separated to face Jaimee.

She slapped her palms against her thighs. "Okay! Tristan is all set and Connell is going back to his bunk. Do you need to see Colton or do you just want to go to sleep?"

"I dinnae need to see him if he doesnae need to see me."

"Okay. Follow me."

She headed off toward the other end of the corridor. More open doors gave Reid a view of Clyde's townspeople bunked down together, more Buchanans, and finally one last bedroom with Colton putting a saber on the chair. He had his back to the door and didn't see Reid and Betty passing.

Jaimee halted by another bedroom. It had a single large bed in it. "Here you go."

She looked straight up at Reid without a shred of a smirk. Her eyes sparkled with knowing, but other than that, she gave no sign that she was doing anything out of the ordinary by putting Reid and Betty in one room.

"Thank ye, lass," he murmured under his breath and he never meant any words more in his life. She knew and that meant that Colton already knew, too. How could they not know after the way Reid and Betty had been acting around each other?

No one had to explain anything to anyone. It was done and it would never be undone. Now Reid could finally rest. All the old pain and hopelessness evaporated forever out of his life.

Jaimee squeezed his arm once and walked off without a backward glance. Reid could just imagine the conversation she would have with Colton when she got back to their room.

Reid stepped across the threshold, but Betty didn't. She glanced up the corridor in Jaimee's direction and then surveyed the room. "Did that mean what I think it meant?"

"Aye. Are ye coming in, lass?"

She hesitated a moment longer, but he didn't try to rush her. She would take some time to get used to this.

She finally stepped in and shut the door behind her. "I guess it's only a matter of time before everyone finds out."

"Aye.... if they dinnae ken already."

She turned bright red and then burst into nervous giggles. "So....is there any kind of secret ritual we have to go through to mate for life?"

"There's no secret ritual. It's already done."

Her head shot up and her eyes widened. "It is?"

"Aye. Ye're here in me own room. What more is there?"

She blushed again and looked at the floor. "Nothing, I guess."

He walked over to her. The air charged with tension and electricity. It set his nerves on fire. He was mated to this woman for life and that simple fact changed everything. It changed him at a root level. He would never be the same after tonight.

He didn't want to be the same. He wanted to be whatever she changed him into. He wanted to be the man who shared her life, the man she relied on, the man whose life and fate hung on her word and her every look.

He slipped his hand into hers and drew her near him. Just feeling her presence made him breathless with so much trembling happiness. He wasn't sure he could get through this night, but he had to. He couldn't wake up tomorrow not bonded with her. He couldn't survive another day without that bond to keep him strong and vital.

He pulled her over to the bed and sat down on it. He drew her between his knees and guided her mouth down to meet his. Her hands fell on his shoulders and her skin touching his bare body exploded his head apart. It was happening. They were bonding.

She didn't fight him when he caressed his hands down her arms and behind her back. She shivered and tensed all over, but those trembling, gasping breaths in his nose and mouth told him that she was excited, not scared.

Her tongue slithered around his and lit his whole world on fire. She was pure magic—every single inch of her. Her golden luxurious hair fell around his face and he floated in a dream that overpowered every memory in his life.

She straightened up and gazed down into his eyes. He read so many layers of meaning and silent communication in her eyes and facial expression. He could spend the rest of his life studying her and never learn all her shades and moods.

His skin ignited in flames when she pushed his tartan off his shoulder. It fell aside and left his chest, shoulders, back, and stomach bare and exposed to her touch. She wasn't even touching him yet and he already felt like she was flaying him alive. She stripped away everything on the surface and left his heart and soul bleeding and fragile for her to do whatever she wanted with him.

Then her hand glided sideways, off his shoulder to his arm, and back up. Was this what she felt when he touched her—this volcanic lava pouring down his body and consuming him in fire?

She barely grazed his neck when she lifted her hand to touch his cheek. That one fleeting instant's touch detonated in his brain. It left him breathless and quivering for what was to come.

She petted his cheek while she kissed him and then her fingers trailed into his hair. She couldn't be taking him apart like this. She couldn't be dismantling all his defenses, only to put him back together as the man she wanted him to be.

She stood up straight and her eyes held him in an impossible hold. He couldn't break away. "Ye're working yer magic on me, lassie," he whispered.

"Really?" She cracked a crazy grin that didn't fit with this life-changing moment. "That was a lot easier than I thought. Maybe I don't have to practice after all."

He blinked at her trying to figure out what she was talking about. Then they both burst out laughing. "Ye're a devil, lass!"

She covered her mouth and blinked back tears of laughter. "I'm sorry! I couldn't resist."

His heart spasmed with so much love for her. He had to have her. He grabbed her hand and pulled her down on the bed next to him. "Get over here, ye vixen, and ye behave yerself. Dinnae make me have to punish ye."

She laughed uncontrollably and she didn't resist when he smothered her under his weight. He rolled her onto her back and kissed her as never before. She stopped laughing and her breathing lengthened as their bodies started moving in unison.

He pushed himself up on his arms and tore off her mouth to gaze down at her. Her eyes burned with some heat and feeling he had never seen before, but he didn't have to worry about it anymore. He knew now what that look meant. He was working the same magic on her.

Chapter 20

B etty and Reid stood around the table in the rebels' underground hideout. Jaimee, Grant, Lily, all the Buchanan Clansmen, all of Clyde's townspeople, and five wizards surrounded the maps while Clyde McKay and Colton explained their battle plan.

Colton pointed to a neighborhood about a mile away from the hotel. "Reid and Betty will lead our lads through the tunnels here. This is the entrance Jaimee and I used to escape from Tyrekirk, so ye'll be taking Jaimee, Grant, Lily, Tristan, and me with ye."

"If the Laird attacks again, I winnae be able to defeat him," Tristan pointed out. "He winnae let us get anywhere near that dome to take it down."

"Ye dinnae need to take down the dome," Grant replied. "Ye're only job is to prevent the Laird from binding me. I'll shift and finish him off."

"With any luck, the Laird will be too busy dealing with the rest of us to ken ye're there." Clyde pointed to another section of the wall surrounding Tyrekirk. "Our lads will assault the castle from the outside. We'll get our own lads up to the dome and take it down if ye dinnae beat us to it."

"If they cannae get the dome down entirely," Colton added, "they may be able to get inside, which will give ye added cover to find the Laird and put an end to him."

"He winnae go quietly," Tristan remarked. "It'll take an army of wizards to take him out."

"We can only try it," Colton replied. "We winnae stand a better chance than now when we're all working together. Do ye all ken where ye're going and what to do?"

Everyone nodded. Betty gazed down at the map. It didn't sound like much of a plan against such a powerful wizard, but Colton was right. Everything depended on working hand in hand with these new allies. The only alternative was going back to Icemeet and waiting for the Creightons to breach what was left of the fortress.

"Let's be off, then." Colton turned to Lily, Grant, Jaimee, Betty, and Reid. "Let's go."

Even after Clyde and Colton gave the word to go, it took a long time for everyone to get out of the basement. The Buchanans and the rebels headed for the stairs only to run into a crowd of Brodies showing up from their own neighborhoods.

Clyde had to explain the whole plan a second time so the Brodies understood what they were supposed to do. Then the Brodies brought in four of their own wizards who had to receive their own orders, not just from Clyde, but from their Clan Chief.

The process took way too long. The little cluster of friends who would be going through the tunnels stood off to one side. The three women checked their weapons and discussed the mission in low tones while they waited.

"What do you think of this idea of distracting the Laird?" Jaimee asked. "I don't like the sound of it."

"Nothing distracts the Laird," Lily told her. "He might be focused on the battle outside, but he's planted boobytraps like you wouldn't believe in those tunnels. You saw what it was like when you were there."

Jaimee nodded. Betty turned to Tristan. "I was going to ask you...."

"It's all clear up here!" Colton called from the stairs. "Let's be off. We're already behind time."

The party went over to the stairs. There was no more time to ask questions about magic Betty wouldn't even be able to use.

The seven friends climbed the stairs to the kitchen yard. It was deserted and the last Buchanans were already disappearing into the neighborhoods.

"Where are we going?" Reid asked Grant.

"Follow me. We'll go north to the city wall and follow that to the tunnel entrance."

The journey to the tunnel took so many labyrinthine twists, turns, and false course changes that Betty long since lost track of where she was.

Grant finally came to a high wall at the far northern edge of Kald. He followed it behind several buildings. "We're nearly there."

"This is too far away from the castle," Betty pointed out. "The dome won't be out here."

"The tunnels will be free from boobytraps until we get nearer to Tyrekirk," Jaimee replied.

Betty surveyed the faces around her. "Are Reid and I the only people here who don't know what we're getting into?"

"I can overcome some of the boobytraps," Tristan added, "but I cannae overcome them all. It's only a matter of time before we trip one of them and then it's all over."

Betty gulped. "What does that mean?"

He laughed easily. "It means we'll have to deal with soldiers the old-fashioned way."

"What about wizards?" she asked.

He laughed again. His casual attitude made her more nervous. He didn't seem to take the danger seriously enough for a man who nearly got killed yesterday, but none of the other four showed any sign that they minded.

Betty's mind raced on her way through the streets. What if the old-fashioned way didn't work? What if it worked against soldiers and then wizards turned up? What if wizards attacked the party and she couldn't use magic against them?

Then she had a terrible thought. What if she *did* use magic against them? That would almost be worse than not being able to. What would happen? What would become of her if that power burst out without her meaning to? What if she became like Duncan—insane and out of control?

Duncan's magic did as much damage to him as it did to everyone else. He probably would have killed Elliot if Duncan's magic hadn't made Elliot shift the way he did. Being a dragon of the Creighton royal line was probably the only thing that saved Elliot's life.

She couldn't stand to lose her mind that way. She would rather not have magic at all, but she didn't have time to learn how to use it before she went down into the tunnels.

She was starting to get extremely shaky about it when Grant turned off into a different street miles from the hotel. He stopped right outside what looked like another broken-down section of a building.

It yawned into a cavernous black hole. It looked from the outside like it led into a destroyed back room of some tavern or storehouse. It didn't look like a tunnel entrance at all.

Grant turned to the others. "Are ye all ready?"

Jaimee drew her saber. "Ready."

"As soon as we get inside, the Laird's boobytraps will increase the farther we go," Tristan announced. "Ye must be ready for anything. Move fast so we get as deep inside the castle as possible before it all goes wrong."

Betty and Lily drew their weapons, too. "We're ready," Lily replied.

Betty couldn't say she was ready because she wasn't. She probably never would be, but at least she had her dirks.

Grant and Tristan went first and broke into a run as soon as they stepped inside the building. The three women dashed after them with Reid in the rear. Betty ran close to Lily and Jaimee. She knew this. Fighting with them and running into mortal danger with nothing but their weapons and their wits—she could do this.

The three women checked every side passage as they passed. How much longer before the Laird's spells caught up with the intruders?

Now Betty really wished she *did* have some magic. Having Tristan's ability to detect the Laird's boobytraps and hopefully dismantle them before they went off—now that would be a really useful skill to have at a time like this.

She kicked herself for not talking to Tristan when she had the chance. When should she have done that—on the roof? She couldn't exactly have interrogated him last night when he was injured and unconscious.

What about Connell? She had been with him at Icemeet for days. She should have at least talked to him.... but she didn't know she had magic then.

She considered jogging forward and catching up with Tristan now, but this didn't seem the best time, either.

She was still trying to decide what to do when a massive explosion ruptured out of the wall right next to her head. Stone fragments erupted from the wall and would have pounded her head and body.

By some miracle, all the debris hurtled past her and hit the others instead. She whirled toward the blast trying to see what caused it.

At the moment when her back was turned, more explosions went off all over the place. She whirled one way and then the other trying to see anything in the confusion.

Shouts and yells drew her out of the dust cloud to find the four men and Lily and Jaimee in a standoff against at least fifty soldiers.

Grant pointed his saber at the soldiers. "Stand aside and let me pass! Ye all ken me. I'm going to the Laird."

"Ye're going to the Laird, all right." The sergeant in charge waved his weapon over his head. "At him, lads!"

The soldiers surged forward in a wave of bodies. The friends closed ranks to defend themselves.... all except Tristan. He stepped away and started bombarding the soldiers from the side.

He fired dozens of spells. Betty didn't have time even to wonder what he was doing before the soldiers collided with the party in an earsplitting crash. Blades met and Betty had to fight with everything she had to hold the enemy at bay.

The soldiers outnumbered the intruders and forced the party back the way they came, back toward that spot where the wall blew out.

A guttural roar broke through the noise. Betty didn't recognize any words in the mayhem, but after a few more minutes of chaos, the soldiers' ranks wavered.

They broke apart and she froze staring at a dozen soldiers hauling Grant up the tunnel. The Creightons parted to let their comrades through and then the ranks closed with the whole enemy force separating Grant from his friends.

"Tristan!" Betty bellowed. "Tristan—they're taking Grant!"

Tristan had his hands full and Betty saw for the first time that he was in the middle of fighting five other wizards. He couldn't get anywhere near his friends, much less help them.

He unleashed a vicious barrage of spells against his adversaries, and in the moment's reprieve that followed, he fired a single twining coil of white light up the tunnel.

It snaked between soldiers and struck Grant who struggled and fought against all the men holding him. Tristan's magic surrounded Grant and then exploded.

For a split second, Grant seemed to swell out of his own skin. Dark scales rippled over his skin and his neck stretched....and then the spell evaporated. He sank down to his normal size and all trace of his dragon nature vanished. He was back to normal. He couldn't shift.

The soldiers fell on him even more furiously. He went ballistic throwing his fists and kicking everyone who came near him, but they overpowered him with numbers. Four men grabbed each of his arms and legs. They hauled him off the floor and carried him away thundering in rage.

"Grant!" Lily shrieked. "Grant—no!"

She charged straight into the soldiers blocking her path. She ran headlong into their weapons and five of them rounded on her to cut her down. Reid and Colton converged on her from the right and left. Their sabers met above Lily's head and deflected the soldiers' assault.

Lily went insane under the brothers' protection. She impaled and decimated soldiers one after the other, but she couldn't get through to reach Grant. His shouts got farther and farther away up the tunnel.

Lily dropped five soldiers while they were still distracted by Colton and Reid. Their bodies hit the floor, and in a flash, Reid shifted into his tiger form. His saber clattered to the floor and he collapsed to a fraction of his size.

His sudden shift confused the soldiers. They didn't realize what happened to him until after he streaked between their ankles, wove through the Creighton ranks, and rocketed up the tunnel to reach Grant.

Half the soldiers looked over their shoulders to see where Reid went and Colton struck with a vengeance. He flattened seven of them while their heads were turned. The rest realized their mistake, but when they tried to defend themselves, Colton shifted, too.

He plunged into the ranks whizzing so fast that no one could keep track of him. He leapt from soldier to soldier, scrambled up their clothes, inflicted mortal damage on each man, and sprang clear before they realized he was on them.

He left the three women standing alone across the tunnel, but Colton's assault sent the Creightons into disarray. They turned in on their own formation trying to locate the demon laying them waste from the inside.

More screams came from farther up the tunnel. Betty caught a moment's glimpse of Reid flying in a whirlwind from soldier to soldier trying to free Grant.

Lily gave another enraged roar of fury and that sound set off Jaimee and Betty, too. All three women plunged in to attack the soldiers who were still struggling to cope with Colton's rampage.

Betty dove in with both dirks flying. One thought consumed her fevered brain. These idiots stood between her and Reid. An unbreakable towing force pulled her toward him. Nothing could stop it. She would kill anyone who prevented her from reaching him.

"Betty!" someone yelled. "Betty—help me!"

She didn't recognize the voice at first. She checked each of her companions one after the other—Lily, Colton, Reid, Jaimee....

Another explosion drew her attention to the tunnel's opposite wall. She had completely forgotten about Tristan. She glanced over and saw him backing farther down the tunnel. He had to keep retreating toward the entrance where the party entered.

The wizards surrounded him pelting him with spells and explosions. All his power came together in a single magical shield. The wizards' spells ricocheted off it, but it couldn't overcome them. Every barrage drove him farther away from his friends.

"Betty!" His frantic eyes darted to her once and then he had to turn all his attention back to his enemies. "Help me, Betty!"

She thought fast, but she couldn't for the life of her think what to do. What exactly was she supposed to do to help him?

She couldn't abandon Jaimee and Lily against all these soldiers. Betty tried to move over in Tristan's direction, but the soldiers adjusted their defense and cut across her path. She couldn't break away.

Three soldiers lunged for her while her head was turned. She spun the other way and raised her dirks over her head to protect herself from their combined downward assault.

Her dirks met and a catastrophic explosion went off somewhere in the tunnel. It boomed out so loudly that she didn't hear where it came from.

When she straightened up to confront her enemies, she, Jaimee, and Lily stared in abject horror at the sight before them. The tunnel floor behind the soldiers was starting to cave in.

It started with a few bricks dropping away. The soldiers in the rear noticed it first and glanced behind them to see what was happening. More and more stones dislodged and the chain reaction spread faster and faster.

Soldiers stumbled, grabbed their comrades, and then plunged headlong into darkness. The cave-in started between this formation and the group hauling Grant away.

Colton and Reid were too busy killing everyone in reach to see what was happening. Another four soldiers grasped at their comrades trying to save themselves and then they screamed as they plummeted out of sight.

"Reid—look out!" Betty yelled.

"Colton, no!" Jaimee hollered.

"Grant!" Lily screamed.

All three women charged forward trying to reach the three men, but too many soldiers barricaded the tunnel. No one could move.

The widening maw engulfed the whole floor. Four more soldiers fell and two who had been holding Grant screamed before falling out of sight.

"NO!!" all three women shrieked, but it was too late. The cave-in escalated faster than thought, and with one last cataclysmic boom, the whole tunnel imploded.

The last soldiers dropped away taking Colton, Reid, and Grant with them. Betty screamed herself hoarse for Reid, but it was no good.

One last crushing blast split her mind in half and then the whole tunnel detonated in a cloud of smoke and dust.

Chapter 21

"Can anyone hear me?"

Betty coughed. "I can hear you."

"Where are we?" Lily whispered from Betty's left.

"Um, let me see if I can put the puzzle pieces together," Jaimee growled from Betty's other side. "We were in a tunnel and it caved in."

"It didn't cave in," Betty countered. "Those wizards blew it up."

"Why did they blow it up with their own men in it?" Jaimee argued back. "Tell me that if you're so smart."

"Isn't it obvious?" Betty asked. "They did it to kill us—all of us. The wizards realized the soldiers wouldn't be able to defeat us by conventional means and they wanted to get Grant away without us stopping them. So the wizards blew up the tunnel with us in it."

"It sounds pretty flimsy," Jaimee countered. "Why would they blow up the tunnel with Grant in it if they wanted to capture him alive?"

"Because they used their magic to take Grant away in the confusion," Betty replied. "Don't you remember them saying they were taking him back to the Laird? He's the Laird's heir. They wanted to make it look like he died in the explosion. They wanted to make it look like he was dead just in case any of us survived."

"So now you're an expert in magic?" Jaimee fired back. "How do you know what the wizards did or were trying to do?"

Betty didn't answer. She didn't know how to answer. She wasn't sure how she knew what the wizards did or were trying to do. She couldn't explain it even to herself, but she was certain that the wizards caused the explosion that ended that battle.

She was also beyond certain that Grant was still alive. No one in that battle wanted to kill Grant. The soldiers wouldn't have gone to so much effort to take him away if they only wanted him dead.

"Well, we're still alive so their plan failed," Lily replied.

"That doesn't tell us where we are or how we get out of here," Jaimee pointed out.

A silence fell over the three friends. Betty listened to the other two. They sat on either side of her in the pitch darkness. Betty could hear them breathing, but she couldn't hear anything else. Not a wink of light penetrated the gloom no matter how hard she strained her eyes.

"We have to get out of here," Betty murmured. "Reid could be in danger out there."

"I lost Colton, too, and Lily lost Grant. We're all in the same boat." Jaimee gasped under her breath. "Hang on a sec. I think I have some matches in my pocket."

"Who carries matches around in the middle of a warzone?" Lily teased.

"Me," Jaimee replied. "You can thank me later."

She struck a match and the three women sat up straighter to look around them. The light reflected off their dusty faces and then all three looked up at a massive wall of rock surrounding them.

A tiny semispherical bubble of safety gave the three women just enough space to huddle under what looked like a mountain of rubble and boulders.

"What the......?" Lily began and then the firelight reflected off a thin shimmer of bluish light gleaming on the underside of the rock.

"Oh, my God!" Jaimee breathed. "Do you realize what this is?"

"What?" Betty asked.

"It's magic—your magic!"

"What are you talking about? I didn't do anything." Betty extended her hand toward the ceiling.

The instant she stretched out her arm, pebbles and small stones dislodged from the ceiling. They fell into the bubble where the three women huddled.

"Stop!" Jaimee howled in pain as a larger stone hit her in the head and bounced off her skull. "Aargghh!"

Betty and Lily both screamed as the whole chamber started to collapse. Betty ducked and covered her head with her arms.

All noise stopped. Then Jaimee cursed under her breath and dropped the match. "Hold on," she muttered. "I'll strike another one."

She struck a match and Betty started to sit up. The rock fall had stopped.

"Stop!" Jaimee yelled at her. "Don't move!"

"Huh?" Betty looked at her friend.

"I said don't move!" Jaimee grabbed Betty's arms and forced her back into the position she was in before. Jaimee pulled Betty's hands together above her head.

"What are you doing?" Betty yelled. "Stop it! That hurts!"

"Don't you get it?" Jaimee fired back. "You're doing this!"

"Me! No, I'm not."

"Listen to me. You crossed your dirks when you made yourself disappear. You did it to protect yourself from the dragon fire. Now you crossed your arms over your head to protect yourself from the cave-in. You had your arms crossed at the wrist and now this magic is keeping all of us alive. The rock started to cave in the minute you uncrossed your hands."

"You're right!" Lily exclaimed. "It has to be true. You were in fear for your life both times."

"You're making this up!" Betty countered. "I'm not doing any of this."

"Really?" Jaimee countered. "Uncross your arms and see what happens."

Betty started to sit up and changed her mind. "Okay, fine. So how am I supposed to get us out of here? I don't even know how to use this magic any other time and I'm not in fear for my life now."

Jaimee yelped, "Ouch!" and dropped the match again.

"Don't light another one," Lily told her. "We can talk just as easily in the dark. Save your matches for when we really need them."

Betty settled down. It was much easier to sit with her head bowed under her arms with her eyes closed. She didn't want to see her own magic at work, but now she had no choice but to think about how to use it. It was her only way to find Reid.

"We can't move this rock," Jaimee pointed out. "It could be miles thick."

"Great," Betty growled. "That should make it impossible to get out of here."

"Look, you might not want to be a wizard," Jaimee went on. "I really don't blame you, but we all have to pull together to make this work. We all have to use our skills to get out of this just like we did in Afghanistan."

Betty nodded in the darkness and sighed. "I know that. I'm willing to try to use my magic. I just don't know how. I didn't get a chance to talk to Connell or Tristan this morning and then all this other stuff happened."

"Okay," Jaimee replied in a much softer tone. "Let's think this through. There has to be a way. We can't be trapped down here with a bonafide wizard and not find a way out."

Lily's hand appeared on Betty's shoulder and she squeezed. "Being a wizard is a good thing. Imagine how happy we would all be if Connell or Tristan was here now."

Betty found herself smiling at her friends in the darkness even though she couldn't see them. "You're right. So.... what do I do?"

Jaimee snorted. "If we knew that, we wouldn't need you at all."

"Any ideas?" Lily asked. "Any ideas at all?"

"Can you remember anything about what you did when you made yourself and Lily and Grant disappear?" Jaimee asked. "Can you remember what you were feeling when it happened?"

Betty thought about it. What did she do when she made Lily and Grant disappear to a spot miles away from where they started?

That was the problem. She wasn't thinking or feeling anything. She was so out of her mind with adrenaline that she didn't think even for a second.

"Anything?" Lily whispered again.

"I think so." Betty hesitated for a second. "Just.... follow my lead."

"What do you mean?" Jaimee asked.

Betty didn't take a moment to let herself think again. She uncrossed her wrists and stood up.

"No!" Lily shrieked, but it was too late. The ball of safety started to collapse.

"Climb!" Betty roared. "Climb and don't stop climbing!"

She didn't know how she was doing this, but she started scaling her way through the crumbling rubble. She clawed hand over hand as the rock toppled all around her.

The collapse left just a few feet of space for her to move through the avalanche. She worked to her utmost and finally scrambled out on top of the pile.

Impenetrable darkness surrounded her, but at least she could stand up and breathe freely. She wasn't trapped anymore.

More sounds of falling rock made her jump to one side. She dove one arm into the avalanche and pulled out her two friends a second later. Jaimee coughed and Lily fell on all fours on the floor.

"Are you okay?" Betty patted them down trying to find any injuries. She didn't know what she would do if she found any.

"We are thanks to you." Jaimee choked again. "Where are we?"

"Light another match," Lily told her.

Jaimee sniffed and shuffling sounds told Betty that Jaimee was moving around a few feet away.

A flash split the darkness, but it didn't come from the same place as Jaimee's noises. Jaimee and Lily spun around and stared at Betty.

She held up her index finger and gaped in disbelief at a light shining from the end of her finger. It reminded her of a firefly's glow. It lit up the tunnel with just enough of a faint shimmer for the three women to see.

"What.... the heck....is going on?" Betty husked. "This can't be happening!"

"It's working!" Lily whispered back. "You're using your magic."

"How can I be? I'm not doing anything! You have to believe me!"

"Maybe it's working by itself, now that it's already started," Jaimee replied. "It must be working in whatever way you need it most."

"That doesn't help me much. What if I want to do something specific and I can't because I don't know how?"

Jaimee squinted at the tunnel surrounding them. "Let's deal with that later. Let's see if we can find a way out of here."

"Which way?" Lily asked. "Are we going on to Tyrekirk to fulfill our mission or are we aborting?"

"You lead us, Betty," Jaimee ordered. "You're the one with the light."

The three women rotated in a circle and Betty's heart dropped into her shoes when the light cast around the tunnel. A massive sinkhole cut off any avenue to Tyrekirk. The whole floor had disintegrated from wall to wall. No one could get through that way.

The three women inched toward the edge of the broken floor. Betty pointed her finger down into the darkness and the bottom fell out of her world all over again.

Far below—what looked like hundreds of feet below—a rushing river of water surged and pounded and tumbled onward into the darkness. It flowed impossibly fast and the light reflected off chopping waves on its surface.

"No!" Jaimee whispered. "No!"

That word ended in a crack of anguished emotion. The sound pierced Betty's heart with more agony than she could stand. Reid couldn't be down there along with Grant and Colton. Betty couldn't accept that.

The three women straightened up. Betty couldn't take her eyes off that hole. The blackness swallowed all light along with any hope of seeing Reid again.

How could she come to care about him so quickly, only to lose him on the very morning when she dedicated herself to spending the rest of her life with him? Was she destined to become a wreck like Edeena after all?

"He can't be gone!" Jaimee choked. "He can't be! He has to be alive somewhere. He has to!"

Betty looked up and her throat constricted when she saw tears streaming down Jaimee's cheeks. Jaimee never broke down—not during the war, not afterward—not ever. She never shed a tear for any of her fallen comrades. She never showed the slightest distress at losing her whole life along with the lives of her teammates.

Now the tears of a thousand deaths poured down her cheeks. She looked up at Betty through swimming tears and Jaimee's lips trembled when she tried to speak. "He can't be gone, Betty! He can't be! He has to be alive somewhere! He has to be!"

Betty gulped down the lump in her throat, walked over to Jaimee, and put her arms around her friend. Jaimee always acted so hard and unfeeling, but that woman was long gone.

"I know," Betty murmured in her ear. "I know he's alive. He has to be and we're going to find him. We're going to find him and Reid. Understand?"

Betty crushed Jaimee in a tight hug and then pushed her back. Betty rubbed Jaimee's arms and kept repeating the same hollow words. Betty had to say them to convince herself as much as Jaimee.

"They're both alive. I know they are. We'll find them. We have to. Okay? We're going back that way. We'll find another way out of here and then we'll decide what to do. Understand?"

Jaimee nodded, but she couldn't talk with her twisted lips pinched together. Betty couldn't look at her. Betty couldn't see someone else expressing the despair and anguish she felt in her own heart.

She had to keep believing that Reid was alive. He had to be. She couldn't survive without him.

She turned to Lily. Lily stared at the sinkhole with her shoulders hunched. Her face registered no expression at all, but the same heavy cloud of hopeless despair hung over her.

Betty walked over to her, but Lily didn't look up. She just stared down into the darkness and Betty knew exactly how Lily felt. Her whole life was down there in that river.

If Colton, Grant, and Reid were lying dead at the bottom of that river, then the three women would lie down there forever, too. They might keep walking around and talking and doing things. They might even succeed in overthrowing the Laird and putting Duncan on the Seat of Armstrong.

None of that meant anything without the men who meant so much to them. None of them could live without Colton, Reid, and Grant.

Betty put her hand on Lily's shoulder and squeezed. "We're going to find him. We *will* find him."

Lily nodded and Betty couldn't delay anymore. She turned away. "Come on."

Chapter 22

Betty led the way back up the tunnel, back toward the entrance. The light shining from her fingertip only illuminated a few feet in front of them, and after just five minutes, the three women came face to face with another cave-in.

"It looks like we'll have to dig our way out," Jaimee observed.

"You know what this is, don't you?" Lily chimed in.

"What do you mean?" Betty asked. "It looks like a pile of rock to me."

"Tristan," Lily murmured. "The wizards destroyed the tunnel to kill Tristan."

Betty rushed forward. "We have to get him out! He could be hurt or in trouble."

"Forget it," Jaimee growled. "If he's under there, he's dead for sure."

"Not necessarily. He could be buried in another magical ball like the one I made. Come on. Help me."

Betty ran over to the rock pile and started pulling stones and blocks off the stack. She threw them aside and clawed more debris aside with her fingers.

"Why don't you just use your magic to move the pile?" Jaimee asked. "I've seen Connell do it a million times."

"Because I don't know how," Betty fired back over her shoulder. "Come on. Help me."

"This will take hours and we don't even know if Tristan is alive under there. We have more important things to worry about.... like finding Colton and Reid."

Betty hesitated and then slumped. "You're right."

Jaimee climbed up on the rock pile next to her. "Let's move some of the rock at the very top. We can probably create a hole big enough for us to crawl through."

The three women scaled to the very ceiling, and as Jaimee suggested, they succeeded in creating a hole by removing just a few large rocks.

"You better go first, Betty," Jaimee remarked. "If anything is waiting for us on the other side, you'll be able to deal with it better than we can."

Betty rolled her eyes. "It's only my first day and I'm already sick of having magic."

She worked her head and shoulders into the hole and clambered out on the other side. She shone her finger around the tunnel and gasped in horror. "Tristan! Oh, my God!"

"Is he there?" Lily called from the other side.

"He's here and he's hurt! Come on! Get through. Hurry! We have to dig him out."

Betty almost fell to her death in her haste to get down the other side of the stack. She collapsed on her knees fighting down panic when she shone her light on Tristan.

A giant mound of rock covered his lower body and his upper body didn't look much better. Ugly smash marks dotted his torso and most of his face had been pulverized by a massive blow.

She touched his shoulder which was one of the only undamaged parts of him. "Hold on, Tristan! We're going to get you out of here!"

Jaimee climbed down and covered her mouth when she saw him. "Jesus!"

"Help me!" Betty sprang to her feet and started pulling the rock off Tristan's legs. She pitched them aside and, after the third large boulder, she really wished again that she knew how to use her magic. This was taking way too long.

"Lassie...." he rasped. ".... help me...."

"I'm trying, Tristan! Just hold on...just a little longer."

"Help me, lassie...." His head lolled to one side before he managed to open his eyes. "Lassie...."

She panted too hard from the effort of moving the rock. She couldn't talk anymore and she had no idea what she would do once she got him unburied.

She, Jaimee, and Lily finally removed enough of the rock to see what was left of his legs. Betty had to fight back the urge to be sick.

"We're getting you out of here, Tristan," she told him again. "We're going to pick you up..."

"How?" Jaimee asked.

"If you won't do it, I will." Betty bent down and tried to pick him up.

She pushed her arms under his torso and he let out a piercing scream that echoed up and down the tunnel.

"Stop!" Lily shrieked. "You'll kill him."

Betty buckled onto her knees by his side and fought back tears. She couldn't watch her only chance die right here in front of her.

"Help me, lassie...." Tristan croaked again.

"How?" she wailed. "Just tell me how."

He grabbed her wrist and pulled her hand onto his chest. "Here.... please...."

She gulped struggling to keep it together. She couldn't let him down. This man might be the only person alive who could show her how to do this.

"Tell me," she urged. "Tell me the spell to heal you."

"I cannae...." His voice trailed off until he seemed to rally again. "Wizards.... we spend years learning all the spells for everything. Ye dinnae have time for that."

"What am I supposed to do, then?" Tears stung her eyes and one escaped. It burned a fiery path down her cheek. "Please tell me, Tristan. I only want to help you, but I've only been able to do this when I'm in danger."

"Ye must find the raw power within ye. Ye must let it flow through ye. Ye must make yerself a river and let it go its own way while ye stand aside out of its path."

She blinked down at him. A river? That blue-black shimmer of death and destruction at the bottom of the sinkhole....it rushed and surged and churned before her mind's eye. Was her power like that river—black and dangerous and hidden? Why not?

Let it go its own way while ye stand aside out of its path. Was that what she'd been doing all the other times? She certainly stood aside out of its path on the battlefield....and then when she climbed out of the rock pile. She didn't think. She just did it.

"You're doing it, Betty!" Lily gasped.

Betty looked up. Tristan had his eyes closed the way he did when Connell healed him last night.

"Don't stop!" Jaimee exclaimed. "Keep going!"

Betty glanced down at Tristan's legs and saw what Jaimee meant. His legs had started to reinflate like a popped balloon someone was pumping full of air, but they stopped as soon as she looked at them.

"Don't stop!" Jaimee repeated. "You're doing it."

"What am I doing?"

Lily tapped Betty on her other shoulder. "Don't look at him. Look away. Think about something else."

Betty blinked. Lily was right. Betty hadn't been thinking about anything when she started healing Tristan's legs.

No, that was wrong. She *had* been thinking about something. She'd been thinking about the river. She had been imagining that river of blackness flowing through her....out of her....in her....

She was the darkness. She was the black heart of Tyrekirk carrying all its deadliest secrets out to the Boundless and onward to the ocean. She carried them where no one would ever discover all the horrible things that Laird Balfour did inside these walls.

That river didn't just move and flow and churn in her and through her. It *was* her. It was all the magic that had been eating her up from the inside all these years. It had turned black and poisonous rotting away in her heart. She never let it out because she didn't know how.

Coming to this country must have released it and now nothing on God's green Earth would put it back in its cage. It threatened to burst forth and she could do little more than steer it in the direction she wanted it to go.

Lily grabbed her and shook her. "You did it! You saved his life! Thank you so much!"

She planted a kiss on Betty's cheek and Betty snapped back to the present. She looked up at Jaimee and Lily smiling at her. Then Betty looked down at Tristan. He looked normal. His legs looked normal except that his clothes were still saturated with blood. His formerly white socks were black with blood and his kilt plaid was totally unrecognizable.

He was also unconscious. "Now what do we do with him?" Jaimee asked. "We'll have to carry him out."

Betty got to her feet. "Stand back. I'll handle this."

Jaimee and Lily exchanged a glance, but Betty didn't care anymore. She had to use this magic. Trying to hold it back would make it explode out of control.

She understood now what happened to Duncan. It didn't take him over and drive him out of his mind because he never used it before or because he didn't know how to use it. It took him over and drove him out of his mind because he refused to use it.

He fought it. He tried to suppress it. It lay dormant and harmless for decades without ever causing him any problems.

Once it woke up and came to the surface, it would no longer be denied its rightful place in his life. He had to use it or it would destroy him.

Now she faced the same problem. This power would destroy her if she didn't use it. That's what Reid said and he was dead right. She just had to direct it where she wanted it to go. Then all she had to do was open the firehose and let it loose.

She looked down at Tristan and felt it…. that unstoppable river of power seething and fighting inside her. It roiled and seethed like some giant monster yanking at its shackles. Was this how Elliot felt when Duncan released the dragon hidden under his skin?

The magical power in her soul felt like that. It felt like an all-powerful demon creature ready to tear her apart so it could unleash itself on the world.

Her hands started to itch. The light shining from her finger felt so pathetic and insufficient all of a sudden. That light could never be enough to satisfy this insatiable devouring monster. It needed out and it needed to use its strength for anything and everything.

"Betty, look!" Lily gasped.

Betty glanced down at her hands. Golden light shone from her palms. It glowed much brighter than the light she'd been using a moment before.

It rippled down her fingers and sparked in the dark air without her even trying. The magic wanted to escape. It would break out any second now.

She aimed her hands at Tristan's motionless body. The magic streamed from her fingertips and surrounded him. He drifted off the floor and started to float the way he did last night when Connell picked him up.

"How are you doing this?" Lily whispered.

Betty didn't answer. It would take too long to explain.

She surveyed the tunnel ahead. She could see more of it, now that the light shone brighter.

Something else made the tunnel clearer to her. Forgotten instincts told her where to go. "We can't go that way. There are too many boobytraps."

Jaimee and Lily stared at her, but she didn't care. She served a different master now. She carried Tristan into another side tunnel. She directed the other two women through several intersections and turnings until they reached another exit.

Betty set Tristan on the floor just inside the threshold. "Let's take a break here for a second. I want to check that Tristan is just sleeping and I didn't miss anything."

"Are you sure about this?" Lily peered out at the city streets. "We're a long way from where we started."

"The sun is going down," Jaimee observed. "We can't do this tonight. We should go back to the hotel and meet up with Clyde's people."

Betty sat down on the floor and picked up Tristan's limp hand. "I can just imagine what Fergus and Boyd will say when we show up without Colton and Reid."

Jaimee didn't answer. She looked out at the city and her eyes narrowed. She didn't cry over Colton now. "He's out there."

Betty looked up. "What?"

"Colton.... he's out there. He's alive. I can feel him."

"Are you sure?" Betty's heart leapt. "Is Reid with him?"

"I don't know about that, but ever since I mate-bonded with Colton, I've always been able to tell where he is and if he's in danger."

Betty gulped. "*Is* he in danger?"

"I.... I don't know, but he's definitely alive. I would know if he wasn't."

Betty surveyed the neighborhood beyond the tunnel. It didn't give her any clues about where Reid might be. Betty's magic didn't give her any clues about whether he was alive.

Jaimee glanced over at her and her expression cleared. "I know what you're trying to do, but don't bother. This isn't magic. It's the mate bond. If you're bonded with him, you should know if he's alive or dead. You should know without even asking."

She studied Betty so intently that Betty jolted....and then she knew. Some other, separate part of her heart already knew that Reid was alive. He had to be, not because she couldn't survive if he wasn't, but because her heart wouldn't yearn for him this much if he was dead.

Her life would be over if he was dead and her life wasn't over—not yet. This driving need to find him and bring him back consumed her heart and soul. It wouldn't leave her alone. She would never be able to rest until she found him. She wouldn't feel this way if he was dead.

Betty's vision cleared and she blinked to find Jaimee studying her with the same unwavering stare. "You see what I mean?"

Betty nodded. Of course. It all made perfect sense now. The mate bond between her and Reid would always lead them back to each other. It couldn't be any other way.

This feeling must have been what made her tell Jaimee that they would find Colton and now it told Betty the same thing. She would find Reid no matter what. They would be together again, and when they found each other, nothing would tear them apart.

Jaimee turned to squint out at the streets again. "The question is how to find him."

"We won't find Grant out there," Lily growled under her breath. "We already know where he is."

Betty gulped again. No instinct or mate bond could get the three women inside Tyrekirk to save Grant. The rebel offensive had been trying to do just that for two days without any success.

Betty tried to think of something encouraging to say, but nothing leapt to mind. The Laird might already have executed Grant and no one would be able to stop it.

Chapter 23

Betty turned away from her conversation with Jaimee and Lily feeling sick to her stomach. Betty would do anything to help rescue Grant from the Laird's clutches, but that wish only brought more firmly into her mind how powerless she was.

She occupied herself by examining Tristan. She touched his chest to see if she could feel how he might be recovering from her healing spell.

The instant her hand touched him, he exploded upright, inhaled a gasp of air, and yelled out in surprise. Betty jumped a foot in the air and Jaimee and Lily both recoiled.

"Holy mackerel!" Jaimee's hand flew to her heart. "What the....?"

"Tristan!" Betty exclaimed. "Tristan.... it's me! It's Betty. See? Lily's here. You're among friends. See? You're okay."

His eyes darted around the tunnel while he gasped and panted for every mouthful of air. Lily stumbled forward and grabbed his hand. "You're okay, Tristan. You're with us."

"Lassie...." he spluttered. He didn't seem to know which of them he was addressing. "Where's......?"

"You're in the tunnels," Lily told him. "We got you out. We're taking you back to the rebels."

"Where's.... where's Grant?" Tristan searched high and low. "I must.... He's in danger."

Lily's features turned to granite and Betty intervened. "Grant isn't here. The Laird recaptured him."

"Recaptured...."

"He's in Tyrekirk...." Jaimee replied. "If he's still alive."

"We must...." Tristan started to get up.

"Take it easy, man," Betty told him. "You're still recovering."

Tristan blinked at her and then at Lily who clamped her lips shut in a grim mask of fury. "How did I.... how did I get healed? I was dying...."

"I healed you," Betty replied. "You helped me use my power. Don't you remember? You asked me to help you and…. you told me about the river. Remember?"

He blinked again and a spark of recognition came into his eyes when he met her gaze. "Aye. I remember now."

She almost asked him how he knew about the river, but she changed her mind. She didn't want to say too much in front of Lily and Jaimee…. or anyone else for that matter.

"We need to get you back to the hotel," Jaimee chimed in. "We need you to get back together with the rebel wizards. These tunnels were a bad idea. They're too dangerous. We need to try again to take down the Laird's dome from the outside."

"We dinnae need the rebel wizards," he replied. "We have Betty's magic now."

"What?!" Betty exclaimed.

"Betty's magic!" Jaimee countered. "She can't take down the dome."

"Do ye remember how all the Laird's wizards worked together to attack me?" Tristan was becoming more lucid by the minute. "They did it just now. Och, they always do it. They never send out just one wizard. They combine their magic to make it more powerful."

Betty frowned. "You can do that?"

"Didnae ye hear Clyde at that meeting this morning? He said they'd work together to assault the dome."

"But he had five wizards," Jaimee countered. "You're talking about using two."

"Aye, but that tells ye naught about which wizards are doing the assaulting."

"Are you saying you and Betty could do the work of five wizards?" Jaimee asked. "Today is the first day she's ever used magic."

"Today is the first day she's ever used magic *on purpose*," he corrected. "All wizards arenae created equal, lassie."

Jaimee snorted. "I realize that. Just look at the Laird."

"I'd wager ye one of Betty against all Clyde's wizards combined," Tristan told her.

"What about Connell?" Betty asked. "He's pretty good for a guy his age."

"Aye. I wouldnae stand the two of us against Connell…or I should say I wouldnae ye stand *me* against Connell, but I'd wager ye Betty could take him."

"No way!" Betty countered. "I wouldn't stand a chance against him."

"What'll ye wager?" Tristan returned.

"Forget it! I'm not…. whatever you're suggesting. What *are* you suggesting—that I fight him?"

"Why not?" he argued. "What better way to find out which of ye is the stronger?"

"Are you saying that Betty and Connell should get into some kind of magical duel or something?" Jaimee demanded. "Kind of like.... like the Highland tigers' matches?"

"I dinnae ken ought about that," Tristan replied.

"You don't want to know," Betty added.

"At any rate, ye'd need to attack each other with spells and see which of ye can best the other."

"So it is like a match," Jaimee concluded. "You'd fight each other to see who's stronger."

"Precisely," Tristan replied.

"Well, forget it," Betty snapped back. "I'm not fighting Connell. We're supposed to be on the same side, remember?"

"Och, ye wouldnae do it in the battle, lassie. Ye'd do it in peacetime—when ye're all friendly and content behind yer own walls. Then ye'd have at each other and may the best man win.... or...." He grinned. "The best lass."

She blushed and turned away. She didn't want to think about fighting Connell or any other wizard. She still struggled even to believe that she had magic.

Jaimee fell silent, too, while she took in everything that Tristan said. Lily broke the silence by speaking up for the first time. "Does this kind of thing happen a lot between wizards? Is it commonplace?"

"All the time," he replied. "We'd blast each other to kingdom come every other day when I was a wee lad."

"You would?" Betty gasped. "Seriously—as in try to kill each other?"

"Och, no!" He burst out laughing. "Nothing as serious as that, but if ye fancied yerself better than the next dobber, why, ye'd challenge him to a duel and take him out behind the nearest shed to prove it."

Jaimee shut her eyes and shook her head fast. "Hold it. You're a Brodie. You come from the slums in western Kald. Colton said so."

"Aye. That's right."

"So.... let me get this straight. Boy wizards out in Brodie country are taking each other out behind the shed and shooting the daylights out of each other with spells and any magical weapons you can cook up just to prove your manhood. Am I getting this right?"

"Something like that, lassie. Aye."

"Wow. And I thought things were bad back in Detroit."

Tristan beamed at them all. "Ye dinnae ken what a charm it is to have all three of ye lassies in one place. Tell me about yer world. Echo wouldnae tell me ought."

"Did she get a chance?" Betty asked.

Tristan laughed again. "No, as it happens. She didnae or I'd have sat her down and wrung her for every detail she could tell me."

"Well, we don't have time for that." Jaimee stood up and approached the tunnel exit. "We should go now before it gets dark."

"Just tell me one thing—just one," he insisted.

The three women exchanged glances. Betty had to bite back a smirk when she remembered her conversation with Reid about emails and airplanes and telephones. This should be interesting.

"You've been in the castle with Lily all this time." Jaimee pointed out. "You should have interrogated her when you had the chance."

Lily chuckled for the first time since Grant disappeared. "He tried. Believe me."

"Grant wouldnae let me," Tristan grumbled. "He threatened to tear me head off if I didnae leave his lassie alone about all that."

Betty and Jaimee laughed. "Now that's what I call a good man." Jaimee squeezed Lily's shoulder. "Come on. Let's get the heck out of here."

"Just one detail, lassie." Tristan scrambled to his feet and hurried over to her. "Please. Put me out of me misery. I've been dying of curiosity ever since I met Lady Lily."

The three women laughed at him again. "All right, Tristan," Betty told him. "I'll tell you something."

Tristan rubbed his hands together in glee. He practically jumped up and down with excitement. "Tell me, lass."

"I can't wait to hear this," Jaimee sneered. "What will it be, Betty—internet dating or the intercontinental Police State?"

Tristan furrowed his brow at her. "The what?"

"Tristan," Betty interjected. "In our time, we sent people to walk on the moon."

He scowled at her for a moment and then exploded in laughter. "Wheesht with yer jokes, lassie! Tell me something real."

"It's true," Lily told him. "We sent them there in a rocket—an explosive-powered vehicle. It landed on the moon and the men got out and walked around. Then they flew home."

Tristan glared at her and then pursed his lips. "Very well, lasses. Have a laugh at me expense. Echo wouldnae pull me leg like this. I'll ask her."

"She'll tell you the same thing," Jaimee replied. "We're telling you the truth."

"Now ye're making me angry." Tristan headed for the street. "I wouldnae have asked if I'd kenned ye were going to mock me. Dinnae ye lassies talk to me again. I'm not yer friend any longer. So there."

He stormed out of the tunnel. Betty almost apologized for offending him. Then she noticed Jaimee and Lily grinning and Betty gave it up. Maybe once Tristan met Echo, Zero, and Liam, Tristan would realize the moon landing really happened.

Then again, maybe he wouldn't. Maybe this war would just keep going on forever and none of them would ever get a chance to talk to each other again.

Chapter 24

Reid kicked and thrashed in the ice-cold water. It kept sucking him under, pummeling him against stone walls, spitting him out just long enough for him to gasp a lungful of air, and then yanking him down into darkness again.

He somersaulted head over heels floundering to reach the surface, but the underground river was moving too fast. He tried a few times to swim with the current to get ahead of it, but he couldn't catch up in time.

Once or twice, he flailed to the surface only to find out that the channel ceiling came right down to the waves. He couldn't breathe. A second later, the current ejected him into open air and he gagged for air before it submerged him again.

He bumped into a body and caught hold just long enough to see Colton. "Laddie....!" Colton roared and then they both went down again. Reid fought to reach his brother, but the current tore them apart and Colton vanished into nothing.

The shock of cold when they first plunged into this underground river knocked Reid back into his human form. That split second probably saved his life. He never would have been able to survive this if he'd still been a cat.

The river plunged down at a steep dive and Reid sailed into the air one more time. An open grate let a shaft of sunshine into the channel. It gave him a fleeting glimpse of a vast plunging pipe dropping deeper underground.

The current thundered over the side and cascaded into the pipe in a deafening waterfall to nowhere. Reid hung suspended over the void for what seemed like hours and then gravity yanked him down hard.

He screamed and contorted in midair, but there was nothing to hold onto and no way to arrest his fall. He twisted around just in time to see Colton soar into thin air behind him. Colton bellowed in shock and terror before he dropped right behind Reid.

A second later, Reid smashed down into a bottomless pool of black seething water. He sank to a stone bottom and then the torrent slammed him hard into a solid wall. It pummeled him all over and he panicked. He needed to breathe, but he couldn't find his way out.

The water roiled faster now. It tumbled him over and over, pounded him into solid objects he couldn't see, and threatened to drown him every time he got near the surface.

Without warning, he catapulted upward, broke the waves, and roared inhaling as much air as he could. The current swirled as fast and as ferociously as ever, but at least it didn't pull him under again.

He floated for a while in a much bigger channel. The walls were farther apart and the ceiling was high enough that he could stay afloat. Thank God.

More grates let daylight into the darkness, but he couldn't see anything beyond the broad flat river in which he swam.

The surface exploded ten feet away and Colton rocketed into the air bellowing for air. "Colton!" Reid yelled. "Laddie!"

Reid stroked toward him and grabbed his brother. Colton clutched at him just as hard. "Dinnae let me go!" Colton panted. "Stay with me! Hold onto me!"

"Aye! Are ye all right, man?"

Colton nodded still gasping and looking wildly in all directions.

"Do ye ken where we are?" Reid called over the noise.

"Are ye mad? We're under Tyrekirk, of course!" Colton started to settle down. He had to swim harder to keep his weight afloat.

Reid clamped one fist on his brother's belt and Colton jammed his fingers down inside Reid's belt so they wouldn't get separated again.

Minutes passed, but the current didn't pick up again. Reid paddled and floated to give his exhausted limbs a chance to relax. If the river stayed like this, he and Colton could just ride it to wherever they were going.

Another grate shone down from above. Reid craned his neck backward trying to see something up there. He saw tall buildings that might have been Kald, but he couldn't be sure.

"Laddie...." Colton growled.

Reid turned around and his blood chilled when he saw Colton's expression. "Aye?"

"Do ye hear?"

Reid strained his ears and every nerve stretched to the breaking point when he heard another thunderous waterfall.

Colton consolidated his grip on Reid's belt. "Ye hold onto me, lad," Colton snarled. "Dinnae ye let me go for ought. Do ye hear?"

Reid nodded. He didn't trust himself to answer. He didn't like the sound of this. It sounded higher and louder and more ominous than the last one.

Reid anchored both his hands deep into Colton's belt. Colton turned to face him and Colton did the same thing to Reid, so the brothers faced each other. "Ye hold onto me," Colton repeated.

"Dinnae ye bother about that," Reid replied. "Ye winnae get rid of me that easily."

The two brothers shared a deep look of understanding. Neither of them wanted to get out of this alive if they had to get out of it alone. If they were going to die, they better die together.

They worked their way closer together, but the sound wouldn't let Reid relax. It built to a catastrophic boom too loud for the brothers to speak anymore. Reid couldn't see anything in the channel ahead. When the bottom dropped out, it would come as a total surprise.

Colton's fierce eyes commanded Reid to hold on, but his hands already ached from gripping Colton so tightly. Reid couldn't lose Colton—not like this.

All at once, both brothers saw it. Another overhead grate lit up the shadowy channel ahead in a blaze of sunshine. Reid caught a single glimpse of a stone wall blocking the channel. A glimmer of light shone on the luminous edge where the water fell away and then the whole river evaporated around him.

Reid inhaled a giant breath of air right before gravity stripped him under. He plummeted into nothing still crushing Colton's belt for all he was worth.

His body crashed into his brother and then they both smashed down against a solid mass of icy water. The impact tore Reid's hands out of Colton's belt and Colton vanished into nothing.

Reid floundered to right himself, but Colton was nowhere near him. Pounding water drilled Reid down deeper into the void. He didn't know which way to swim to get out of this torrent or even if he could get out.

All at once, a cannon shot blasted him out of the water with a bone-crushing boom. He cartwheeled through the air and slammed down hard. He huddled there panting and whimpering in pain, but at least he was outside in the air. He dug his fingers into sand and gravel. Yes, he was on solid ground at last.

He gagged the water out of his lungs and hugged the blessed earth letting the last tremors leave his body. He didn't want to get up to find out where he was.

Then he heard Colton coughing nearby and Reid looked up. Colton lay curled on his side a few yards away. Was he hurt?

Reid forced himself onto his hands and knees and crawled over to his brother. "Lad...."

Reid succumbed to another retching fit and keeled over at Colton's side. Colton rolled the other way and spat on the ground. He looked all right.

"Reid...." Colton choked. "You're alive!"

"I'm all right.... Are ye?"

Colton collapsed on the sand and shut his eyes. "I'm all right."

Reid shuddered and just concentrated on breathing for a moment. He didn't want to move. He didn't want to think.

An explosion booming in the distance brought his head up fast. He looked toward the sound and Colton looked up at the same time.

They were outside Kald on the banks of the Boundless and continuous concussions echoed out of the city. Reid couldn't lie around and rest anymore, now that he saw where he was.

He dragged himself to his feet and Colton stood up, too. The gate through which the Buchanans entered Kald had been blasted to smithereens. A large breach gave a segmented view of the streets beyond, but Reid didn't see any people running around in there. The battle must be happening somewhere else.

Reid and Colton stood on a gravel bar jutting into the Boundless and Tyrekirk's turrets rose straight up from where the two men stood. Reid had never been this close to the castle before and his instincts told him to get away from it at all costs.

The estuary flowed into the sea only a few dozen yards away and a large pipe exited the castle just here. Water poured from it and drained into the ocean. That must be where the brothers left the channel and ended up here.

The sun was going down and the wind chilled Reid's wet skin. He didn't usually feel the cold, but this creeping sensation came from somewhere deeper inside him. The last glow of sunset gave just enough light to see the surroundings.

Reid glanced across the Boundless toward the Buchanan side. Icemeet waited for him up there. He couldn't see the fortress from here with all the rubble blocking the entrance, but it was still there. He could climb up that mountain and go home.

Except that he couldn't. His whole family was in Kald and Betty was in Kald. If she was in danger, he had to go find her.

"She's in there," Colton muttered.

"Who?" Reid asked.

"Jaimee. She's in there. She's alive and she's searching for me." Colton narrowed his eyes toward the breach in the walls. He went very still for a second and then spun around to confront Reid. "Listen to me, laddie. I'm going back in there to find Jaimee and finish the job of conquering the Laird. Ye must go home. Ye must go back to Icemeet and look after our Clan at Stronghold."

"No!" Reid exclaimed. "Dinnae ask me to do that!"

"Ye must! The Laird will defeat all these invaders and ye must return to Icemeet to take over the defenses. A son of Neill Buchanan must be Clan Chief, and if it isnae me, it must be ye. Go on. If anything happens to me, I need to ken ye're safe inside the walls. Ye've a straight run up the mountain and all the Creighton scum are inside the city. No one will see. Go."

"And where do ye think ye're going without me?" Reid countered. "I winnae run home like a wee bairn and leave all me Clan and kin in Kald to die. Clan Buchanan needs its chief and that's ye."

Colton lowered his voice to a murmur like he might be talking to a child. "Listen, lad. Jaimee's in there. I cannae go back until I find her and get her to safety. Clan means naught compared to this. Ye'll make a good Clan Chief. Ye're more a man than I am even if ye dinnae ken it."

"And what about Betty?" Reid heard the words coming out of his mouth, but he didn't try to hold them back. They felt good to say. "I'm mated to Betty for life and she's in there, too."

Colton's expression changed in a flash. He blinked in surprise and then burst out laughing. "Ye saucy wee lad! Ye didnae!"

"Will ye shut yer mouth and listen a moment? This isnae any joke. Och, she's with Jaimee. If we find one, we'll find the other."

"Aye." Colton laughed again and clapped Reid on the shoulders. "Me own wee laddie—all grown up!"

Reid slapped his hands away. "Get on with ye! It isnae as if ye didnae already ken."

Colton wouldn't stop chucking. "Aye, but I didnae ken ye'd made her yer own for good."

"Well, I have. Ye do as ye please, but I'm going back in to find Betty no matter what ye do. If she's alive in that city, she needs me help and I winnae turn tail and run home now."

Colton only beamed at him. "All right, lad. Let's go, then."

They headed toward the breach. Reid kept glaring at his brother on the side, but Colton only grinned at him. Reid wished Colton wouldn't act so delighted about this, but at least Reid got the news off his chest. All of Clan Buchanan would know in a few hours and then he wouldn't have to think about it anymore. He just had to find Betty and make sure she was safe.

Chapter 25

Lily, Jaimee, and Betty stepped out of the tunnel into the dusky Kald streets. "Where do we go?" Jaimee asked.

"This way." Tristan headed off to the left.

The three women advanced much more cautiously, but all the sounds of battle came from miles away. Tristan didn't act concerned about anyone attacking them, but Betty couldn't stop herself from checking every corner and shadow.

The city got darker with every passing moment. She didn't want to get caught out on the street at night.

"Maybe we should skip working on the dome tonight," she suggested. "We should get back to Clyde's hideout. If Colton and Reid are anywhere in this city, they'll go back there, too."

"I agree with you," Jaimee murmured back. "We're too exposed out here."

Lily didn't answer. She kept glaring at everything, but Betty didn't mind. Betty would be just as disturbed if she knew Reid had been captured and taken before the Laird.

"Here it is." Tristan turned into a different avenue and the three women pulled up short in front of the giant magical dome.

It glowed with an eerie light in the gathering darkness. That light gave Betty the shivers. How could someone wield such magical power to create something like this? What on earth was she thinking trying to counter that?

Tristan acted as nonchalant about this as he always did. He strolled right up to the dome. "Don't touch it!" Lily hissed.

"Won't trying to dismantle it trigger the Laird's alarms?" Jaimee asked. "Won't it tip him off to what we're trying to do?"

"Quite likely. We'll just have to succeed and get inside." Tristan looked over his shoulder toward Betty. "Are ye ready to give it a go, lass?"

She didn't want to, but she had to try if there was any chance of success. She tiptoed over to his side. "What do I do?"

"Ye ken what to do." He raised his hand. "On the count of three."

She swallowed hard. "This is some way to test a theory on my very first day."

"Ye'll be grand. Dinnae concern yerself about it. One...."

"Don't concern myself with the Laird coming after me? You'll excuse me if I concern myself with that."

"Two...."

Jaimee and Lily backed away to the other side of the street. Betty's eyes slipped out of focus. That dark river boiled and hissed deep in her being. It wanted to come out and fight the Laird. It wanted to pit its strength against a wizard stronger than itself. It wanted to vent its great power on something to see just how strong it was.

She raised her arm and all that magical energy flowed down to her hand. Sparks fired from her fingertips. The river chomped at the bit just itching to come out and do something serious.

Tristan took her hand and placed it on top of his own. The monster sensed Tristan's power building to an epic pitch just under his skin. He must have felt the same thing coming from her. Their power combined into an even bigger, deadlier, more explosive force.

"Three!"

Tristan touched the dome and the monster exploded from both their hands. It closed its jaws on the field to wrestle with the Laird's essence buried deep in the magical ether.

A whipcrack stung back, struck Tristan, and sent him flying backward to crash into the wall near Jaimee's position.

"Tristan!" Betty ran over to him and Lily bent down to help him.

"Look out!" Jaimee bellowed and she sprang between them and the dome.

Betty spun around as dozens of soldiers charged through the dome's gleaming perimeter. The street beyond the dome looked empty and harmless a second ago. The soldiers appeared out of nowhere.

Betty stared at them as Jaimee raised her weapons to defend the party, but at that moment, a fork of lightning cracked from somewhere behind her. She glanced down to see Tristan firing magical barrages from the ground.

That one crackle of electricity blasted five soldiers away and Betty remembered. She had magic, too.

She raised both her arms. She wasn't sure what to do so she just let the river off its leash. She let it pour out of her and crazy energy erupted from her hands. It came from her skin and hair and eyes the way she'd seen it happen with Duncan in the forest.

She barely constrained the monster enough to direct it at the soldiers. It would have scattered wildly at anything and everything if she didn't strain every ounce of concentration to keep it under control. Where did it all come from? How did it get so strong so fast?

Tristan scrambled to his feet unloading spells and bombardments everywhere. Jaimee and Lily retreated to the corner to keep out of the way as Tristan and Betty wiped the street with dozens of spells.

Betty didn't see herself casting any spells that she could distinguish. She just turned the monster loose to destroy everyone it wanted to destroy. She hurled soldiers back against the dome and they vanished inside where they came from.

She kept blasting away out of all control until Tristan grabbed her. "Lassie.... That's enough! Stop now! LASSIE!!"

She snapped out of her trance to realize he was bellowing in her face. She barely heard him. Only an almighty effort dragged the monster back inside its cage. She had to summon all her effort to bury it under the surface where it couldn't break out again.

Tristan's voice quaked and his eyes flickered with something like fear for the first time since Betty met him on the rooftop.

"Can ye hold him, lassie?" he panted. "Can ye keep him down?"

Her addled brain took a minute to realize who he was talking about. The "he" that Tristan meant must be the monster.

"You.... you know about him?" she gasped.

He nodded quickly and pursed his lips. "Aye. Are ye all right, lassie? He winnae beat ye?"

She opened her mouth to ask what he meant, but some part of her already knew. That monster—the black volcanic river bubbling in her soul—it would overcome her strength and break out if she didn't keep a constant watch on it—on him.

"I'm...I'm okay," she rasped. "I have him now."

Tristan cocked an eyebrow at her and finally nodded and turned away. "Ye tell me if he gets the better of ye, lassie. He's naught to trifle with."

She was starting to realize that. She might have thought at first that she'd bitten off more than she could chew by letting the monster out of its cage.

She knew now that she could hold it back. She could release it when and where she wanted to. She could pull it back in line when she finished. She just needed practice.

She looked around at bodies littering the street. Jaimee and Lily plastered themselves against a wall far away from the fight. How many of these men did Betty kill with her magic? Could she live with that?

She never hesitated to kill the enemy with any other weapon. How was this different?

It was, though. This power came from her. It *was* her. This darkness.... She was the darkness. The monster's fury was her fury. The monster fed off of blood and destruction. Should she hate herself for that?

She couldn't bring herself to feel that way. The monster's rampages felt too good. She didn't want to hold it back. She could barely even think about holding it back. She wanted all the death and destruction the monster could inflict.

"Lassie!" Tristan snapped and Betty struggled to come back from that deep, black pit inside herself.

Lily inched forward to Betty's side. "Are you okay? You don't look...."

"What?" Betty asked. "I don't look what? I feel fine."

"You look.... different." Lily shrugged and averted her eyes. "I can't explain it."

"I think I know what she needs," Jaimee replied. "Let's get back to Clyde's hideout and then we can think about finding Colton and Reid."

The four friends turned away and went on their way keeping an eye out for any soldiers. Betty didn't ask what Jaimee meant by finding what Betty needed. Betty didn't have to ask.

She needed Reid. She needed his presence to ground her. She wouldn't keep fading out and getting swept away by her magic if he was here.

They set off through the city as it sank deeper into darkness. Fewer people moved around on the street, but the party had to dodge and hide in corners and dim alleys to avoid getting caught by more patrolling soldiers.

At least none of them attacked the townsfolk anymore. The soldiers trooped around making a show of standing guard over the city, but at least they didn't blow up any buildings or slaughter people the way they did before. Betty wouldn't be able to stand that. She would have to step in and do something to stop them. She didn't think she would be able to restrain herself from doing something really drastic then.

She didn't see any dragons in the air, either, but that might be a trick. The Laird might be keeping his dragons in reserve for the right time to strike.

All her hopes evaporated when they got nearer to the hotel. Explosions and yelling got louder as they drew nearer to the rebel hideout. Gold and yellow light flickered brighter in the skies.

"I don't like the sound of this," Jaimee muttered.

Tristan steered the three women into an alley. "This way. We must keep out of sight."

Betty had no plans to show herself, especially when Tristan pulled them into a corner and everyone looked out at the hotel.

Flames licked from the upper windows while a hundred soldiers surrounded the building. Soldiers stood guard over a long line of the townsfolk who had been in the basement last night. They were all Clyde's people.

All the townsfolk had been disarmed and bound hand and foot. The soldiers guarded the rebels in such numbers that no one could get away.

The soldiers lined their prisoners up in a row, marched them forward, and some huge guy beheaded the rebels one after another. The pile of bodies mounted higher by the second.

"Holy crap!" Betty breathed. "This is bad!"

"I don't see Clyde," Lily remarked. "He might already be dead."

"The offensive is over," Jaimee whispered. "We have to get out of here. We need to find somewhere to hide for the night—somewhere no one will find us. Maybe tomorrow we can think about getting back across the Boundless."

Betty looked up and recognized that anguished convulsion in Jaimee's face. She didn't want to leave Kald as long as Colton was somewhere inside the city, but what choice did they have?

"Follow me," Tristan replied. "I ken a place."

Chapter 26

Reid and Colton made their way through Kald heading back to the rebel hideout. Reid paused to check around a corner and his blood ran cold when he saw another squad of soldiers.

They stood outside a house talking to a man in the doorway. Their voices escalated to shouts and then half the soldiers marched around the house to its back side.

Screams came from inside, and a second later, five soldiers stormed back into view hauling two young children by their arms. The children shrieked and struggled as the soldiers dragged them to the front and threw them on the ground.

A woman who had to be their mother attacked the soldiers screeching to wake the dead. They grabbed her and threw her down, too. The soldiers pointed their weapons at the woman and the two children and the man in the doorway exploded.

He lunged for the soldiers drawing a saber from inside the doorway. The soldiers raised their weapons to strike him down.

Reid turned away grimacing in disgust. "I cannae watch this. Come on, laddie. We can find a better way to get through the city without being seen."

He didn't wait for Colton to answer. Reid shifted and streaked away into the darkness. He skimmed the edges of walls and sprang onto the rim of a rain barrel standing next to a tavern.

He vaulted up to the roof and dashed from one building to the next as silently as a ghost. All of Kald lay spread out below him and he found his way back to the hotel with no trouble.

He tiptoed along a high parapet and crouched low when he saw soldiers surrounding the building. Flames engulfed the upper stories and bodies covered the nearest square where the soldiers were still busy executing everyone from inside.

Reid flattened himself to the roof, but none of the soldiers looked up. They probably wouldn't have been looking for a cat anyway.

Colton showed up a second later. He slithered his furry body next to Reid's and they both watched for another moment. The brothers couldn't go down there now. In a few minutes, there would be no one left to talk to anyway.

Reid sincerely hoped that Betty and Jaimee were nowhere near here right now. He sent up a silent prayer that they hadn't been in the basement when the soldiers showed up.

Reid scanned the surrounding buildings and roofs and his instincts told him that they hadn't been. Betty was still out there somewhere. She wasn't here.

Colton meowed in his ear and Reid understood. The two brothers slipped away into the darkness. Reid had no idea where to go, but at least he didn't see any Buchanans among the dead. His Clansmen would all be sleeping on roofs and in shadowy corners tonight.

He sprang from one building to another until Colton called to him again. Reid found his brother on a different roof with a low wall surrounding the parapet. Colton touched his nose to Reid's.

Reid didn't want to stop here. He wanted to keep looking for Betty, but she wouldn't be out in the dark, either. Wherever she was, she and Jaimee would find a place to hide until morning. Then he would see what he could do about finding her.

Colton tiptoed to the corner of the parapet and turned around in a circle. He purred to Reid once and then curled up in a furry ball. His striped, yellow eyes flashed in Reid's direction once and then Colton closed his eyes.

Reid didn't want to settle down, but in the end, he went over to his brother and curled up, too. He sighed and wrapped his tail and body around Colton's. Colton purred much more deeply and Reid shut his eyes.

His mind immediately switched to Betty. Where was she? Was she thinking of him the way he was thinking of her?

He drifted back to last night—their first night together. Just thinking about her skin and hair and eyes relaxed him and he floated away into a blissful dream. She was here with him. She was curled up in his arms asleep. Her presence flooded him with peace and contentment. Nothing else mattered.

He woke up with a start when Colton jolted awake. Sunshine spread across the sky and made Reid squint. Colton shot out of a sound sleep and sprang to his feet even before Reid completely woke up.

Colton growled under his breath, paced the roof, and his yellow eyes flashed. Reid stood up more slowly. He blinked the sleep out of his eyes and strode over to his brother to touch noses. What was wrong?

Colton ignored him, sprang lightly onto the parapet, and peered down into the streets below. Reid didn't bother to join him. He could hear tramping feet and voices calling orders up and down the neighborhood. The city would be crawling with soldiers today.

Reid retreated to the same corner where the brothers spent the night. He sat down and shifted so no one would be able to see him over the parapet. "Listen to me, laddie," he began. "I've an idea."

The tiger on the parapet sniffed at him and turned his eyes toward the north. He blinked at Icemeet in the distance.

"Ye can go home, but I'm staying to find Betty," Reid told him. "I dinnae care if I go alone. I dinnae care if the rest of the Buchanans fall back to the mountains. I winnae leave Kald so long as she's in it."

Colton jumped down and sauntered over to Reid. Colton shifted and squatted across from his brother. "Do ye realize what ye're saying? Betty and Jaimee would be out of their minds to stay in Kald now. Do ye see what's going on out there? This offensive was a disaster!"

"I saw."

"And ye still mean to stay behind? The Laird's men will hunt ye down. The Laird and his wizards can track ye anywhere."

"Ye ken as well as I do that both Betty and Jaimee are still in Kald, but that's neither here nor there. Icemeet winnae be safe, either. I ken what ye're going to say. Ye're going to say we'll retreat back to Stronghold, but that winnae win the war, lad. There's only one way to end the war and that's to get inside Tyrekirk and do away with the Laird once and for all."

"We're as likely to get captured or killed if we stay," Colton replied. "Betty and Jaimee are as likely to get captured and killed as well."

"If they get captured, they'll be taken to Tyrekirk, lad," Reid pointed out.

"And how do ye propose we get inside the castle? We've tried every other way."

"We havenae tried any way but one. Betty, Jaimee, and Lily tried the tunnels and now they're at large somewhere in Kald. Either they've already been captured or it didnae work and they had to run for it."

"All the more reason we'd be bloody mad to try it. Betty has magic and she was with Tristan. Clyde had Connell and five other wizards. If they couldnae get inside the dome with all that magic, what hope do we have? We're naught but tigers, lad."

"I have an idea."

Colton snorted. "I cannae but hold me breath and listen. It'd best be a good one to beat all that."

"Do ye remember the drainpipe—the one that took us out of Tyrekirk in the first place?"

Colton gaped at him with his mouth open. "Have ye lost yer blimmin' senses, man? Ye want to go back in *there*? Not a bit of it, lad. We barely made it out with our lives."

"We didnae ken what we were doing then. We were in fear for our lives and all turned upside down. We didnae ken about the river until we were in it. We can make it back, now that we ken what we're up against."

"Ye're daft!"

"Perhaps." Reid turned his eyes back to the city. "I ken one thing. The Laird is the one thing threatening Betty. She winnae be safe so long as he's alive and he's inside Tyrekirk so that's where I'm going. Ye can stay behind if ye like."

"Dinnae give me yer lip!" Colton snapped. "Ye're me own wee brother! Do ye think I'd let ye go alone?"

Reid grinned at him. "Aye. Ye play the protective older brother and look after me."

Colton didn't take the joke. He ran his fingers through his hair and blew out a shaky breath. "I cannae believe I'm agreeing to this. Ye want to swim all the way back up that channel? How do ye say we should find the one outlet to take us where we want to go?"

Reid shrugged. "I dinnae ken, but I'm doing it. Did ye see the grates in the ceiling? Ye could see which ones led outside and which ones inside."

Colton shook his head. "I must be as mad as ye."

Reid stood up, scanned the neighborhood one more time, and gripped his brother's shoulder. "Come along, laddie. The day's wasting."

Colton got to his feet, but he didn't make any move to leave. He sidestepped in front of Reid and caught his brother's eye. "Ye're a different man than I thought ye were."

"I'm a fool for love," Reid growled.

"No. Ye're a leader. She's turned ye into the man ye were meant to be. I wouldnae have believed ye'd ever be ought but me wee bairn brother, but ye are. Ye're the leader ye were born to be. Ye're a man fit to be Clan Chief in me place."

Reid blushed and tried to look away. "Dinnae spin me a yarn...."

"I'm dead serious, man." Colton squeezed the back of Reid's neck. "Congratulations. I should have said that yesterday when ye first told me. It was crass of me to turn it into a joke. It's the best news I've had in weeks."

Reid gulped down the lump in his throat. He couldn't think of anything to say to match Colton's words.

Reid never dreamed that his brother's support would mean so much. Did Reid ever congratulate Colton on marrying Jaimee? Not like this. He should say it now, but he couldn't get his voice to work.

Colton stepped back and nodded toward the east. "This is yer mission. Ye lead the way and show me where to go. I'll follow ye."

Those words set off a reaction in Reid even more powerful than the one from Colton's congratulations. *Ye lead the way. I'll follow ye.*

Colton was stepping aside as the leader—for now at least. Colton had always been the leader, even when they were boys. All of that changed.... because Reid changed. Colton was right. Everything changed when Reid mated with Betty.

Clan meant nothing compared to his bond with her. Colton was right about that, too. Of course he was. Colton knew all about it.

Reid would go to the ends of the earth to find Betty. He would abandon his brother and everything else he knew. What did swimming up that river matter if she was on the other end?

He shifted and took off at a fast run back the way he came last night. He covered the distance much more quickly. An irresistible force pulled him back to the Boundless and the beach.

He halted in front of the drainpipe and shifted again. Colton skidded to a stop next to him and his black eyes flashed toward the pipe when he shifted. "We both need our heads examined for this."

"It will make a good story to tell the lads when we get back home." Reid clapped his brother on the shoulder. "Let's go."

He marched up the beach to the pipe. The flow streamed out of the opening, splashed on the gravel, and gushed down to join the estuary. The water left half the pipe clear so at least the two brothers would be able to breathe once they got inside—for as long as that lasted. Eventually, they'd be swimming underwater with the current against them.

Reid climbed onto the edge. Water pounded his body and splashed in his face and eyes. He gripped the upper rim with his fingers and hung on. The water already felt incredibly powerful and that was saying nothing about the waterfalls and the main sections of pipe where he wouldn't be able to breathe at all.

He wasn't about to back down, though. He peered up the pipe as far as he could. It vanished into the dark. He would never get a better chance than now.

He dove in, plunged headfirst into the water, and started clawing his way up it.

Chapter 27

Pounding water bombarded Reid's face and blinded him. He fought to the limit of his strength just to hold his position. If he slackened his efforts even once, the torrent would sweep him away. He couldn't let that happen.

Something tugged his belt. Reid struggled to the stone channel wall, raked his fingertips across it, and found an anchor point. He dug his raw, aching fingers into it and held on.

He couldn't remember now how he and Colton had worked out this system, but it was just as well that they did. It was the only way they could fight their way up the worst parts of the channel without losing their lives.

As soon as Reid got into position, he gave Colton another tug. Colton let go of his own anchor point, swam with all his might to pass Reid, and anchored farther up the river. Once he did, he signaled Reid and it was Reid's turn to go forward.

This method gave each brother a few precious minutes to rest and, if nothing else, it ensured that they never got separated. This might take forever, but at least the brothers were making some headway.

Reid anchored himself again and his head broke the surface. Just enough space between the water and the ceiling let him catch a breath of air....and then he heard it.

Colton popped up next to him and spluttered for air. His hair plastered his face and he coughed before he heard it, too. "Blast it! How do we get up that?"

Reid searched the tunnel up and down, but there was nowhere to go but down. He swam the rest of the way to the waterfall and squinted up at the thunderous torrent. "Do ye see that grate at the top?"

"That's miles up!" Colton protested.

"It's inside the castle. We get up there and we'll climb through into the castle. We'll be there. We winnae have to swim any further."

"How do we ken we winnae crawl out at the feet of a thousand soldiers?"

Reid cracked a grin at his brother. Reid was really starting to enjoy being the leader for a change. "Who better to handle them than ye, lad?"

Colton humphed. "Remind me not to put ye in charge ever again."

Reid laughed. "Watch and learn how it's done, laddie. Ye need a few lessons, I think."

He pushed off the wall, swam to the other side of the channel, and moved hand over hand toward the waterfall.

The water pounded into the river with such force that the spray itself stung his cheeks and eyelids. It threatened to rip him away any second now. He wasn't even sure he could climb with so much water hurtling inches away from him. One slip would mean plunging all the way back down and maybe getting swept all the way back to the beach.

He worked his way to a spot he thought he might be able to climb, but it was too close to the falls. Then he realized that the water swept several feet away from the wall when it blasted out of its upper channel. It left the rear wall clear underneath the falls.

Reid migrated underneath the falls to the back wall. "Ye're out of yer mind!" Colton hollered from below, but Reid didn't listen. As soon as he got behind the flow, he was safe.

"Come on!" he yelled back. "We can get in through here."

Colton grumbled under his breath, but Reid couldn't wait any longer. He started climbing toward another open grate sixty feet above the pool. Light shone from the other side and it looked like soft, shadowy light. It must be coming from inside Tyrekirk.

This would be perfect if he was right. He had nothing to lose at this point so he started climbing. His heart hammered in his ribcage and he hardly dared to breathe. He couldn't fall. He couldn't get swept into that river again.

He reached the grate and clung to the wall for all he was worth. He didn't dare to let go to open the grate. He didn't even know if he *could* open it. He hung there panting and made the mistake of looking down.

The waterfall boomed right next to his head. Tons of gallons of water rocketed past his ear and drove him out of his mind. Colton clung to the rock twenty feet below him and hauled himself up one painstaking foothold at a time.

Reid couldn't wait any longer or his fingers would weaken and he would fall. He couldn't ask Colton to go back down the river, either. Reid had to get this grate open one way or another.

He thought fast. He had no weapons or any tools at all. All he had were his tartan, his belt, and his wits.

He dragged himself the last few inches to the grate and crammed his fingers into it. He could hold onto it to anchor himself while he got his belt off. Maybe he could use that to yank the grate loose.

He shifted his weight to hold on with his right hand while he unfastened his belt with his left, but as soon as he put the slightest weight on the grate, it popped free in his hand.

It came loose so fast that he almost went tumbling off into the falls. His arm whipped back and the grate struck the torrent. The force stripped the grate off his fingers and it vanished into nothing.

He screamed in surprise and Colton bellowed, "Reid!"

"I'm.... I'm all right.... I'm all right...."

"Dinnae do that, lad!" Colton growled.

"It's...." Reid peered into the hole where the grate used to be. "We're in. Come on!"

He jammed his head and shoulders into the hole and scanned the surroundings. He was in some corridor and it was deserted.

He slithered through and fell down sopping wet on the stone floor. He made double sure no one else was around and then leaned back into the hole to help Colton through.

Colton crouched on the floor dripping water from his saturated tartan. His eyes darted around and he whispered low. "Well, laddie, ye've done now. The fox is in the henhouse. Now how do we find the Laird and put an end to him?"

"The first part should be easy."

Colton chuckled. "I wouldnae have come with ye if I'd kenned ye had such a death wish."

Reid kept looking around everywhere. "At least Betty and Jaimee arenae here."

"Did it ever occur to ye that they'd want to get in here to save us if we got caught?"

Reid didn't answer. He didn't want to think about that. "Let's find the Laird."

He straightened up, wrung as much of the water out of his tartan as he dared without taking it off entirely, and set off down the corridor. He had never set foot in Tyrekirk before. He had spent his whole life hoping he never would and now he didn't recognize where he was. He didn't even know which level of the castle he was on.

Colton inched after him. They checked every passage and room they passed. "It's too quiet," Colton murmured.

"Aye. I have an idea. Follow me."

Reid shifted and tiptoed down the passage in his tiger form. He paused to listen and sniff the air at the next intersection. He emerged on a high landing overlooking a huge cathedral-sized gallery many stories high. Miles of staircases surrounded it going all the way up and all the way down.

He cocked his head and twitched his ears while Colton did the same thing. He stiffened when his sensitive cat ears picked up screams in the distance......or roars......or screams mingled with roars.

A second later, he realized what that sound was. It was a man bellowing and howling in excruciating pain and Reid recognized the voice. It was Grant.

Reid wheeled sideways and took off down the stairs with Colton right on his heels. The two cats dashed down the staircases in a flash and skidded to a halt on a different landing.

Reid listened to locate the noise. It sounded much louder now. It sounded like the two Buchanans were right on top of it. It wasn't coming from directly below them, though. It only sounded that way because Grant was yelling so loudly.

Reid streaked downward again and slid on a polished marble floor at the very bottom. The stairs ended in an even bigger lobby or court of some kind.

Reid whipped around and saw two enormous double doors not far away. Grant's howls and roars in pain came from right behind those doors.

An old man stood outside the doors with his head bowed. He had his back to the two cats and the man's shoulders quaked with suppressed emotion.

Reid didn't think twice. Grant was behind those doors, and if he was in that much trouble, Reid could think of only one person who could be causing it.

He took off running at his top speed. He sprang along the tiles on silent paws, but he didn't care if he made any noise or alerted the old man of his arrival. Reid would take down the old man and anyone else who got in his way.

The old man didn't see him coming. Reid launched himself off the floor. He got halfway to the doors, but the old man still didn't turn around.

Reid adjusted his position in midair and slammed all his weight into the doors. They flew open and he sailed into a gigantic audience hall full of soldiers. Grant lay on the floor in a pool of blood. He thrashed and flopped in his own blood while he roared and thundered in agony, but he couldn't get up.

Another old man with lanky white hair and floor-length robes stood over Grant's prostrate body. The Laird grinned down at Grant with a sick, twisted leer of savage triumph. The old man clenched his fingers in midair like he might be squeezing the life out of something.

Reid hit the ground and Colton touched down a second later. Reid took in the scene in a flash and charged straight for the Laird.

A dozen soldiers rushed in to block Reid's path. So much the better. He collided with the first soldier he came to. Colton gave a shriek of fury and plunged in to attack another group closing from the left.

The two Buchanans laid waste as many soldiers as they could. Reid sprang from one falling body to the next. He tasted blood and it drove him insane. He saw everything the soldiers planned to do a split second before they did it.

He rode another dead soldier to the ground and leapt clear before the body hit the floor. Another man rushed him with a saber raised on high. The soldier planned to hack the tiger out of thin air and Reid couldn't adjust his flight now.

The soldier's eyes widened and he planted himself for the killing stroke when, without warning, Reid contorted his body hard to the right. He couldn't stop his forward momentum from carrying him the rest of the way into the soldier's range.

Reid barely managed to flip aside and the saber whistled past his head. He started to drop. He had one chance to save his own life, so he rotated his claws the other way and slashed down the soldier's leg from thigh to ankle.

The soldier bellowed in pain, doubled over to clutch at the gash, and blood gushed from the wound. It splashed Reid and bathed him in battle mania.

He slammed down sideways on the tiles, vaulted up, and caught his jaws around the man's neck. The soldier shrieked in terror, reared back, and carried Reid with him.

Reid released at the height of that arc and flew off in another direction. In that fleeting instant between one soldier and another, he spotted the Laird and Grant behind the battle.... except that they weren't there anymore.

They receded into the distance getting farther and farther away. Neither of them had moved. Grant still lay on the floor with blood all over him, but he and the Laird got smaller and smaller until they vanished through the back wall.

Tall windows towered over the throne at the far end of the hall. The Laird, Grant, and even the pool of blood seemed to fade through the wall and drift off into the sky.

Reid stared at them in astonishment. How could he hope to kill or even attack a wizard like this? How did Reid even know that Grant and the Laird had ever been in this room at all? Maybe the whole thing was a vision the Laird concocted to trap Colton and Reid in this hellhole.

An instant later, a crushing blow slammed Reid to the floor. He crashed down on the tiles and someone kicked him in the body. He flew backward, struck the wall, and the impact shocked him into shifting back into a man.

He tried to stand up and fell under dozens of blows. Soldiers surrounded him pummeling him with their fists and feet. How soon would they start using their weapons?

He spotted Colton not far away. He had shifted back into his human form and he was down on his hands and knees with soldiers going to town on him, too. Colton tried to stand up and they struck him down.

Reid tried one last time to shift, but another punishing strike to his head sent him reeling off into semi-consciousness. He couldn't find the pathway in his mind to shift. He was doomed.

Chapter 28

Jaimee, Betty, Lily, and Tristan hunkered at the very back end of an alley and hid behind a stack of barrels piled against the wall. "How much longer do we have to stay here?" Jaimee whispered.

Tristan cupped his hands one on top of the other to create a space between them. Light and color swirled between his hands, rotated in a vortex, and then congealed to reveal a scene from some Kald neighborhood.

Soldiers and dragons moved around some building. The dragons bombarded the walls with fire and explosions while the soldiers drove anyone who tried to escape back into the inferno.

"They're nearly finished," Tristan whispered back. "Just a moment longer and we can go."

"How did you do that?" Betty gasped.

"It isnae difficult, lassie. Ye should try it once in a while."

She could only stare at him. She didn't know half of what she could do with her magic. She didn't even think to try using her power to find out what was going on in other parts of the city.

Could she use her magic to find Colton and Reid? How exactly should she go about it?

She almost asked Tristan to show her, but he was already standing up. He peeked over the nearest barrel. "It's clear. We can go now."

He crept to the end of the alley and the three women dared to look into the open. The same building Tristan had shown them crackled and popped in flames at the end of the block. No one tried to come out of it now. Everyone inside must already be dead.

Jaimee glared at the building, but the soldiers and dragons were gone. Tristan led the way into a different street, but the three women stood there staring at the building for longer than they should have.

No magic had to tell Betty that her two friends were thinking the same thing she was. Were they really going back to Icemeet now when the Laird's forces were devastating Kald and killing all these innocent people?

Betty didn't want to leave. She wanted to make the Laird pay for all of this. The Last Division came to Scotland to stop him, but they couldn't do that on their own, not even with Tristan's and Betty's magic.

Tristan came back. "Is anything wrong?"

No one answered. Everything was wrong. Colton and Reid were both gone. Grant was gone. Betty and Jaimee didn't even know where any of the other Buchanans were. They might all be dead in this catastrophe of an offensive.

Jaimee turned away first. "Let's go."

Betty followed her and then Lily joined them. The four friends moved off through the city in a daze. Where were they going? No one had discussed their plan to fall back to Icemeet. Betty didn't want to go there. She wasn't even sure if they *were* going there.

No one asked what Tristan was doing or where he was taking them. No one questioned Tristan's loyalty. Grant and Lily trusted Tristan. Beyond that, no one knew the first thing about him.

He woke Betty from her thoughts. "There's the breach ahead."

She followed his gaze to a destroyed section of the city wall. It opened onto the beach bordering the Boundless. Nothing moved out there besides the estuary itself. No one would stop the three women from crossing to the Buchanan side and climbing up to Icemeet. They would be safe up there.

Betty didn't want to be safe at Icemeet. She didn't want to leave Kald without Reid and every passing second made her more certain that he was here somewhere.

Jaimee kept looking around at the surrounding neighborhood, too. She must be thinking the same thing about Colton.

Betty surveyed the city around her as she kept getting closer to the breach—closer to the moment when she left Kald behind. She'd never seen any city so destitute and oppressed. Afghanistan didn't come close to this.

Was she really leaving it like this? Had she really done everything possible to free this city from the Laird? Was that just a convenient lie she told herself to save her own skin?

She hardly even noticed the city anymore. She kept looking around for Reid....and then she saw it. The dome gleamed down a different street. The way gave her a perfect view of the glowing sheen surrounding Tyrekirk.

Jaimee came over to her. "What's wrong?"

"Do you see that?" Betty whispered.

"I don't see anything. What do you see?"

"It's Reid—and Colton!" Betty took off at a fast walk toward the dome. She didn't know how she could get through it, but she had to find a way.

She stopped in front of the bluish field. It towered over her throbbing with energy. The black monster in her soul stirred and growled to engage with its enemies.

"There's nothing in there," Lily remarked. "It's deserted."

"Reid's in there and so is Colton. They're in a fight—and Grant is hurt! He's in trouble. They're in some kind of audience hall. The Laird is doing something to Grant. Oh, my God! They're about to kill Colton!"

"No!" Jaimee took a step back and drew her saber, but there was nothing there to fight. "We have to get to him!"

"We cannae," Tristan added from somewhere behind Betty. "We've already tried."

"We have to." Betty raised her hand, but she hesitated to touch the dome.

"Hurry, Betty!" Jaimee cried. "Don't let anything happen to Colton!"

Betty moved her hand closer to the dome. The black river seethed out of its bed, reared its ugly head, and flexed its power to do what had to be done.

The vision playing out behind the dome shone before her eyes. She couldn't miss a single detail. Soldiers raised their sabers over Colton. One move and they would cut him down right in front of her eyes.

Then another soldier raised his weapon to strike down Reid and Betty's whole being snapped. She touched the dome and an explosion went off as her power collided with the field.

The Laird's magic knitted into a solid fabric constructing this barrier and the power inside Betty grappled and wrestled and cartwhipped in a desperate struggle against the Laird. She couldn't see him or even sense him, but his rotten soul filled every magical filament of that dome.

The reaction came swift and sure. The moment she touched the dome, hundreds of horsemen charged up the street beyond. They came out of thin air and they looked nothing like the kilted Creighton soldiers who had been leveling Kald for the last three days.

These horsemen wore black tartans over black jackets and even the parts of their skin that Betty could see seemed to be black. Some kind of black masks covered their faces and heads, but as soon as she saw them, she knew they weren't wearing masks.

These horsemen came from the Laird. The Laird's magic conjured these otherworldly attackers to destroy his enemies. He must have cast some spell on the dome to unleash these defenders if ever a wizard came along who was powerful enough to take down the dome.

Jaimee and Lily definitely saw them, too. Both women drew their weapons to defend themselves, but they backed away in a hurry. They couldn't defeat this enemy. No one could.

"Do something, Betty!" Jaimee roared.

Betty reacted in a heartbeat, but she barely saw the horsemen. She still saw Colton, Reid, and Grant in the Laird's audience hall. The whole scene slowed to a snail's pace. She could see every twitch and breath of everyone in the room.

Her hand shot out, but she never moved on her own. The monster—the river—did it all for her. Reid. Only Reid mattered.

Her hand plunged through the field and it exploded in a ground-shaking crash. She never knew how she did it and it didn't matter. The four friends whooshed through space, and a split second later, they materialized in the audience hall.

Betty extended her hands toward the Laird and let the monster off its leash as never before. She let all the rage and blood lust flow out of her. God, it felt good! She blasted the Laird with dozens of shots.

Tristan raced to her side and they bombarded the Laird with everything they had. The party's sudden appearance distracted the soldiers from Colton and Reid. Jaimee dashed over to them and started hacking her way through the soldiers' ranks.

Lily raced forward trying to reach Grant, but another magical shield blocked her path. Grant lay sprawled in blood on the floor. Was he already dead?

The monster told Betty that he wasn't. She broke off attacking the Laird just long enough to aim a blistering shot at Grant. She spared one instant to think about healing him and releasing whatever hold the Laird had on him.

That spell struck him full force and he exploded off the floor. He swelled bigger and bigger and his skin turned black. His body stretched to a colossal length and the dragon reared onto his hind legs.

He let out a bellow that shook the whole castle, extended his wings in an almighty thump, and cracked his tail around the audience hall.

He sent all the soldiers sprawling and then turned his fury on the Laird. The Laird returned Betty's and Tristan's fire, but the tide turned when Grant lowered his head, cocked back his neck, and unloaded a vicious jet of fire on his grandfather.

The Laird fired another volley of spells at Betty and Tristan, and at the moment when Grant's fire hit him, a massive explosion went off right at the point of impact. It detonated and then ruptured outward until the supernova of heat and blinding light filled the hall.

It imploded just as fast and the Laird rocketed off the floor with incredible force. He shot upward at supersonic speed, smashed through the castle roof, and launched into the stratosphere before anyone could think twice.

Betty, Tristan, Lily, Grant, Colton, Jaimee, and Reid all stared up at a blue sky dotted with clouds beyond the hole in the roof. Was it possible for skies like that to still exist in this warzone?

At that moment, just when peace and silence descended over the scene, four black dots crossed the sky beyond the roof. They looked like birds.... but they weren't birds.

In front of Betty's eyes, they tilted downward and zoomed straight for the breach. She caught one glimpse of long scaly necks, leathery wings, and bright green scales flashing in the sunshine.

The dragons shrieked as they dove through the hole flying at breakneck speed. They spat fire everywhere and Grant erupted in murderous rage.

He shot out his neck, snapped his jaws, and chomped one of the dragons in half, but he wasn't fast enough to get them all. Seven more dragons bombed through the breach and attacked the invaders at once.

Grant rose on his hind legs again and let out a long, spine-chilling shriek of rage. The monster lurking under Betty's skin understood him. "Everybody out! Get out!"

She whirled away and started herding her friends toward the only exit. Reid grabbed her hand and the friends raced to escape from the castle.

"Grant!" Lily screamed and tried to fight her way back into the audience hall.

Grant screamed again. Betty caught hold of Lily and wrestled Lily toward the door. "He's telling you to leave! He says he'll occupy them while we get out."

"No!" Lily roared. "Grant!"

Jaimee grabbed Lily's other arm and, between the two of them, Betty and Jaimee dragged Lily out of the hall. The three men went in front, but in only a few minutes, they ran into more soldiers advancing to intercept them.

Betty let go of Lily and rushed to the front to help Tristan clear their path. She leveled as many soldiers as she could while her mind spun in a thousand directions. She knew where to go now, but she didn't have to tell anyone. Tristan already knew.

They ran down more stairs to the ground floor and out through the castle's front entrance. The party burst into a large courtyard and nearly got mowed down by a mob of combined Buchanans, Brodies, and ragtag townspeople all fighting for their lives against Creighton soldiers.

The soldiers drove the invaders into the courtyard from the city. Connell and a few of Clyde's wizards did their best to protect the Highlanders, but so many soldiers converged on the spot that the battle looked hopeless.

The friends charged in to help, but nothing seemed to stem the tide of more and more soldiers. Where did they all come from?

The rebel army overran the friends and drove everyone deeper into the courtyard. There was no way out.

Betty and Tristan combined their magic and Betty gave her power full rein to devour everyone in sight, but nothing worked. Was the Laird protecting these soldiers somehow?

A deafening boom distracted her as another explosion went off somewhere inside Tyrekirk and the highest turret blasted outward in a rain of stone and mortar.

All the dragons from inside rocketed into the sky followed by Grant's enormous black form. He picked up speed to hunt them down, but they separated in a dozen directions and came sweeping back toward the battle on the ground.

The soldiers saw the dragons coming and started to fall back. They retreated into the city as six dragons banked low over the streets and zoomed straight for the courtyard.

The rebels shrank inward even further, but the courtyard walls hemmed them in. The soldiers had driven the rebels into a death trap.

Betty and Tristan charged forward and Tristan grabbed Betty's hand. They raised their joined hands and another dome erupted from them to protect their comrades.

The dragons whistled on the wind getting closer all the time. They didn't slow down or divert at all. Did they know something Betty didn't? Would the Laird's magic let their fire penetrate her dome? Would Betty die here along with all the people she cared about most in the world?

The dragons narrowed their eyes and wound back their necks to breathe deadly fire on their enemies. They pumped their wings to pick up speed when, without warning, a massive dragon shot out of the city behind them. The monster rose huge and menacing and a hint of gold gleamed on his black scales.

Betty blinked once struggling to get her brain to function. It wasn't Grant. It was Elliot.

He didn't fly toward the dome. He didn't move at all. He hung suspended there in the skies over Kald with his gargantuan wings covering the horizon.

He squinted at the dragons targeting the rebel army. Those pathetic little dragons didn't even see Elliot.

He flicked his wings once—just a little bit. He tilted forward and fired a cataclysmic fountain of flame at the Creighton dragons—his own cousins.

He was too far away to burn them all. He didn't have to. He hit them so hard that the impact caught them in the torrent of fire. He smashed them into Betty's dome and pulverized them.

An ear-splitting roar erupted out of the city as a fresh wave of fighters poured out of streets and alleys and from behind buildings. None of them wore any tartan that Betty recognized.

The new attackers laid into the soldiers at the back of the Creighton force. A ferocious battle broke out...and then Betty did recognize someone. Echo Boxwood charged out of the mayhem and started cutting her way through the Creighton line. Echo and Elliot came after all.

The rebels from the forest reached the dome. Tristan startled Betty out of her shock by releasing her hand and the dome blinked out. The forest rebels overran the courtyard and now the forest rebels and the defenders from Kald closed the soldiers in a death trap of their own.

Betty worked fast rotating her power in all directions to help her friends. She ambushed soldiers who came close to threatening the invaders. Highlanders fought soldiers everywhere. Tigers shredded their enemies fighting side by side with Clan Brodie and the townsfolk.

Dragon shrieks echoed over the noise and Betty looked up to see another ten dragons sweeping in from the east. They fanned out over Tyrekirk with Grant driving them off the sea.

The Creighton dragons aimed downward to assault the courtyard. They opened their mouths to torch everyone, Creighton and rebel combined.

Grant folded back his wings and bombed out of the sky at terminal velocity. He cracked his jaws and exhaled a sweltering barrage of fire, but the dragons only picked up speed to outrun him.

They streaked over the courtyard, and at the moment when they would have made their escape, Elliot rose from the other side and opened up with a cannon blast of his own fire.

His breath smashed into Grant's and the two infernos ignited the dragons between them. The dragons shrieked in their death throes, but they couldn't escape.

The sight of the last Creighton dragons meeting their end in the skies above set off a fresh surge of energy in the invaders on the ground. The two forces charged each other cutting down the last soldiers until not one Creighton remained to stop the rebel advance.

Jaimee raised her saber and bellowed over the noise. "Buchanans—take the castle!" A groundswell of cheers and war cries resounded off the walls and all the rebels flooded inside. Tyrekirk was theirs.

Betty set off to follow them when a low grumble drew her attention to the skies. Two dragons remained aloft in the clouds above Tyrekirk. Grant and Elliot swooped around each other patrolling Kald, but they were the last dragons left alive.

Elliot's scales flickered golden-black in the sun, but Grant's enormous body seemed to swallow all light. She could barely see him from so far below.

She wasn't thinking about anything in particular when Grant cocked his head and looked down at her. His smoldering eyes narrowed and she smiled.

She didn't know how she understood him in the audience hall, but this enormous creature spoke to some hidden dark place deep inside her. One monster recognized another. They spoke the same language even if she couldn't understand it herself.

She waved to him and he screeched again. He banked out of the clouds, turned another revolution over the castle turrets, and descended to land in the courtyard. She had to move out of the way to make room for him.

He shifted in front of her, collapsed in on himself, then he had to scramble out of the way when Elliot touched down behind him.

Elliot shifted, too, and the two brothers embraced each other laughing and clapping each other on their backs. "Brilliant, laddie!" Grant exclaimed. "Absolutely brilliant!"

"Did ye save me some sausages?" Elliot teased. "This place always had the best sausages. That's the only reason I came back, not to see yer ugly mug."

Grant laughed again and then noticed Betty standing there watching them. He came toward her beaming. "Lassie—thank ye. I cannae thank ye enough. Ye saved me life."

She gulped. "I'm sorry it took me so long to find you. I would have come sooner, but...."

"Och, no! Ye came...and ye saved Lily. I cannae tell ye how grateful I am."

Betty blushed and tried to wave it away. "I was just ......doing my job."

"That's what makes ye lassies special. Come along before Elliot decides to eat us both instead."

"I can hear ye, ye droog!" Elliot thundered from behind him.

The brothers laughed and grabbed each other. Grant started pulling his brother inside, but Betty couldn't leave yet. She stepped out into the courtyard and looked up at the sky.

"What is it, lassie?" Elliot asked. "What do ye see out there?"

"Not out there.... He isn't out there."

"Who?" Grant asked.

"The Laird.... he's somewhere, but he's hiding from us. He won't leave us alone."

"What can we do to stop him from coming back?" Grant asked.

"I'm not sure. I'm not sure we can do anything to stop him from coming back."

She raised her hand and watched from a distance as her fingers swirled through the sky. She didn't know what she was doing, but she had to do something.

Then she remembered and let the monster out of its cage. It slithered from her guts, snaked through the air, and wove a giant glowing dome over Tyrekirk. It surrounded the castle.

"There." She breathed a sigh of relief as the monster settled back into its hiding place. "Now no one can get inside."

"Not even the Laird?" Elliot asked.

"Well, maybe *he* might."

Both brothers laughed and Grant waved to her. "Come along, lassie. We're late for a celebration."

Chapter 29

Reid, Colton, Jaimee, Echo, and Lily stepped into the audience hall. All the tapestries and coats of arms that had been hanging on the walls had been burned to a crisp. Every soft furnishing in the place had been incinerated and the giant windows behind the Laird's throne had been blasted out completely.

Most of the roof had been obliterated when Grant flew through it to drive the smaller dragons out. Now the hall stood open to the air.

Jaimee murmured low under her breath. "I never thought we'd actually make it. It doesn't seem real."

"We arenae home yet, lass," Colton replied. "We dinnae ken how many of the Laird's troops are still at large in the city."

"And wizards," Tristan added. "We must be on watch for them to mount a counteroffensive against us."

Reid turned to Fergus and Callum who stood nearby. "Go rally our lads and post a watch around Tyrekirk. Do what ye can to guard the place in case the Creightons make another move."

"Take the Brodies with ye," Tristan told him. "Ye dinnae have enough Buchanans to patrol the whole perimeter. Ye'll need more men."

"Thank ye, lad," Reid replied. "The Brodies are a staunch Clan."

"What do we do now?" Lily asked.

Just then, Grant, Elliot, and Betty strode in. Reid rushed Betty and caught her in his arms. "Lassie! I thought I'd lost ye!"

She melted in his arms and he caught the others beaming at him behind her back. He didn't have to hide anymore that he and Betty were bonded for life.

Lily hugged Grant and they kissed in front of everyone. Reid didn't care as long as he had Betty. He could make up for all the lost kisses later.

Elliot surveyed the audience hall and curled his lip. "This place is a mess! What did ye do to it?"

"Your dear brother did this," Jaimee told him.

"Guilty as charged," Grant replied. "I'd do it all again if I had a chance. I'd bring the whole place down if we didnae need somewhere to sleep tonight."

"We were just talking about what to do next," Lily began again.

"I dinnae ken about the rest of ye, but I'm going to the kitchens," Elliot announced.

"How can you think about food at a time like this?" Lily demanded.

"I can think about food anytime, lass," he replied. "If we're to get into a counteroffensive against the Laird's men, I'll need strengthening."

"I hate to be the one to tell you this, pal, but you don't need strengthening," Jaimee replied. "You're plenty big enough the way you are."

"Ye cannae go down to the kitchens anymore, lad," Grant told his brother. "Ye're the Laird's grandson. Ye must stay upstairs and let the servants wait on ye hand and foot."

"Stow that tripe! I winnae!" Elliot snapped back. "I've been eating out of the kitchens since the day I was born. I winnae stop now."

"Ye try it," Grant told him. "Ye see what Mary and the other cooks say. They'll drive ye out with their ladles and cleavers as sure as I'm standing here."

The whole group burst out laughing. Reid could finally appreciate all these people, now that he had his arms around Betty. They had accomplished what they set out to accomplish. They had driven the Laird out of Tyrekirk.

"Well!" Grant exclaimed. "That's all settled, then. I'll get to work calling all the soldiers back out of the city. We'll need to count them up and see who's dead and who's unaccounted for." He turned to his brother. "See if ye can find Maxwell anywhere."

"Aye." Elliot turned toward the exit.

Colton dodged in front of him. "Hang on right there, lad. What the devil do ye think ye're doing?"

"Someone has to run the country," Lily replied. "The whole place will descend into chaos with no one in charge."

"Aye," Reid replied. "We agreed we'd put Duncan on the throne."

"Duncan isnae here," Elliot countered. "Even if he was, we dinnae ken he'd be able to run the country. Grant's the next in line."

The Buchanans all started talking fast. "I dinnae think so, laddie," Colton fired back. "We didnae fight and die out there to put another Creighton on the throne."

"Who'll ye put on instead of me—yerself?" Grant asked. "The city winnae follow any Buchanan."

"We wouldn't have won the battle at all without Grant helping us against the dragons," Echo pointed out. "He's the only one with the authority to take the Laird's place. Grant is the logical choice."

"The rebels from the forest winnae follow a Buchanan, either," Elliot added.

"So you plan to turn the forest rebels to the Creighton side?" Jaimee fired back. "We wouldn't have asked you to help us if we'd known you were going to do that."

"We cannae let the place fall into Clan fighting Clan," Grant explained. "Ye've already taken the Brodies...."

"To help you defend the perimeter," Betty cut in, "the perimeter we just fought to win back for you. You aren't going to take it away from us."

"No one is taking anything away from anyone," Lily argued. "We just want to put someone on the throne until we can...."

"Duncan is the only man who will sit on that throne," Jaimee declared. "We'll take our men and restart the war if any Creighton takes over."

"Who do you say should rule in Duncan's place until we find him?" Echo asked.

"No one," Reid replied.

"That's impossible," Lily told him. "Someone has to make decisions. You just heard Grant. He wants to do a headcount of the remaining soldiers so we know who's who. We can either execute or banish anyone who doesn't swear fealty."

"Fealty to whom—ye?" Colton snorted and turned toward Reid. "Go get our lads and prepare to withdraw across the Boundless. We must rearm and prepare for the next incursion."

"Don't do this, Colton," Echo urged. "Don't turn against us now."

"It's ye that's turned against *us*." He jabbed his finger at Grant. "I was right not to trust ye. Ye're as conniving and underhanded as yer grandfather before ye. Ye deserve to sit on that throne."

He waved to Reid, Betty, Jaimee, and the remaining Buchanans and they strode out of the audience hall.

Grant, Elliot, Echo, and Lily stood stunned like they really didn't understand what they had done that was so bad. They were utterly clueless as to why this was such a big deal to the Buchanans.

Betty hesitated, but Reid pulled her away. The four women just reunited after organizing a successful campaign. Now circumstances tore them apart again, but Reid couldn't feel anything but hatred and betrayal toward Echo and Lily.

Clan Buchanan sacrificed more than anyone to win this victory. The Buchanans had been fighting and dying for generations to stand up to the Laird. How dare Echo and Lily side with the Creightons now? How dare they snatch Clan Buchanans' victory from them at the last second?

His fury escalated with every passing minute. Betty was the one who healed Grant. She was the one who made him shift into a dragon and forced the Laird to flee.

Her magic allowed Grant and Elliot to destroy the dragons. Grant and Elliot wouldn't be standing in that audience hall right now if not for her. Her dome protected Tyrekirk right now. Her magic alone prevented the Laird from counter-assaulting and retaking the castle.

Colton spotted a few more Buchanans on the way down to the great entrance foyer. "Gather all our lads from the perimeter," he told Fletcher. "Take them to the northern gate and assemble them on the beach. We're going back to Icemeet."

"That will leave the castle undefended," Fletcher pointed out.

"Good," Reid told him. "Pass the word to the Brodies to fall back to their own territory. Tell them we dinnae need them guarding Tyrekirk any longer."

"Good thinking," Jaimee added.

"I'll need to take down the dome," Betty pointed out. "I should go do that now."

"Is there any way you can stop the Creightons from following us?" Jaimee asked. "How do we know they won't pull a sucker punch on us while we're trying to withdraw?"

"I'll reverse the dome instead of taking it down. As soon as we get through, I'll switch it so none of the Creightons can leave. They won't be able to get out of the castle."

"What about any soldiers out in the city?" Reid asked.

Betty frowned thinking about it. "I could send out some kind of order to make them come back to Tyrekirk. I can make them think Grant is ordering them to return, and once the soldiers get inside, they'll be stuck here."

"You can do that?" Jaimee gasped.

"I can do a lot worse." Betty shot Colton a sidelong glance. "*Do* you want me to do worse? I could...." She broke off. She didn't want to say it.

"Not yet, lassie," he replied. "We arenae there yet. Wait until we get across the Boundless first."

Colton started to turn away, but Reid stopped him. "Lad...."

"Aye?" Colton asked.

"I have an idea."

"What is it?"

Reid shifted. He dropped onto all fours and trotted back toward the stairs. He turned to look back up at his brother. Jaimee and Betty both stared at him, too.

Reid swished his tail and darted upstairs. He knew what he had to do, and when he reached the audience hall, he slowed, tiptoed to one of the remaining tapestries, and slipped behind it.

He inched closer to the audience hall, but he found it empty. A few servants worked in there sweeping up and tearing down the burned tapestries. Grant, Elliot, Echo, and Lily were gone.

Reid returned to the landing and sniffed the floor. He picked up a scent trail for Lily. That was good enough for Reid.

He sprinted up the stairs following her trail. Grant and Elliot would be wherever Lily and Echo were.

Reid finally found the landing where Lily left the stairs. He tiptoed down a carpeted corridor lined with bedrooms. They were empty, but this had to be where Grant and Lily lived which meant Elliot and Echo would be staying here, too.

Reid heard men talking up ahead and he found another tapestry to hide behind. It came all the way down to the floor and hid him from prying eyes while he pushed his way closer to the speakers.

He crouched in the dark sniffing dust out of his nose and strained to hear. One of the speakers was definitely Elliot, but Reid didn't recognize the other man's voice. It wasn't Grant.

Reid pushed to the edge of the tapestry, but he didn't have to put his head out in the open. Elliot and another man stood in an alcove off the corridor. They spoke in low tones, but Reid could make out every word.

The unknown stranger wasn't a common Creighton soldier. Reid had never seen the man before and he was wearing Armstrong tartan.

He had to be one of the Laird's blood relatives which meant this man was another dragon shifter. How the holy hell did he get inside Tyrekirk with Betty's protective dome in the way?

Reid could think of only one explanation. This intruder must have had the Laird's help. The Laird must have spirited this shifter into the castle to drop a bug in Elliot's ear....and maybe in Grant's ear.

"It's perfectly simple, laddie," the stranger whispered. "Attack the Buchanans and be done with them before they have a chance to get out of the castle. It will solve all our problems and leave no one to contest the Creighton line."

Elliot shrugged and looked away. "We didnae agree to that. Our agreement...."

"Ye agreed to put a Buchanan on the throne," the stranger cut in. "Is that what ye want—to turn over yer fathers' and grandfathers' legacy to the Buchanans?"

"I dinnae say that. Duncan's a Creighton...."

The stranger snorted. "Do ye think he'll treat us any differently?"

Elliot threw up his hands. "I cannae speak to that. Ye take it up with me brother...."

"*Ye* take it up with yer brother. Convince him. He'll listen to ye."

"Ye dinnae ken what ye're asking. If we attacked them, we'd have to attack their women, too. It's asking too much."

"Ye cannae stand by and allow them to live," the stranger whispered even lower. "They ken about Duncan Buchanan. All trace of Duncan's claim to the throne must be removed for this to work. It's the only way."

Reid didn't stick around to hear anything more. He wriggled around behind the tapestry and took off at a run to tell Colton what he just heard.

Chapter 30

Betty crossed the courtyard, looked up at the protective dome she created to guard Tyrekirk, and raised her hand. Her fingers traced a pattern in the sky above. The sun was going down. It would be night again soon, but that didn't matter.

In a few minutes, the Buchanans would leave here, cross the Boundless, and return to Icemeet. They would unpack the weapons that Betty and Jaimee worked so hard to stash in Neill Buchanan's old apartment.

Then Clan Buchanan would start to rearm for another war against the Creightons. The same old hostilities would go on and on forever.

They wouldn't be the same old hostilities, though. Jaimee and Betty would still be here. They would keep fighting for Clan Buchanan and Betty would use her magic in that fight. She would never go home to modern-day America. That life no longer existed for her.

She let the power flow from her fingertips. It threaded into the dome's magical fabric. She could switch it in a second to trap the Creighton bastards inside Tyrekirk.

She and Jaimee would fight on the Buchanan side. Echo and Lily would stay here and fight for the Creightons, but in the end, none of the four old friends would be able to change anything. Not even Betty's magic would change the hatred and hostility between the two Clans. They would keep hating each other forever without end and they would keep killing each other.

How did this happen? How did the Last Division come to this country to help save it and wind up doing absolutely nothing? If anything, their efforts in mounting this offensive had only made life worse for the people of Kald *and* the people of Icemeet. Nothing changed except that it got worse.

She sighed, but she startled to high alert when a door opened in the castle wall nearby. She spun around and glared at Echo and Lily emerging into the courtyard.

Betty's power went cold and she turned around to confront the two women who used to be her friends. "What do you want?"

"We want to talk to you about this misunderstanding that just happened in the audience hall," Echo replied.

"It wasn't a misunderstanding," Betty snapped. "We all understood perfectly."

"You didn't understand our intentions. We never planned to put a Creighton on the throne."

"Grant is a Creighton. You want to put him on the throne. What part of that did I not understand?"

"We know you're loyal to Clan Buchanan," Lily began.

"Then you know why I can't ever go along with this. Whatever it is you came here to say, I'm not interested. If you can't find a way to put Duncan on the throne, then the throne should be left vacant until we find him."

"How *can* we find him?" Echo asked. "His magic conceals him from everyone. He has to stay hidden to protect him from the Laird."

"I don't care about that," Betty replied. "If you really care to make it up with us, you should be as anxious to find him as we are."

"We are," Lily replied. "We just don't know *how* to find him and someone has to run the country until we do find him."

"It doesn't have to be a Creighton."

"Can't you talk to Colton and Reid?" Echo countered.

"And tell them what, exactly?"

"Tell them to cool down. Tell them not to restart hostilities when we're all working toward the same thing."

Betty turned away. "I'm not sure we're all working toward the same thing anymore."

"Just talk to them,' Lily replied. "They'll listen to you."

"I have a better idea," Betty countered. "Why don't you two talk to Grant and Elliot and tell them to put aside this ridiculous idea of Grant taking the throne—or any other Creighton taking the throne? They'll listen to *you*."

Lily started to say something else when a different door opened across the courtyard. Jaimee stepped out and her expression turned stony and hateful when she saw the three women together.

She snorted as she sauntered over to Betty's side. "Let me see if I can guess what's going on here."

"We just want to talk, Snowflake," Echo told her.

"Don't call me that," Jaimee snapped. "Whoever you think that person was doesn't exist anymore. I'm just as much a Buchanan as Colton and Reid. If you don't have the spine to say it to them, don't say it to me."

"We already did," Lily replied. "They wouldn't listen."

"Then what makes you think that Betty and I will listen? You coming out here and isolating Betty by herself is an insult. You two are sneaking around conniving and scheming. You're as bad as we thought. In fact, you're worse."

"How can you....?" Echo countered and broke off right away when the same door opened and interrupted her. All four women fell silent as Colton and Reid appeared.

Colton's expression went through the same transformation as Jaimee's when he saw Lily and Echo talking to Jaimee and Betty.

He and Reid walked over to them and Colton eyed Echo and Lily with his coldest glare. "Ye lassies arenae welcome to make yer opinions kenned any longer. I'll thank ye to run along inside and leave us alone. We were just leaving."

"Colton...." Lily began.

"Save your breath, Lily," Betty cut in. "It's over. Just leave us alone."

Lily gulped and then she turned and hurried away. Echo followed her and dead silence fell over the courtyard.

Jaimee broke it by blowing out a shaky breath and covering her eyes. "How did this happen?"

"It's worse than all that, lassie," Reid murmured. "I've just overheard Elliot scheming with one of the Armstrong dragons to hit us before we escape from this pit."

"Get out to the perimeter with the lads," Colton told Jaimee. "Tell them to arm and prepare to fight their way out of the castle if need be. If we strike the first blow, we can swing it our way and get out before they retaliate." He turned to Betty. "Lassie, we'll need ye to wait until the very last and switch the dome once we're all through."

"I'm staying with ye, lass," Reid added. "I winnae leave ye alone."

She slipped her arms around his waist and hugged him. "Thank you. I wouldn't want to do this without you. I don't want us getting separated again."

"If ye get separated from the rest of us," Colton added, "ye get across the Boundless at any cost. Ye dinnae have to fall back with us so long as ye get home." He turned back to Betty and his eyes flashed with black fire. "I'm trusting ye to bring me laddie home. Ye dinnae let any harm come to him. I'm trusting ye, lass."

Betty's heart spasmed and she gripped his arm with more warmth than she'd ever felt for him before. Colton was her brother-in-law now—and her Clan Chief. She couldn't let him down.

"Don't worry. I'll bring him home. You have my word on that."

"Good lass. Let's go."

He started to turn away and froze when a different man stepped into the open. This one came from the same door where Lily and Echo had disappeared, but this man wore Brodie tartan. He had been fighting on the street a few minutes ago.

He advanced eyeing all four of them with sharp, clear, unwavering eyes. Then he nodded to Colton. "Sir."

"What is it, lad?" Colton asked. "What do ye want with me?"

"I'm here to bring ye a message from Grant Ritchie. He'd like to speak to ye—all four of ye and only the four of ye."

Colton pursed his lips. "Go back and tell him I dinnae speak to Creightons unless he'd like a taste of me claws. Tell him that."

"He asks ye four to meet with him—not as a Creighton but just as a man. He asks ye to meet him in the stables."

"The stables!" Jaimee exclaimed. "What for?"

"He asks ye to speak to him man to man—and woman to woman—and he says to tell ye that he and his will come unarmed. He asks ye to come unarmed, too—just to talk—before ye go."

The four Buchanans exchanged glances. Colton motioned the other three aside. "I dinnae like this. It could be a trick."

"Tell him to stuff it," Reid snarled. "We've already heard everything he has to say."

"Why would he be calling us to talk to him if he just wanted to repeat the same things?" Jaimee asked. "Maybe he has something new to say."

"I have an idea," Reid countered. "We tell him we're coming, and while the four of them shuffle their feet in the stable, we slip away."

Colton laughed. "Excellent. I like it."

"I have a better idea," Betty whispered. "If anything goes wrong, I can put the whole castle into a deep sleep—kind of like in *Sleeping Beauty*. We can slip away unopposed and the Creightons won't be able to stop us."

"Could ye do that fast enough to put Grant and Elliot to sleep before they shift?" Colton asked.

She shrugged. "Probably, but I think it's worth the risk to see what they have to say. They might have something in mind that could avoid any further bloodshed. Isn't that worth it?"

"I dinnae like going before them unarmed," Colton growled.

"We winnae be unarmed," Reid pointed out. "We've got Betty which is a sight more than the four of them have got."

"At least we know they won't attack us in the stable," Jaimee replied. "I agree with Betty. Let's give them one last chance. None of us wants to go on with this war."

"All right," Colton decided. "We'll do it yer way, lassie, but ye be ready to act if anything goes wrong."

Chapter 31

Betty stepped into the stables and paused to let her eyes adjust to the shadows. Sunlight peeked through cracks in the walls and horses stamped in the stalls. The place smelled like hay and manure. It was as far from the Laird's audience hall as any of the Buchanans could wish.

Grant, Elliot, Echo, and Lily stood at the far end of the stables waiting for the four Buchanans to arrive. Colton and Reid both stiffened when they saw Grant and Elliot both wearing Ritchie tartan, but that didn't set Betty's mind at ease.

She measured Lily and Echo down to the inch. She knew all their strengths and weaknesses. She knew exactly what moves to make and where to hit to take them down if this came to a fight.... but it wouldn't come to a fight.

She would cast a spell to put all four of them to sleep if anything went wrong at this meeting. None of these people had a shred of power that could stop her. She would even kill the four of them if she had to. She wouldn't hesitate if that's what it took to get the Buchanans out of Tyrekirk.

Colton and Reid pulled up in front of Grant and Elliot. Jaimee and Betty faced off against Echo and Lily.

Colton raised his arms and let them drop. "Well? Here we are."

"Listen to me, man," Grant began. "We all want Duncan on the throne. We only need to find him."

"If ye have a plan for that, I'm all yers," Colton countered. "None of us can find him."

"What about Betty?" Lily asked and then turned to Betty. "Have you tried to use your magic to find Duncan?"

Betty never had thought of that, but as soon as the thought crossed her mind, she knew the answer. "I can't find him. He's too well hidden. If he can hide from the Laird, he can hide from anyone."

"That's neither here nor there," Grant interrupted. "What matters is that we find him. I'm offering ye a compromise."

"What could ye possibly offer us that can take the place of our own brother on the throne?" Reid fired back.

"Duncan is our brother, too," Elliot cut in. "We want him on the throne as much as ye. None of us wants to carry on the Laird's rule."

Grant held up his hand. "Just listen, ye lot. I'm offering to run the country, not as Laird in my grandfather's place, but as Duncan's steward. As soon as he's found and brought back alive, he'll take over and I'll step down."

"How do we know you won't violate your word the first chance you get?" Jaimee demanded. "You might be using this as a ruse to find Duncan and kill him to remove your only competition."

"That's why I propose we send out two teams—one Creighton and one Buchanan. They'll leave Tyrekirk separately with orders to find Duncan and bring him in alive. Neither team will ken where the other is going nor what they're doing. I dinnae care if it's the Buchanans that find him so long as he comes in and rules us all. It's the only way to stop the war."

Betty glanced over at Reid. He and Colton exchanged glances. Maybe Grant was sincere after all.

"I ask ye only one consideration," Grant went on. "I'd ask ye to stay in the castle until he's found. We'll need ye lot on hand to restore him to sanity once he comes in." Grant turned to Colton. "I cannae run this country without ye. Dinnae let us throw all this away. We've worked too hard to turn against each other now."

Colton regarded him with a stern glare and finally nodded. "All right, lad. I accept. We'll post our team and send them out and ye do the same. If yer lot finds him first and he refuses to come in, we'll send out our own to bring him back. We'll work together to put him on the throne in yer place."

"Thank ye," Grant breathed.

Colton nodded again as much to himself as to the others. "Where do ye want us to go, then?" He glanced over at Jaimee. "Tell the lads...."

She nodded back at him. "I'll tell them."

Betty couldn't let the matter so easily. She still held herself stiff and alert. She could see too many problems with this plan, but what other option was there?

She searched again in that black river of power, but she couldn't locate Duncan anywhere. She could detect other wizards—weaker wizards. They couldn't mask their presence and location from her.

More powerful wizards than herself were a different story. She couldn't locate the Laird, either, but his menacing aura hung heavy over the landscape.

"Before ye disarm yer lads," Grant interjected, "ye may want to reconsider. If the Laird's forces counterassault, we'll need yer lot on our perimeter....and I called back the Brodies. If we're all to stay together in this castle, we'll need our own men together so no one gets the upper hand."

"I can accept that," Colton replied. He paused, but he didn't move or speak for a second. "So.... which of us will leave first?"

"We will." Grant motioned to the other three and they filed out of the stables.

"So.... we're staying after all?" Jaimee murmured as soon as the four Creightons got out of sight. "I don't trust them."

"That's what so brilliant about it," Betty replied. "He didn't ask us to. He understands. I think he's telling the truth about putting Duncan on the throne."

"Whether he's sincere or not doesnae matter at all." Colton turned to Jaimee. "Ye come with me to the perimeter and help me tell Connell, Fergus, Callum, and Fletcher what's going on."

Jaimee nodded. "Sure. I'm certain they'll be delighted to go find Duncan."

Colton grimaced at Reid and Betty. "I'd send ye out to find Duncan, lassie, but I couldnae torment me wee laddie that way."

"Send us both," Reid told him. "We'll find him and we winnae let any Creighton near him."

"I cannae," Colton told him. "I need ye with me—both of ye. If anything happens...." He trailed off, jutted his chin toward the door, and left with Jaimee.

Betty looked up at Reid, but she couldn't think of anything to say to him. This was the first time they'd been alone together since.... since their first night in the hotel basement. That night seemed so long ago, but it had only been two days.

He moved toward her at the same moment she moved toward him. She put her arms around him and all the tension and fear of the last two days dissolved. She couldn't forget it and she didn't have to. She was safe from it all, right here in his arms.

She didn't even want to kiss him. Kissing him seemed so pointless compared to just holding him and feeling him here against her. What peaceful bliss he was!

He rested his cheek against her hair and heaved an almighty sigh. He didn't have to say the words. She felt the same relief and contentment spread through him. Whatever ordeal he had been through, it was over now.

She gave him the same sanctuary and safety that he gave her. She could be his rock in the storm. She could hold him like this forever. She would overcome any obstacle to get back to this, to him.

She didn't need to go back to Ironforge or the modern world. She didn't need Icemeet or even Tyrekirk. He was her only shelter, her only home—the only home she would ever have for the rest of her life. What a relief it was to know that at last.

She didn't know how long they stood there just holding each other. It might have been hours for all she knew.

She finally straightened up and raised her eyes to gaze at his beloved face. He gazed down at her and his fingertips trailed her cheek. He cupped her chin to bring her lips up to his.

At that moment, a deafening bell clanged in the distance. Shouts echoed off the walls and then a massive explosion went off somewhere.

Betty whirled away, every nerve tensed, but she couldn't see anything in this stable. "What the...?"

Before she could move, Colton and Jaimee rushed back into the stable, grabbed her, and dragged her out into the yard. "Come on!" Jaimee bellowed.

"What's going on?" Betty yelled back.

"The counteroffensive! The Laird's troops are overrunning Tyrekirk!"

"What about the dome? It should have stopped them."

"What dome?!" Jaimee roared. "It's down! It isn't there anymore!"

Betty skidded to a halt gaping at her friend. Then Betty's eyes snapped to the high turrets standing tall against the evening sky. Betty could see everything all the way to the stars coming out in the east. Jaimee was right. The protective dome was gone.

Another devastating smash rocked the castle. It vibrated the paving stones underfoot. "Can ye get it back up?" Reid yelled in her ear. "Can ye reestablish it?"

"I...." Betty broke off as fifteen dragons whistled overhead. They flew in low shooting fire all over the castle. They zoomed southward and back to the west.

Betty's blood ran cold as her gaze traced the dragons' route to the western mountains. She couldn't see anything besides more explosions rupturing all over Kald, but something far on the western horizon chilled her heart.

"Betty!" Jaimee roared in her ear. "Can you put the dome back up?"

"The Laird!" she whispered.

"What?" Jaimee hollered.

"The Laird!" Betty screamed. "He's doing this! He's over there! He took down the dome! We have to evacuate—now! Get everyone out of Tyrekirk! It's a matter of life and death!" She whirled back to Reid. "Get inside and...."

"I'm going, lassie!" He turned to charge back inside the castle. Betty couldn't think of anything but getting everyone out, including Echo, Elliot, Lily, and Grant. What the hell difference did it make if they were Creighton or Buchanan?

Chapter 32

Betty rushed after Reid while Colton and Jaimee took off in the opposite direction. Betty froze all over again as two giant black dragons rocketed out of the audience hall. Grant and Elliot flew straight up into a swarm of smaller dragons and they all piled in to attack each other.

Deafening screeches ripped the air apart. The smaller dragons ganged up on Grant and Elliot, but the Creighton attackers couldn't do as much damage against two of them.

Grant and Elliot coordinated their attack the way they did in the courtyard. They veered wide to the east and west, separated the Creightons from each other, and then converged to trap the smaller dragons in a vise.

Grant and Elliot unleashed their fire to plaster their cousins in a blazing inferno when a starburst erupted in the sky surrounding them. The Creighton dragons vanished in a blaze of light and the two enormous black brothers changed in a split second. They shifted back into men hanging in midair hundreds of feet off the ground.

Lily and Echo screamed the brothers' names at the same instant. Betty had become so engrossed in the battle that she didn't see Reid go inside and come back with her two friends.

Lily and Echo charged forward, but there was nothing anyone could do. Grant and Elliot plummeted on an impact course for.... somewhere. They were nowhere near Tyrekirk. They would smash to earth somewhere out in Kald. Would the friends ever find them in time before the whole world went up in flames?

Betty's heart spasmed. She didn't realize she had released the monster until it ruptured from the center of her chest. It streaked upward in a river of light to surround the two brothers. She caught them and started lowering them to the ground.

Reid collided with her out of nowhere and nearly toppled her. "Move, lassie!" he thundered and would have tackled her to the ground.

She staggered and he jostled her sideways just as one of the highest turrets detonated in a catastrophic boom. Rock, rubble, and spinning shattered timbers twirled through the air and then pounded the yard in a rain of destruction.

Betty didn't recover fast enough. He grabbed her in his arms and carried her away. She almost lost track of where Grant and Elliot were until Echo's scream pierced Betty's confusion. "Elliot—no!"

Betty scrambled to reestablish the connection just in time. She held the brothers suspended a dozen feet above the outer castle wall. She set them down and then a crowd of Buchanans surrounded the party.

Fergus, Callum, Fletcher, and Connell rushed over to Colton and he started yelling at them on the run. "Ye four break away and get out of Kald to the west. Dinnae come back until ye find Duncan and bring him in alive and unharmed. Do ye understand?"

The four men nodded. there was no time to say anything else. So many blasts and pounding explosions shook the castle that Betty couldn't think or see anything anymore.

The remaining Buchanans raced for the only exit left to them—a small wooden door in the outer castle wall. They dashed through it and found Grant and Elliot lying unconscious on the pavement outside.

Echo and Lily ran over to them and Colton and Reid bent down to pick up the Ritchies. "They're out cold," Colton observed. "We'll have to carry them."

"I'll take them," Betty told them. "Get to the Boundless. Get everyone across the water and up the mountain. We don't have much...."

Another bone-crushing boom struck the wall right behind them. Stone and brick smashed into the fugitives.

"Get us out of here, Betty!" Jaimee shrieked.

"Run!" Betty roared. "Run and don't stop running—all of you!"

Colton stood up and pointed to the north. "Go, lads! Get to the breach and get over the Boundless—now!"

The last surviving Clansmen took off through the labyrinthine streets. Betty didn't have to think. She surrounded Grant and Elliot with so many tendrils of magical energy that the next blast deflected right off them.

They floated off the ground and she bolted on Jaimee's heels. Reid stayed at her side, but she kept pushing him and the rest of their comrades ahead of her. "Go! Go!"

Continuous concussions shattered the street and blew up houses and buildings all around them. Betty couldn't turn around. If she saw or even felt the Laird watching from the distant hills, she would lose her nerve and forget what she had to do.

She widened the net surrounding Grant and Elliot. It created a shield covering the Buchanans' retreat, but she couldn't do anything more. She couldn't fight this enemy. The Laird was just too powerful.

She let Grant and Elliot trail out behind her. She felt the Laird's strikes pummeling the brothers and her and all her fleeing comrades—her Clansmen. The Laird could rain spells on her all day long, but he couldn't penetrate her protections. That was all she could do. She couldn't do more than defend their retreat.

She ran on and on until Reid grabbed one of her arms. Jaimee grabbed the other and they pulled her into a side street. She had been so out of her mind with fear and confusion that she didn't see where she was going.

They charged the breach. The rest of the Clan were all outside on the banks of the Boundless—all except Fergus, Callum, Connell, and Fletcher. They were long gone—gone to the west to search for Duncan.

Betty gulped hard when she saw all the Buchanans streaming down to the Boundless, wading across, and scrambling up the mountain. Most dropped their weapons, shifted, and streaked up the hillside on their fleet paws.

Heavy bombardments smashed all over the mountain. They pounded the high cliffs, split granite boulders off the peaks, and sent projectiles hammering into the slopes below.

Cats veered back and forth dodging blocks and thunderous explosions ripping the mountains to a moonscape. Betty hesitated to go out there and someone grabbed her from the side.

Reid and Jaimee towed Betty behind the wall. Lily and Echo huddled there and Jaimee pulled Betty down with the others.

Betty lowered Grant and Elliot to the ground. None of the fugitives could see the battle going on, but that meant nothing. "We can't stay here!" she yelled to her friends. "The Laird knows where we are. He'll attack us sooner or later."

"I have to take Elliot back to the forest!" Echo called back. "How badly is he injured?"

Betty rested her hand on Elliot's chest and then on Grant's. "They've only been knocked out. I can revive them."

"Do it," Colton ordered. "Ye cannae climb that mountain with them hanging out like a flag for the Laird to shoot at."

Betty nodded. "Of course not. I wasn't thinking."

"Don't apologize," Lily told her. "You saved their lives. You saved all our lives."

"Revive Elliot," Echo went on. "We have to get out of here."

"Come to Icemeet with us," Jaimee insisted. "You'll be safer there, especially if the Laird is in the western mountains."

"He won't be," Betty countered. "As soon as we get under cover, he'll come back to Tyrekirk. He's driving us out and then he'll consolidate his rule exactly the way he did before. Everything will go on the way it was except that he'll be even more interested in hunting us down."

"We can't have Grant and Elliot in the same place," Echo pointed out. "If anything happens to Duncan, Grant and Elliot are our only chance of getting a decent person on the throne."

Colton made a face. "I didnae like Duncan's chances before. Now they're all but nonexistent."

"Then splitting up Grant and Elliot will be the best way to take the Laird's attention off of Duncan. Revive them, Betty," Echo told her. "Do it now."

Betty touched both brothers. She barely had to think about it before they both shot upright. Grant sat up so fast he knocked Betty's hand away. He jerked right and left searching for something. "Where....?"

Lily squeezed his shoulder. "You're all right. You're safe. You're among friends."

"Ye're among friends, but ye arenae safe," Reid muttered.

Elliot woke up more slowly. He glanced around at the faces staring at him and his eyes widened. "What happened? Where am I?"

"I'll explain everything later," Echo told him. "Get up. We have to go."

"Are you sure you guys will be all right?" Jaimee asked.

"Don't let him shift, Echo," Betty told her. "You have to stay hidden."

Lily pointed down the beach. "Run along the wall over there. Keep to the Boundless until you get west of Kald. Then you can get into the forest."

Elliot rubbed his head. "Dinnae concern yerself on that, lassie. I ken how to get to the forest."

"Don't shift, Elliot," Lily countered. "You have to stay out of sight or the Laird could kill you."

He nodded. "Aye. I understand, lassie."

Echo took his hand. "Come on. Let's go."

"Echo...." Jaimee began.

The two women exchanged a glance and then pulled each other into a hug. Betty didn't want to hug Echo. She wanted Echo and Elliot to reach safety now and hugging Echo would only put them in more danger by delaying them.

Echo shot Betty a knowing smile and pulled Elliot away. He seized his brother's hand once, made eye contact with the others, and then he and Echo took off running down the beach.

"That was the easy part," Reid observed. "Now it's our turn."

"I'll protect you as best I can," Betty told them all.

"We cannae shift, either," Colton ordered. "None of us."

"Of course no," Reid replied. "We'd outrun the lassies and Grant...."

"I winnae shift, lad," Grant replied. "Ye dinnae need to tell me why."

"Let's go." Betty launched herself toward the beach, spun backward, and projected the same shield charm between herself and the western mountains.

A single blaze of light shone on the highest peak as though the sun might be going down, but it wasn't. That light cast the whole landscape in shadow.

"Run!" Betty roared and the other five sprang out of their hiding place.

They sprinted down the beach making for the Boundless. Betty didn't dare to look back. She concentrated everything on keeping that shield in place while she and her friends made their escape.

Deafening concussions smashed the shield from behind and the Laird's power devastated Betty's energy. She poured more and more of her own reserves into keeping that defense in place as her friends waded across the Boundless.

Her foot touched the Buchanan side and she staggered under another punishing blow. The Laird crushed her under the weight of brutal fire and he hadn't even tapped his own strength yet. He could keep this up all day.

She charged up the hill, but she only made it fifty feet before another catastrophic blast knocked her to her knees. She couldn't keep this up much longer.

Colton and Grant were almost to the gates of Icemeet. Colton scrambled up first and then extended his hand to pull Grant to safety. Lily made it a second later.

Someone grabbed Betty's arm and started picking her up. "Get up, lassie!" Reid hollered in her ear. "Ye must get up!"

That crack of desperation in her ear woke her from her daze. He needed her....and he was scared. She dragged her awareness back to the battle—except that it wasn't a battle.

Only one side was attacking. The Laird rained hammer blows on the fleeing Buchanans while they couldn't shoot back at him.

Betty glanced over her shoulder and her stomach dropped. Her magical shield had disappeared. She tried to summon it again, but it didn't work. The Laird did something to her so she couldn't defend herself or her people.

Jaimee materialized on her other side. "Get up, Betty! Come on! We're almost there!"

Jaimee and Reid forced Betty to her feet, but when she tried to take a step, her knees sagged. She buckled, but they caught her and started dragging her up the mountain. She couldn't stand that and she rallied the last of her strength.

Another bone-crushing blast thumped her in the back and she fell sprawling on her face. She heard voices yelling in her ears, but she couldn't make them out. She started to slip into unconsciousness.

Then she felt herself floating. Something soft and magical surrounded her and suspended her off the ground while she drifted through the air. Was someone using magic to carry her home?

It almost felt like her own magic was transporting her, but that couldn't be right. She didn't have any magic. She was just an ordinary girl—nothing special.

In a few minutes, she would wake up in her bed at Ironforge. Then she would go back on rotation with her training, kitchen duties, rifle range practice, hand-to-hand combat—all the daily chores that made Ironforge her home. Nothing would ever break that routine and she didn't want it to.

Chapter 33

Betty's eyes drifted open. She gazed through tall windows at sheer mountain peaks outside. Snow flurries swirled in the chilly air and a steel-grey sky blocked out any sunshine. The whole landscape looked grey and cold and forbidding.

She floated with the snowflakes for a while. She was warm and comfortable in a soft bed and everything sounded quiet.

Then she remembered and looked around the room she was in. She wasn't at Ironforge. She was in some random bedroom at Icemeet and Reid sat in a chair by her bed.

She smiled up at him and he smiled back down at her. "Hi," she breathed.

"Good evening, lassie. How's yer head?"

"My head? My head is fine. Was there something wrong with it?"

"Ye got hit in the head. Ye were bleeding all over the place, but ye seem fine now."

He put aside a stack of papers he had been reading and swiveled over to sit on the edge of the bed. He beamed down at her and then pushed her hair off her forehead. His eyebrows came together in the center like he was looking for something.

"Aye. The wound has healed up completely."

"What wound?" She touched her forehead. "There's nothing there."

"There isnae ought there now, but there was last night. Ye're whole head and face were stoved in. We all thought ye'd die."

"So.... what happened? How could I be about to die and now I'm fine?"

He shrugged. "I suppose yer magic healed ye. I cannae explain it any other way. It just...went."

"Went...how?"

"I dinnae claim to understand it. Ye healed yerself and ye came right. That's all—a bit like yer magic transporting ye up here. Ye wouldnae be up here if ye hadnae. Jaimee and I would have been dead along with ye."

"I don't understand you. I was out cold on the mountain. The Laird knocked me down and stopped me from using my magic."

"He knocked ye down and ye were out cold, but he couldnae stop yer magic. I was there, lassie. I saw the whole thing, and if ye dinnae believe me, ye can ask Jaimee. She was right by yer side the whole time. Ye went down and then ye started to float. Yer shield went down, but as soon as the Laird knocked ye out, the shield came back stronger than before. We didnae even need to carry ye home. Ye floated on yer own and ye protected us until we got inside."

"Wow!" She sank back on the pillows and rubbed her head. "I had no idea I was doing all that."

"Aye. Ye were gone."

She squeezed his arm. "I'm sorry. I never meant to worry you."

"Dinnae ye apologize to me, lass, nor to anyone else in this place. It's thanks to ye we made it at all. None of them can stop talking about it."

She pushed back the covers. "I have to get up. I have to go see them. I have to...."

"No, ye dinnae." He pushed her down. "Ye'll stay where ye are and sleep it off. Ye've already been asleep for two days. Ye're too weak to rush back into the battle and all."

"Two days! Why didn't you wake me up?" She tried to shove him away.

"I wouldnae wake ye for all the gold in these mountains, and if ye dinnae lie down and be quiet, I'll bring Colton in here to restrain ye. Ye arenae going anywhere, lass."

She glared at him for a minute, but he only glared back with just as much determination. He wouldn't back down.

She collapsed and looked out the window. "I can't believe I've missed so much time. What's been going on while I've been asleep?"

"The usual business. Colton and Jaimee sent up to Stronghold to bring most of the archers back. We're down so many men, we need every hand to help defend the place against the Creightons."

"Are the Creightons threatening again?"

"Who kens?" He got up and paced over to the window. "The Laird is back at Tyrekirk just as ye said. If he isnae arming for another incursion now, he will be soon."

"So what are Colton and Jaimee doing about the defenses?"

Reid sighed and then came back to sit next to her. "I can see ye winnae keep quiet about this so I suppose I have no choice but to tell ye all. Ye'll only hound me about it until I do."

She laughed and touched his cheek. He meant so much to her. She wouldn't want to see any other face when she woke up.

He caught her looking at him like that and the words died on his lips. He didn't tell her about the defenses. He gazed down into her soul and then his mouth smothered out every other thought.

He sank onto the bed with her and her arms enfolded him—the way it should be. She was safe behind these walls....and she was home. The wider conflict might return to Icemeet, but it would never touch the bond between her and Reid.

The dream she had of returning to Ironforge was just that—a dream. Everything she cared about was here and now the Last Division was here, too. Only Zero remained behind, but she would be coming to Scotland soon, too, if she wasn't here already.

None of that mattered. Nothing outside this room mattered. Betty was with Reid and she would stay that way.

His body crushed her into the mattress and the passion of their first night in the hotel basement flooded back. She could release that passion here, now that she knew she was home.

He tilted off to one side and pulled her over next to him. They swam in delicious kisses for a long time, but it would never be long enough. A lifetime wasn't enough to spend with him and share all the delights of love and belonging.

They'd lost so much time already and the war would take even more of it. Fears and demands and work waited for her outside this room, but all of that could wait while she enjoyed the blessed peace of his....

A knock on the door startled both of them into pulling away. Reid twisted around and yelled, "Go away!"

A muffled voice replied from out in the corridor. It was Colton, but Betty couldn't understand what he was saying through the door.

Reid growled under his breath. "Och, for the love of God! What now?"

He heaved himself off the bed, went over to the door, and opened it. Colton handed him another pile of papers and started talking fast about inventories and supplies at other locations and preparations and a whole lot of other stuff Betty didn't understand.

Reid kept saying, "Aye," and "All right," and "Of course," but he didn't budge from the doorway or even take his hand off the latch.

Colton finally finished saying everything he had to say, asked, "How's yer lassie?" and glanced into the room.

His jaw dropped when he saw Betty looking at him. She smiled and waved. "Hi, Colton."

"Lassie.... I didnae ken...."

"It's all right." She started to push back the covers. "You might as well come in. I was just getting up."

"No, ye werenae." Reid stormed over to intervene.

"I might as well. I feel fine and we'll only keep getting interrupted. I can see how it is."

She sat up and swung her feet to the floor. She was wearing a white linen night dress she had never seen before. It looked like something out of an antique store.

"Lassie.... I didnae mean to...." Colton stammered.

"Go on back downstairs. We'll be down in a bit and we can talk about this then." Reid waved the papers that Colton had just handed him and gave Colton a stern glare that Colton read loud and clear.

"All right." Colton bolted and Reid shut the door.

"You didn't have to be so hard on him," Betty chided. "He couldn't have known that I was awake."

"I've made a grave mistake, lassie. I told him I wanted to help him run the Clan and now he winnae stop loading me with work. I didnae ken it took so much. I dinnae ken how he's managed on his own all these years."

"Then it's more important than ever that you help him." Betty looked around. "Where are my clothes? Where are we, anyway? I don't recognize this room."

"Of course, ye do. It's the guest room I gave ye when ye first arrived in Icemeet. Ye stayed here for three days before the assault."

"What? No, it isn't. It looks completely different."

"I changed some of the furnishings. Dinnae ye recognize the view over the Boundless? It's the same room."

She went over to the window. He was right about the view, but the room itself looked nothing like she remembered. "Why did you change it? It was so fancy before."

"Too fancy. It wasnae as comfortable as it could be and we dinnae want to live in a guest room all our lives."

She frowned at him. "What do you mean?"

"It isnae a guest room anymore. It's our room. Ye couldnae join me in the men's barracks, could ye? Colton gave me this one, but it wasnae comfortable the way it was.

I brought up some of the goods from Father's old apartment and changed it round. If ye dinnae like it, ye can fix it up any way ye please. It's ours now to make our own."

She blinked at the room and then at him. "So.... we're...."

"That's the way it is when a couple mates for life. They move up here. Colton and Jaimee are just down the hall as I told ye before."

She strode over to him and put her arms around him. "Thank you!"

"Why are ye thanking me, lass? It's the way of things."

"Thank you for being you....and for being mine." She lifted her face to kiss him. She would have kissed him a lot longer if all the business outside this room didn't keep calling her away.

"And thank ye for being mine." He kissed her, too, but he didn't linger the way he did before. He seemed to understand that they couldn't hide in this room forever. Too many people were depending on them.

She turned away. "Now what am I going to wear?"

He pointed to a dresser across the room. "Over there, lass. It's all in there. Jaimee and Lily sorted it all out for ye. It's a mercy they did for I wouldnae have kenned how to do it meself."

She dug into the dresser and found everything she needed—pants, clean shirts, underwear, a jacket, socks, and new boots. The clothes she'd been wearing since she first came to Scotland had disappeared. Jaimee and Lily had replaced them with the same leather clothes all the women wore now.

Betty got dressed and was starting to feel ready for more action. The dark river of magic still roiled and tumbled inside her. It wanted to get out and get to work. Whatever the Laird did to her, he couldn't rob her of her magic entirely. It was a part of her—a part she would never lose again.

She was just pulling up her hair in front of the mirror when another knock drummed on the door.

"Blast it!" Reid muttered. "It doesnae ever stop, lassie. I'm warning ye."

"Who knew you could be so popular?" she teased.

He opened the door and Jaimee barged in without waiting for an invitation. She carried a tray of food in one hand and a pitcher of water in the other. "I brought your dinner and make sure you eat it this time or your brother will kick your.... Betty!"

Jaimee barely got the tray set down on the table before she charged Betty and hugged her. Betty laughed. "Take it easy or Reid will kick something of yours. He thinks I'm fragile."

"Are you all right?" Jaimee gushed and pushed Betty's hair back to study her forehead. "God, you scared the crap out of all of us! We all thought you were dead!"

"So I hear."

Jaimee grabbed her and hugged her again. Then Jaimee spun away and raced for the door. "I have to tell Lily and Colton. They've all been waiting for you to wake up....and make sure Reid eats something, will you? He's been half-starved while you were unconscious."

"You don't have to tell Colton," Betty called after her. "He already knows."

Jaimee didn't hear her. She walked out and vanished. Reid shut the door. "Ye see how it is, lassie?"

She put her arms around him and kissed him again. "I see that you haven't eaten in two days because you were worried about me. I love you for that."

He melted into her kiss, but when he straightened up to meet her gaze, he wasn't smiling. He furrowed his brow in concern. "I cannae tell ye how much I love ye, lassie. I couldnae sleep nor eat so long as ye were in danger."

She collapsed into his arms. She didn't want to be anywhere else and now she didn't have to be.

Chapter 34

Reid and Betty descended the stairs to Icemeet's big entrance foyer. Betty stopped and looked around. "Where is everybody? I thought they would all be here preparing the defenses."

"They were." Reid peered into the dining hall. "I dinnae ken where they've gone, but they cannae be far away. I'm going up to Colton's office to see about the...."

He broke off when Grant, Lily, Colton, and Jaimee approached from the kitchens. They were in the middle of a conversation when Lily spotted Betty.

"Betty!" she exclaimed and rushed over to hug her.

"I'm okay," Betty told her. "You don't have to make such a fuss."

"We do," Grant told her. "We most certainly do."

Betty beamed around at them all. "It's good to be back. So what are we doing first? I was thinking...."

"Don't," Jaimee interrupted. "Don't think. That's my number one rule nowadays."

Everyone laughed and Betty waited for them to finish. "I was thinking I could get started repairing the damage to the outer wall. I can reconstruct it pretty easily with my magic and then...."

"Leave it as it is," Colton told her.

"Why? It's a pile of rubble."

"That rubble is the only thing protecting us from the dragons," Jaimee replied. "It's better protection than anything we could have come up with."

"Perhaps we should have blown it up ourselves years ago," Reid observed. "Then we wouldnae be in this situation at all."

"What do you want me to do instead? What are we doing about the defenses?"

"If you really want to help us," Jaimee told her, "you can help us build some new siege machines. All of ours have been destroyed and we have no other way to build them."

"Didn't you say your blacksmith built them—what was his name—Boyd?

Colton and Jaimee exchanged glances. "Boyd's dead," Colton finally replied. "We dinnae have a blacksmith nor a forge nor any other way to make them."

"Okay," Betty replied. "I can do that."

"You're our only wizard, now that Connell's gone," Reid told her. "It means ye'll be called on to heal all the injured and repair nearly everything that gets broken."

"Hey, at least I don't have to run the Clan, right?"

Colton and Reid both laughed. Betty started feeling like things were getting back to normal—as normal as possible.

She was just about to ask Jaimee where she should go to work on these siege machines and how to go about it when heavy footsteps advanced from the north keep.

The Buchanans who had been in Kald appeared out of the long corridor leading to Stronghold. Betty burst into a grin and opened her mouth to greet them, but she stopped short when she saw their faces.

All the men she'd gotten to know during her first stay in Icemeet had either fallen or gone off to search for Duncan. She knew these people by name, but that was about it.

Three thick-set Highlanders named Craig, Donald, and Sloane halted in the foyer and glared at the six friends. At least twenty more Buchanans assembled behind them and none of them looked at all happy.

Colton stepped forward and shoved his way between the three couples and his Clansmen. "Can I help ye lads with something?"

"Ye can help us rout *that* out of our house." Donald jutted his chin at Grant. "It's a dark day when our Clan harbors a Creighton under our own roof after the work he's done on us."

"He isn't a Creighton," Jaimee countered. "He's a Ritchie and he's our friend."

"Ye lads are as blind as ye are dim if ye didnae see him save all our lives in Kald," Reid chimed in. "Ye must have had yer heads buried in the ground while the rest of us were fighting to free this country. He's done more to help us than anyone else and he's the only reason ye lads are standing here alive. He's the only reason any of us are standing here alive."

"He's one of the enemy," Sloane countered. "It's thanks to him and his brother that we're defenseless against his kind and ye'd allow him to walk amongst us as one of our own. We winnae stand it, laddie."

"Then ye ken what to do." Colton waved toward the passage leading to where the courtyard used to be. "If ye dinnae like it, ye can go and no one will shed a tear." He waited for someone to say something. "Go on, then, the lot of ye. Be off."

No one moved or breathed. Betty checked in with her magical power just to be sure it was still there. She could call it up in case something went terribly wrong. How did she get to the point of preparing herself to use her power against the Buchanans—the people she had come to consider her own Clan?

Colton breathed an almighty sigh. "We've been over this already, lads, and I winnae keep going over it again and again. I've stated me piece as Clan Chief and Reid agrees with me."

"Ye've got that right," Reid snapped.

"Ye lads have three choices," Colton went on. "Ye can get on board with helping this Clan defend our borders from the Laird's forces that are arming across the Boundless as we speak. Ye can lend yer blades to defend yer families or ye can pack yerselves off to whichever one of your enemies will have ye. Ye winnae ever be welcome here again.... or at Stronghold.... or at Easthollow or any other Buchanan fortress. Yer only other option is to get yerselves a new Clan Chief from the pack of glaikit cows that gather in corners and whisper behind me back."

His words ricocheted through Icemeet's empty halls and corridors. His voice boomed loud enough to wake the sleeping ghosts of ancient Highland warriors and those words called them to come out and back him up.

Then he lowered his voice to a menacing half-whisper and spat between gritted teeth. "I warn ye, though, lads. Ye come out against me and ye'll have all six of us to cope with. Ye go on back to yer holes and think on that before ye come near this man with yer mouths open again."

Betty stood up a little straighter and her resolve hardened. If any of these men—or anyone else—laid a finger on Grant or Lily—or Colton or Reid—the attackers would never see her coming. She would put them down before they had a chance to think twice.

Colton dragged his fierce eyes away from his Clansmen and turned to Betty. "Ye take these lads down to Stronghold and start repairing the siege machines. Put them to work doing something useful for a change."

"I'll go with you," Jaimee volunteered.

"I'll go, too," Reid offered.

Betty stepped forward and slipped in front of Colton to confront the Buchanans. "Let's go, guys. We have work to do."

Donald and Sloane glared at her and then they looked past her shoulder to scowl at Colton. The tension spiked into the stratosphere. Was this homecoming going to explode into an internal conflict with Buchanan fighting Buchanan and cousin fighting cousin?

Sloane turned away and Craig snorted, but none of them argued. They turned to the Clansmen who stood behind them. "Let's go, lads."

Betty stood her ground and waited while they all trooped back into the corridor heading for Stronghold. Jaimee and Reid came forward to join her. The three of them blocked the corridor so none of the Buchanans could return to threaten Grant and Lily.

The Buchanans filed into the tunnel and Betty turned back to make sure everything was all right behind her. Colton was talking to Grant and he noticed Betty watching him.

He gave her a single nod of acknowledgement and she went on her way toward Stronghold. That one glimpse told her all she needed to know. Grant and Lily faced an uncertain future surrounded by hostile people who blamed them for everything the Buchanans had lost in this war.

Grant and Lily had no way of knowing where they would be tomorrow or where their next threat would come from. No one did. All of Clan Buchanan and the whole country hung in the balance. Their only hope was for the two teams to find Duncan before the Laird dragged everyone into another catastrophic disaster.

<u>End of Book 4.</u>

Sign Up Once--Get all Theo Mann's free books including brand new releases

S ign Up Once--Get all Theo Mann's free books including brand new releases

Ian Wallace is tall, muscular, magnetically handsome, heroic, and passionately in love with the lady of his dreams--Lady Ada Ross.

Too bad he's just a character in a romance novel......or is he?

When Dayna Roberts finds a mysterious letter tucked between the pages of her favorite book, she decides to write Ian back to warn him of his enemies sneaking up on him. Little did Dayna know that one act would sweep her into a world of the past--a world of danger, intrigue, and powerful forces she never imagined possible. Disaster strikes when Ian's archnemesis Gavin Macauley intercepts her letter and conquers Grimlock Castle with Dayna inside it--but how could he intercept the letter when she wrote it in the twenty-first century?

If Dayna refuses to marry Gavin in Ada's place, he'll take drastic measures that could leave this whole mysterious world in ruins. Forget about Dayna finding a way to get back to the modern world. She'll be lucky if she survives long enough to escape from the castle. Is there any way out--much less a way to get back to the family and the modern life she knows?

Sign up at www.theomann.com to read it for free

About Theo Mann

I write 70 books per year—and yes, before you ask, all these books are my original creative work. Nothing written under my name is AI-generated or ghostwritten because I write better than AI and any ghostwriter out there.

People don't read fiction for entertainment or to escape from reality. People read fiction to see their humanity reflected in another person's character and story.

This is my promise to you. When you read my books, you'll see your own humanity reflected in the characters and stories. I take this commitment to my readers very seriously. My books are an intimate form of communication between us. I would never disrespect my readers by turning that over to a machine or another writer. This is my bond between me and you as my reader.

I write 20,000 words per day as my daily work output. If anyone with a public platform would like to challenge me to prove this in a controlled environment, feel free to contact me on this website's contact page.

I worked as a professional ghostwriter for fifteen years. Now I'm on a mission to set a Guinness World Record by writing 700 books over the next ten years and 1400 books over the next twenty years, all originally written by me. See my website for the full book list.

I'm also the author of *Proof for the Existence of God* and the *Crimes Against Fiction* blog. You can find all my nonfiction work at www.crimes-against-fiction.com.

If you have a story idea, or if you would like me to explore a series in more depth, or if you'd like me to explore a character by writing a spinoff series about that character or world, leave me a message on my website's contact page. I answer all reader emails, so ask me anything, tell me what you liked and didn't like, and let me know where you'd like your favorite series to go. I would love to hear your ideas and find out what you'd like to read next.

Find out more at www.theomann.com.

Also by Theo Mann (so far)

<u>Standalone Novels</u>
Kingdom of Heaven
The Verge

<u>Series</u>
Onyx Series
Prideland Series (Books 1-5)
Ultra Meridian Series (Books 1-7)
Hellhounds Series (Books 1-7)
Battlefleet Series (Books 1-4)
Highland Heroes Series (Books 1-5)
Battalion 1 (Books 1-5)
Corrupted Coil (Books 1-6)

www.ingramcontent.com/pod-product-compliance
Lightning Source LLC
Chambersburg PA
CBHW061504030726
47503CB00005B/1807